ABOVE
BEYOND

ABOVE & BEYOND

JAMES A. LANDRY

ISBN   978-1-951913-09-0   (Paperback)
ISBN   978-1-951913-10-6   (Digital)

Lettra Press books may be ordered through booksellers or by contacting:

Lettra Press LLC
30 N Gould St. Suite 4753
Sheridan, WY 82801, USA
1 303-586-1431 | info@lettrapress.com
www.lettrapress.com

DEDICATIONS

Friends

Mike Wentworth, may he Rest in Paradise

Tim Finnemore, may he Rest in Paradise

Saint Anthony said he sometimes encounters

Angels who look like devils

And he encounters devils that look like

Angels

You can only tell them apart

By the way you feel

After either

Encounter.

PREFACE

<u>Astral Projection</u> (or astral travel or journeying) is an interpretation of out-of-body experience (OBE) that assumes the existence of an "astral body" separate from the physical body and capable of travelling outside it. Astral projection or travel denotes the astral body leaving the physical body to travel in an astral plane. The idea of astral travel is rooted in common worldwide religious accounts of the afterlife in which the consciousness's or soul's journey or "ascent" is described in such terms as "an out-of body experience, wherein the spiritual traveler leaves the physical body and travels

in his/her subtle body (or dream body or astral body) into 'higher' realms." It is frequently reported in association with dreams, and forms of meditation.

Patients have reported feelings similar to the descriptions of astral projection induced through various hallucinogenic and hypnotic (including self-hypnotic) means. There is no scientific evidence that there is any measurable manifestation of a consciousness or soul which is separate from neural activity, and there is no scientific evidence for the contention that one can consciously leave the body and make observations. Attempts to verify that such has occurred have consistently failed in spite of the variety of pseudoscientific claims to the contrary.

Western beliefs

According to classical, medieval and renaissance Hermeticism, Neo- Platonism, and later Theosophist and Rosicrucian thought, the astral body is an intermediate body of light linking the rational soul to the physical body while the astral plane is an intermediate world of light between heaven and Earth, composed of the spheres of the planets and stars. These astral spheres were held to be populated by angels, daemons and spirits.

The subtle bodies, and their associated planes of existence, form an essential part of the esoteric systems that deal with astral phenomena. In the Neo-Platonism of Plotinus, for example, the individual is a microcosm ("small world") of the universe (the macrocosm or "great world"). "The rational soul is akin to the great Soul of the World" while "the material universe, like the body, is made as a faded image of the Intelligible". Each succeeding plane of manifestation is causal to the next, a world-view called emanationism; "from the "One" proceeds Intellect, from Intellect Soul, and from Soul - in its lower phase, or that of Nature - the material universe".

Often these bodies and their planes of existence are depicted as a series of concentric circles or nested spheres, with a separate body traversing each realm. The idea of the astral figured prominently in the work of the nineteenth-century French occultist Eliphas Levi, whence it was adopted and developed further by Theosophy, and used afterwards by other esoteric movements.

Bible

Some have claimed that The bible contains mentions of astral projection. Carrington, Muldoon, Peterson, and Williams claim that Above Beyond 11 the subtle body is attached to the physical body by means of a psychic silver cord. The final chapter of the Biblical Book of Ecclesiastes is often cited in this respect: "Before the silver cord be loosed, or the golden bowl be broken, or the pitcher be shattered at the fountain, or the wheel be broken at the cistern." Scherman, however, contends that the context points to this being a metaphor, comparing the body to a machine, with the silver cord referring to the spine.

Paul's Second Epistle to the Corinthians is more generally agreed to refer to the astral planes; "I know a man in Christ, fourteen years ago, (whether in the body I know not, or out of the body I know not, God knows) such a one caught up to the third Heaven." This statement gave rise to the Visio Pauli, a tract that offers a vision of heaven and hell, a forerunner of visions attributed to Adomnan and Tnugdalus as well as of Dante's Divine Comedy.

Islamic Mysticism

Many sects and offshoots belonging to Islamic mysticism interpret Muhammad's night ascent—the Isra and Mi'raj—to be an out of body experience through nonphysical environments, unlike the Sunni and Shia Muslims. In view of the references from the Qur'an and Hadith, the Sunni and Shia Muslims reject this saying the Isra and Mi'raj, the night journey – mentioned in the Qur'an and Hadith was physical yet spiritual. He was taken to the Masjid Al Aqsa, where he performed prayer leading all previous prophets and then taken to the Heavens in a journey. The mystics claim Muhammad was transported to Jerusalem and onward to seven Heavens, even though "the apostle's body remained where it was."

Ancient Egypt

Similar concepts of soul travel appear in various other religious traditions, for example ancient Egyptian teachings present the soul as having the ability to hover outside the physical body in the ka, or subtle body.

China

Taoist alchemical practice involves creation of an energy body by breathing meditations, drawing energy into a 'pearl' that is then "circulated". "Xiangzi ...with a drum as his pillow fell fast asleep, snoring and motionless.

His primordial spirit, however, went straight into the banquet room and said, "My lords, here I am again." When Tuizhi walked with the officials to take a look, there really was a Daoist sleeping on the ground and snoring like thunder. Yet inside, in the side room, there was another Daoist beating a fisher drum and singing Daoist songs. The officials all said, "Although there are two different people, their faces and clothes are exactly alike. Clearly he is a divine immortal who can divide his body and appear in multiple places at once." At that moment, the Daoist in the side room came walking out, and the Daoist sleeping on the ground woke up. The two merged into one."

India

Similar ideas such as the Lin'ga S'ari-ra are found in ancient Hindu scriptures such as the YogaVashishta-Maharamayana of Valmiki. Modern Indians who have vouched for astral projection include Paramahansa Yogananda who witnessed Swami Pranabananda doing a miracle through a possible astral projection and Osho (Bhagwan Shree Rajneesh) who practiced it himself. The Indian spiritual teacher Meher Baba described one's use of astral projection: In the advancing stages leading to the beginning of the path, the aspirant becomes spiritually prepared for being entrusted with free use of the forces of the inner world of the astral bodies. He may then undertake astral journeys in his astral body, leaving the physical body in sleep or wakefulness. The astral journeys that are taken unconsciously are much less important than those undertaken with full consciousness and as a result of deliberate volition. This implies conscious use of the astral body. Conscious separation of the astral body from the outer vehicle of the gross body has its own value in making the soul feel its distinction from the gross body and in arriving at fuller control of the gross body. one can, at will, put on and take off the external gross body as if it were a cloak, and use the astral body for experiencing the inner world of the astral and for undertaking journeys through it, if and when necessary. The ability to undertake astral journeys therefore involves considerable expansion of one's scope for experience. It brings opportunities for promoting one's own spiritual advancement, which begins with the involution of consciousness.

The Yogic tradition is an elaborate system of meditation and astral projection and most other Chino-Tibetan systems are derived therefrom through Buddhist channels. Astral projection is one of the Siddhis considered achievable by yoga practitioners through self-disciplined practice.

Japan

In Japanese mythology, an ikiryō (生霊) (also read shōryō, seirei, or ikisudama) is a manifestation of the soul of a living person separately from their body. Traditionally, if someone holds a sufficient grudge against another person, it is believed that a part or the hole of their soul can temporarily leave their body and appear before the target of their hate in order to curse or otherwise harm them, similar to an evil eye. Souls are also believed to leave a living body when the body is extremely sick or comatose; such ikiryō are not malevolent.

James A. Landry

Inuit

In some Inuit groups, people with special capabilities are said to travel to (mythological) remote places, and report their experiences and things important to their fellows or the entire community; how to stop bad luck in hunting, cure a sick person etc., things unavailable to people with normal capabilities.

Amazon

The yaskomo of the Waiwai is believed to be able to perform a "soul flight" that can serve several functions such as healing, flying to the sky to consult cosmological beings (the moon or the brother of the moon) to get a name for a new-born baby, flying to the cave of peccaries' mountains to ask the father of peccaries for abundance of game or flying deep down in a river to get the help of other beings.

"Astral" and "Etheric"

The expression "astral projection" came to be used in two different ways. For the Golden Dawn and some Theosophists it retained the classical and medieval philosophers' meaning of journeying to other worlds, Heavens, hells, the astrological spheres and other imaginable landscapes, but outside these circles the term was increasingly applied to non-physical travel around the physical world.

Though this usage continues to be widespread, the term, "etheric travel", used by some later Theosophists, offers a useful distinction. Some experients say they visit different times and/or places: "etheric", then, is used to represent the sense of being "out of the body" in the physical world, whereas "astral" may connote some alteration in timeperception. Robert Monroe describes the former type of projection as "Locale I" or the "Here-Now", involving people and places that actually exist: Robert Bruce calls it the "Real Time Zone" (RTZ) and describes it as the non-physical dimension-level closest to the physical. This etheric body is usually, though not always, invisible but is often perceived by the experient as connected to the physical body during separation by a "silver cord". Some link "falling" dreams with projection.

According to Max Heindel, the etheric "double" serves as a medium between the astral and physical realms. In his system the ether, also called prana, is the "vital force" that empowers the physical forms to change. From his descriptions it can be inferred that, to him, when one views the physical during an out-of-body experience, one is not technically "in" the astral realm at all.

Other experients may describe a domain that has no parallel to any known physical setting. Environments may be populated or unpopulated, artificial, natural or abstract, and the experience may be beatific, horrific or neutral. A common Theosophical belief is that one may access a compendium of mystical knowledge called the Akashic records. In many accounts the experiencer correlates the astral world with the world of dreams. Some even report seeing other dreamers enacting dream scenarios unaware of their wider environment.

The astral environment may also be divided into levels or subplanes by theorists, but there are many different views in various traditions concerning the overall structure of the astral planes: they may include Heavens and hells and other after-death spheres, transcendent environments or other less-easily characterized states.

Notable practitioners

Emanuel Swedenborg was one of the first practitioners to write extensively about the out-of-body experience, in his Spiritual Diary (1747–65). French philosopher and novelist Honoré de Balzac's fictional work "Louis Lambert" suggests he may have had some astral or out-ofbody experience.

There are many twentieth century publications on astral projection, although only a few authors remain widely cited. These include Robert Monroe, Oliver Fox, Sylvan Muldoon and Hereward Carrington, and Yram.

Robert Monroe's accounts of journeys to other realms (1971–1994) popularized the term "OBE" and were translated into a large number of languages. Though his books themselves only placed secondary importance on descriptions of method, Monroe also founded an institute dedicated to research, exploration and non-profit dissemination of auditory technology for assisting others in achieving projection and related altered states of consciousness.

Robert Bruce, William Buhlman, and Albert Taylor have discussed their theories and findings on the syndicated show Coast to Coast AM several times. Michael Crichton gives lengthy and detailed explanations and experience of astral projection in his non-fiction book Travels.

The soul's ability to leave the body at will or while sleeping and visit the various planes of heaven is also known as "soul travel". The practice is taught in Surat Shabd Yoga, where the experience is achieved mostly by meditation techniques and mantra repetition. All Sant Mat Gurus widely spoke about this kind of out of body experience, such as Kirpal Singh.

Eckankar describes Soul Travel broadly as movement of the true, spiritual self (Soul) closer to the heart of God. While the contemplative may perceive the experience as travel, Soul itself is said not to move but to "come into an agreement with fixed states and conditions that already exist in some world of time and space". American Harold Klemp, the current Spiritual Leader of Eckankar practices and teaches Soul Travel, as did his predecessors, through contemplative techniques known as the Spiritual Exercises of ECK (Divine Spirit).

In occult traditions, practices range from inducing trance states to the mental construction of a second body, called the Body of Light in Aleister Crowley's writings, through visualization and controlled breathing, followed by the transfer of consciousness to the secondary body by a mental act of will.

Scientific Reception

There is no scientific evidence that astral projection as an objective phenomenon exists, and pseudoscientific claims to that effect are not accepted as reliable scientific evidence in the relevant fields of study.

Robert Todd Carroll writes that the main evidence to support claims of astral travel is anecdotal and comes "in the form of testimonials of those who claim to have experienced being out of their bodies when they may have been out of their minds." Subjects in parapsychological experiments have attempted to project their astral bodies to distant rooms and see what was happening.

However, such experiments have produced negative results.

According to Bob Bruce of the Queensland Skeptics Association, astral projection is "just imagining", or "a dream state". Although there is rigorous mathematical support for parallel universes, Bruce writes that the existence of an astral plane is contrary to the limits of science. "We know how many possibilities there are for dimensions and we know what the dimensions do. None of it correlates with things like astral projection." Bruce attributes astral experiences such as "meetings" alleged by practitioners to confirmation bias and coincidences.

The psychologist Donovan Rawcliffe has written that astral projection can be explained by delusion, hallucination and vivid dreams.

Arthur W. Wiggins, writing in Quantum Leaps in the Wrong Direction: Where Real Science

Ends...and Pseudoscience Begins, said that purported evidence of the ability to astral travel great distances and give descriptions of places visited is predominantly anecdotal. In 1978, Ingo Swann provided a test of his alleged ability to astral travel to Jupiter and observe details of the planet. Actual findings and information were later compared to Swann's claimed observations. According to an evaluation by Bruno Randi, Swann's accuracy was "unconvincing and unimpressive" with an overall score of 37 percent. Wiggins considers astral travel an illusion, and looks to neuro-anatomy, human belief, imagination and prior knowledge to provide prosaic explanations for those claiming to experience it.

PART ONE
THE CHOSEN

CHAPTER ONE

We know it's all about love, don't we? Bruno thinks himself to sleep.

We either fall in love, dream about love, recover from it, wish for it or reflect upon it. No matter what, truth is that it is what everything and everyone are made of. Love is the atomic value of every being and creation in our universe: God is love. Throughout our lives, it gets pulled apart. It is reformed. The realists and believers realize love has no parameters and does indeed make up the world supreme – the universe. These are the people who keep the world turning.

What about time and space? When one breaks down, say, fifty years into manageable little units, such as decades, it makes it easier to realize how short the span of a lifetime really is. Time really does fly. It is coined that time is but a man-made device with which we measure our agony. This was once said the same of God Supreme, a measurable intangible being; a gift residing in, and used by most to measure earthling pain. Chronology does not capture the earth's natural timekeepers, the sun and moon. And heavenly time differs from both greatly. Love eventually breaks our linear walk of life and forms a divine circle of life and via love all is connected. All roads lead to here.

Space is, and will ever be, an ever-changing aura of different depth, breadth, size and shape all controlled by each of our own diminutive universes, the focal point being our own mind's eye. To believe is to strengthen, yet not driven by doctrine or theology. Verse by verse, we walk the roads of space barefoot if not with divine purpose. Some tend to gather their space for fear of losing it. Others share and seek to expand upon it. Some invite their God to join them. Mclaughlin the Guru hears eternity's breath call.

"Oh Lord Supreme, Supreme

Let me fulfill Thy will

Let me fulfill Thy will."

* * *

"I wake every day a man looking over my shoulder," the old man says from his hard finished, molded yet uncomfortable subway seat, syllabic as he rocks back and forth, "There will always be another man out there who once loved her, and will always hate me. Some days I wonder if it was all worth it.

You say God will let me know when I have paid my due. Confession has never eased the pain, so which God are you talking about, kid?"

"The only God, my friend, your father, mother, mine. Our very conscience, Faithfulness, Hope; the Holy Spirit who reads the writing on the walls of our souls and cleanses with pure, white grace from the heavens; the God who monitors our every thought, our struggles and wishes," replies Bruno. "The Trinity takes a step in your direction even as you sin. Always. That sacred Trinity are the one who knows and governs us with that discomfort in our wrenched and wretched gut when we lie and sin, have done something outright wrong to ourselves, another, or to our planet; the Earth – all living things and beings. There is only one God, rider, whether we call him our supreme being God, Allah, her Goddess, The Great Spirit or Buddha, and so on."

"I'm sorry, but you appear damned lost, young sir," the old man declares.

"No… No, I am not lost, elder brother. I am found. In fact, I've never been lost, in any sense of the word."

"How old are you, anyway?"

"I am, in terms of the chronological year, thirty-four."

"Well, I'm seventy-four, and I can tell you this. You have to stand for something, for someone; have faith. …And hope, right."

"Oh, I have faith and hope, my senior friend. Have you not been listening? Faith and hope guide me, strengthen me. I trust what I feel." Young Bruno asks, "Are you now with me, sir?"

"Don't tell me you're one of those friggin' secular atheists!"

"I am a Christian, sir," Bruno answers. "I intuitively act upon all things presented here, before me...around me," motioning a sweep across his forehead and mid-section. "...before me, knowing I am free, and as well, righteous. I simply realize my personal bill of rights, and yours." Bruno looks into the palms of his own hands held twelve inches in front of his chin as he speaks.

"You speak in vague terms, young man, and you are becoming too pious for me."

The thirty-four year old stands, leaning against the train's centrifugal force as it screeches around a bend.

"They think they know who God is," Bruno spits loudly. His pleasant smile disappears, "Just like you."

People are looking at him.

"what would you say or do if I told you

that I have seen the Goddess?" Bruno bellows again. "Too many of us think they know the one God almighty is gone, but it is only fear of God that actually has. Fools! For if she is naught, then, how do you explain all of this?"

As the young man's arms wave - almost violently one-hundred degrees - the lights dim, blink, and then finally go out. The rail precariously takes a lengthy, jerky left curve, and runs through a very dingily, tiled tunnel. The older gentleman sits back in his seat and holds on tight in somewhat fearful silence. He trembles. At the other end of the short tunnel, he sees the younger man is gone…Vanished.

The old man sits quaking on the bench seat. He has been taking this train in and out of the city for over thirty years, but has never felt so shaken by the ride, that left curve. He thinks he has seen it all, however, he can't get the vision of the younger fellow out of his mind. The image of Bruno is tattooed there on the walls of his memory, nicely like a portrait of Jesus, Elvis or JFK.

Bruno falls gently back onto his bed, not sure whether he should feel guilty over the incident, or revitalized. He knows he had to let it out. He feels weak, but in thought he is justified, qualified enough now too. He had to relay something of a message to an adult. He knows now, without a doubt that he can make his earthly self be seen in the living dimension while projecting into the heavenly one.

It is quite a milestone for Bruno to reach, and that familiar voice of late is right there to tell him so. "Although you relayed emotional trauma through your message, that journey proves you can do that what you question," the voice softly acknowledges.

"You proved you can indeed keep visible in being while projecting. Very, very good Master Bruno. I am your patron Saint Bruno. You have overcome the most difficult of all journey-related tasks." The Saint smiles.

The thirty-four year old seems at peace, yet also appears frustrated and hurt, like he wants to relay more but is not yet ready, able or welcome to do so. He is so confident in his resolve and his beliefs, but seems also damn angry at the world and what it is turning into before everybody's eyes. Not a word about America's failed march to spread freedom and democracy. Not a word about the shanghai of the good book by the Middle East extremists. Not a word about the silent poor, the bourgeois or the committed middle class of the world.

Frighteningly, he does not feel or appear finished, either. Bruno looks down at the four or five books on his night stand, bed side table. He chooses one of them and reads from it. He absorbs and retains all he reads and intends to read a bit from another. However, Bruno is sleepy and so he falls off to rest… books on his chest.

CHAPTER TWO

"If I may, my almighty Goddess," Saint Peter begins and asks for continuity at the same time. "The proverbial carrot rots. For our offers of hope inside lives on the planet — hope for the (better) afterlife, based on faithful beliefs in their current one, seem to fall short up against modernism. For they are intangible things and the spirit is too often misunderstood altogether. The Holy Spirit simply must step-up alongside technology in a divine marriage for the genuine good of all. That is, they must follow the laws of this one existence to get to the next. However, fear of God, dare I say, is none existent altogether on your father's Earth.

Why, some believe the Earth is purgatory, while others believe it is hell itself!" Saint Peter exclaims in a raised vocal. "Most people misinterpret the bible, or now at worst, ignore the teachings and commandments therein by and large. The originators wrote much too metaphorically, admittedly, so you might realize discrepancies by such misreading, misinterpretation and misunderstanding. Finally, in sadness, I can see that even the Earth's high and mighty, most, have managed to bastardize the teachings instead. We must realize that our population shall not further guess, or ever believe honestly that they have arrived. The simple truth is that simple step of purpose, which lay beyond what is an achievement. Having been rewarded materialistically, most, at that point, lie back and wallow in their private, perverted empire. They grow fat and lazy. Their spirit becomes one of greed. They boast and ride on their so-called accomplishments."

The board is rarely worthy to speak directly to her, nor do they must, yet she has spoken to them with invitation, so her word shall be considered sacredly done. Goddess has the disposition and patience of the supreme angelic being that she purely is. Yes, sadly, gods do get old, too, and eventually forge themselves untouchable beyond prayers heard.

Jesus' young sister inherited responsibility of Earth upon her brother's death. He performed his deed nobly, at the word of his father. It helped save the species and planet for many centuries, with some violence, nonetheless, and convolution between religious doctrine and political governments, but now she faces her own challenge, for her father grew tired after sacrificing his very son Jesus to win the battle against the fallen Lucifer, Satan, who had no way to trump him. God realizes it is all he could do to win the draw, but it exhausted the multimillennia old creator. He did beat the devil and Jesus saves us from our own sins.

She and her board meet in timelessness on all pressing matters for the sake of the earthbound inhabitants, give it an earthly century, millennia or beyond. For, a moment in heaven, as it is a timeless space, may span a moment, day, week, month, year or century, or millennials, on the planet Earth. If all those who joke about God being a woman, or wish it were true, or everyone alive there now were introduced to the truth today…Oh, what a world it would be. The world is still not exactly ripe with women leaders of its own, save a few, let alone hearing the news of Jesuette and the liberated heaven. Not to forget plans for mother Earth that she churns about. Earth is fallen far from the present stuck in a time of old. The Lordess attentively, delicately and fully nudges humanity forward.

"I concur." Saint Paul begins. "We maintain theological flaws, as discussed by the board previously. People on your planet are indeed becoming too psychologically sophisticated to any longer fear God. With no presence of God, there is practically, sad to say, no law either and certainly no safety in law enforcement. Any law. All laws." He becomes quite animated as he continues "No end to war. And, there appears no end to corruption at every given level, to any given degree." Saint Paul stops there.

"If not for the sheer resiliency of youth, I fear, and I feel the end could, just may be, ever near." Saint Peter raises something suggestive and also questionable.

Tears fall from the corners of both Jesuette's eyes.

A light rain drizzles down all over the Earth.

"And now, once again, this...this…this degeneracy abounds. Fortunately, we seem to have caught the atrocity of evil in the early stage." Saint James offers. "Yet alas. No?"

The entire board knows to what he refers and recognizes it now with solemn agreement and in murmured side discussions. But, Saint Peter feels the need to repeat the severity and symptoms. And so he asks Jesuette for her permission to review with the table their initial plan for abolishment and recovery, from Satan's latest threat. It is granted.

"We now face a demon," Saint Peter commences. "It is a demon that haunts our innocent children in adolescence, and young adults alike. He talks to them, terrifies them and manipulates them in what they want to believe is a dream state. He threatens to bring them to face with their worst fear. He has risen from the ashes yet once again, from those smoldering ashes of his hell below us.

His visits in the night invariably lead to suicide, homicide or apparent psychosis. Satan uses his power to deliver the nightmares of each. Unbelievably, the beast delivers them to vividly dream the violence, if not come true to be. The common innocents do have the option to follow along with the fallen instead, fear free. And many do opt for just that. However, that option shall, little do the victims know, in the end reach martyrdom nonetheless. It simply must. And, we simply must see to it. We shall, in the blessed of God's heaven. We shall!" Saint Peter rests.

"I have gathered as much and more from

the children's prayers," the Goddess shares. "Thank goodness prayer hasn't vanished all-together, even when recited in naked desperation."

"Pity…" says Saint Peter. "It is a pity indeed."

"It has grown in impact fold and fold over, eh sirs, sisters?" Jesuette rhetorically asks.

"As described, recorded in childhood, in description – horrendous and gruesome," she continues. "And so wistfully, once again, doth stay forever in mind."

"One by one, night by night, he visits and then revisits and does even again, to toil and spoil the poor tortured souls," Jesuette reminds, then continues, "As needed and by virtue of his many ugly failures and hideous visions.

"And so then, we shall not worry about the representative flaw, my brothers and sisters, we will continue to work on awakening our earthly representative." She declares in finality.

"Amen?"

"Amen… Amen." The table resounds.

The Lordess continues.

"We need a gentle man, yet one who has faced the death of loved ones, been defeated during life on Earth and recovered. A man who has experienced triumph, achievements, accomplishments as well, and can once again. On grander a scale, he would call by each with the same strength and non-eventfulness of an angel uppermost. Draw upon experience and be open for instruction. He has faith in, and accepts the realism of all of us. His character is learned of in catechism.

Is there really such a soul, Saint Bruno?" She wonders aloud.

"I truly believe there is," Saint Bruno answers quietly. "As you know, I have been visiting with my apprentice, training and testing him for such a time."

"I shall wander soon with you to experience the earthly subject of yours. I want to see an example of at least his power to journey in soul." Jesuette confirms.

"That will be an honor, Lordess Jesuette." And then Saint Bruno smiles, and adds to his superior, "He longs to meet you, you know." His comment and grin reflects calm and relief. Thankfully, the saints softly chuckle for a moment, and Jesuette smiles. Then they quietly cheerdown as they take that cue from their goddess, as well.

"The last time heaven had to step-in,

my father sacrificed his only son in the miserable, unblessed, filthy deal with the devil. He will not lose me in this one," she declares.

"We once inseminated a preferred and proper young woman to bear a child-god, a savior, a messiah, altogether God's son. We can certainly and at the least serve an earthly man up some heavenly strength and power in this extreme circumstance." She once again drives forward.

"We could have had the misled bin Laden's and inhumane Hussein's plan together we could have let all the Western coalition troops through to Baghdad with their shock and awe and then simply killed them all! Or, something quite the opposite if we were to choose a side explicitly. But, we're equally with the west, as well, now, are we not? And we do not control; we know. Earth people do not consider the possibilities. They may believe in God, yet not of me, thus they use me. Bless them, my God, and forgive their sins, for they know not what they do, as this has been prayed out loud before, when Jesus saves Mary Magdalene."

Everyone makes the traditional sign of the cross and in just above the decibel of a whisper respond, "Lordess hear our prayer."

The board has not ever heard Goddess this animatedly. "Contrary to the outdated joke, 'If God were a woman, men would be the child bearers,' God is so now, and she knows women are just as right in every way for the job and tasks. Year by year and ever more-so, adeptly built to perform and give thanks for the privilege. So fortunately earthling females possess a high tolerance for pain.

And remember also everyone that black

Africans were persecuted long before they were delivered to America.

Homosexuals were around when Jesus walked the Earth and prior.

People should know they talk to God every time they walk the virgin sod of the Earth. People should know that sometimes change, rights, enablement, and even equality take time for the species, races, governments, society and religions to grasp, tolerate the ensuing pain, accept and uphold. For, experiments, exercise and adaptation can last many, if not thousands...millions of Earth years.

Consider the human race God delivers to his reshaped Earth. Consider the United States of America. Long, complicated experiments in government mixed with Christian-Judaism humility. The modern scientists do not understand. The heavenly, unfortunately, are too far removed from their fact-based, simpleton reach...Shame.

How can people not believe in miracles when African babies live a full life despite being born with terminal disease? Many do. Children... God's greatest miracle and gift. What else, if ever lost, could ever bring a parent closer with God? Oh, I know...sad is the reality. But, as the world grew too greedy the first time, God shows up with a man-like revolutionary and miracle worker.

And the world grew fatter yet.

The Jews with the Romans executed one of their own. The Catholics use that as part of their theology. Make no mistake, the doctrine rings true, my father had to reconcile with the death of his own son to win the war against the fallen one."

Jesuette breathes deeply and sighs.

The jet stream wind cycles and blows harder below.

She continues. "And now, society is again beginning to deteriorate. The West grows more politically correct and greedy once more, the more 'American' they become, the less American they turn. The Middle East abuses the Koran for the sake of radical Islam, and a good many, no surprise have fallen to temptation. A lifelong struggle from here, eh?

The East is under constant scrutiny of each other. I confirm the rumors; I near the decision to handle this myself, as I see the fallen is in harness again charging toward his prey. History has such a way of repeating itself, trying to teach the world's people a lesson. Native aborigines, including those in North America wiped out by a Queen, white Anglo-Saxon Protestants or other religious zealots or progressive governmental or citizen militia. The Black plague, the wake of the great flood, AIDS, et cetera, et cetera, et cetera. Oh children...

Now, a new power heaving in the holy land; will they never learn? Sometimes I think not. They cannot know what will have really gone on, could they? The final answer, the only answer, for harmony is unbridled love and peace, which create that joyous heart and mind."

The Goddess finally brings her oration to an end. Tears roll down her cheeks as the near entirety of the Earth is drenched. Some downpours, some short showers, some regions more than others.

"The only thing, alternatively, would be for us to blatantly let ourselves be known; no, be seen, like the spirits in heaven we are. And we all know what that would do for our planet in this day and age, do we not? Besides, that is against our rules of engagement for this experiment. They'd first shoot, then later ask… wonder, no? A trifle shame that vociferousness will have met fear instead," says a sad participant from the table.

"Not that we could ever die again," replies Saint Paul humorously.

All the saints grin and slowly shake their heads.

"Listen to me. We must rid the Earth of the fallen one, and save as many children as we can. Asmodeus has surfaced once more, and so we must thwart his very plan, and the time is now. He discovered the limit of God's patience once. And now, the beast has already depleted mine. We shall find the man of Saint Bruno's and, hopefully, deliver forth a soldier. A commanding soldier. This time he will not be born of their kind from ours. He shall be an adult talent, prophet, warrior and holy man – one of them – a human Earth specimen with faith and promise, worthy to be fortified by us. We shall make it so."

She lets the current announcement digest around the board.

All the Saints and Angels hum out an "Amen."

"Saint Bruno, tell us please, more of your candidate."

CHAPTER THREE

"Hey, Mr. Ryan," Bruno greets his English II teacher. "I hear you're selling your 240z."

"Oh, hello Bruno," answers Ryan. "Please, call me Mike. That's right. Why?" Mike continues. "Are you interested?"

"Yeah, I am looking for a car," Bruno says. "But, I don't have a lot of money."

"Well," Mike says. "You'll get a lot of car for the money I'm asking."

"When can I come over to look at it?"

"Any time after school would be good,"

Mike declares. "Actually, I'll be home every evening this week."

"Great! I'll be over tonight," Bruno is excited at the thought. "After supper. How about 7:00?"

"Sounds good to me," Mike replies. "See you then. I'm right around the corner from the entrance to the country club in Greenland, Back Bay Terrace. Turn in to Country Club Drive, then take the first right. I'm the fifth and last house on the right."

"I got it. Thanks!"

Bruno is beside himself with the prospect of driving a 240Z. It's a tough little sports car, he knows. He thinks it will be pretty cool seeing Mike outside of the classroom, too. See him on 'the other side.' Maybe, Bruno thinks, he'll invite me to visit a little while. Bruno caught easily the good vibe off

Mike the first day of school. He wears his hair kind of long, he has a beard, and he does not speak or teach from the text book. He wears casual clothes, too, no suits. His assignments and lesson plans are equally cool. He has the class reading and dissecting rock & roll bios, music lyrics, reading science fiction, and, he manages to cover all the literary must-knows by semester end.

Bruno rings the doorbell to the right of Mike's front storm door.

"Well, hey there Bruno," Mike greets him. "I suppose you're here for the big test drive, huh?"

"Yeah," Bruno chuckles. "You know, I am genuinely interested."

"I gathered that. I'll grab the keys," Mike says, then adds, "I'll come along!"

When Mike returns, he hands the car keys to Bruno and leads him to the driveway.

On the stroll to Mike's car, Bruno says "It isn't fair that I use my mother's car every day."

Bruno unlocks the passenger side car door for Mike, then walks around the front of the car, unlocks the driver's side door, then seats himself in the driver's seat. The vehicle, to him, felt deceivingly larger inside than it looks from the outside. He is in a cockpit of sorts, seated way down low, with his legs straight out in front of him, like he is in a kayak.

It is intimidating to Bruno, but he does not mention it to Mike, who is sitting quietly and patiently waiting while Bruno checks the layout of the dash board. He learns where all the controls and switches are located. He adjusts the mirrors, pushes the clutch in to the hilt, and starts the car. He turns the headlights lights on in the dusky mid-eve, his stomach churning with excitement as he does.

"Starts right up," Bruno remarks.

"Oh yeah," Mike says. "She runs great. I'm only selling it because my wife is pregnant, and we're planning on having each a more familyfriendly vehicle, if you know what I mean." Singing 'Fat Man in the Bathtub,' by Little Feat, Mike changes the words to "there's a fat man, in a mini-van… who's got the blues."

Bruno laughs out loud at that, hard, it hit him so funny.

"Oh," Bruno replies. "I get it. Too bad you'll lose your toy, here, but you got to do what you got to do, right? You know…Do the right thing?"

"You got it, my friend. Let's drive!"

Bruno yanks the stick shift into reverse, and then accelerates slightly as he eases off the clutch. He is surprised, and a little scared, as the car jumps backwards with such impetus, so that he involuntarily and instinctually brakes, then stalls it. He is embarrassed, but Mike assures him that he did the same thing the first time he set the sports car in motion, too.

On a second try, Bruno doesn't stall it, but the vehicle still jumps into motion, and before he knows it, he is in the road right next to his own car parked at the curb. He has no recollection of actually navigating to that point. It all just happened so fast.

"Holy shit, Mike," Bruno exclaims. "This thing goes when you tell it to, don't it?"

"I should have warned you," Mike replies

with a grin, though somewhat sorrowfully. "Yes, she goes when you tell her too. It's incredibly difficult to ride slow, but it sure is fun driving."

"Oh, Christ, almighty," Bruno replies rolling his eyes, as he performs the sign of the cross. He shifts to first and goes.

"Wow," Bruno calls out. "This thing is fuckin' powerful!"

"Like I said, Bruno," Mike says. "She goes when you tell her."

"Nice. Amazing, actually," Bruno says. "I'm only a dite fearful, though."

Bruno drives the sports car, and he tries hard, sometimes to no avail, to keep to the speed limit. He goes out from Back Bay Terrace out to Route 1A and drives toward Route 287, via the Route 1 Bypass. He wants to swing around the rotary a few times to check out the handling, and he tells Mike so. After that exercise, Bruno bears right heading up to Woodbury Avenue. He has a hard time bringing the automobile to a stop at the top of the off ramp, and lets out a little gasp as he stands on the brake and clutch.

"Are you okay, Bruno?" Mike asks, but he already knows the answer. He is slightly, yet genuinely concerned, because he knows Bruno had trouble on the stop.

"Yeah, yeah, I'm okay," Bruno answers. "I lost it a bit coming off the ramp. This car is too hot."

"Yes, she is," Mike says. "I hate to let 'er go."

Bruno decides to return to Mike's after taking Woodbury to Islington Street. He drives straight up Islington, hits Route 1A, and then drives to Back Bay Terrace. He handles the car great after the one incident at the off ramp, but he is thinking that it's probably way too much car for him. Besides, he thinks, it's but a two-seater, and, it would not be good in the snow. Here up north gets a lot of snow during winter, even some in the off-season. Ice…

They talk topicality and esoteric items on the way back, however, just as Bruno had hoped, Mike invites him in for a beverage after parking the car back in Mike's driveway. Bruno is happy to accept the invitation; he thinks it is pretty cool hanging out with Ryan. He wonders what Mike does for fun… Mike wonders the same about Bruno. Neither guy breaches the subject.

"Come on in!" Mike happily commands. "Follow me. We'll sit in the living room for a bit."

"Okay, Mike."

"What would you like," Mike asks. "I've got milk, juice, water, Diet Pepsi… I'd consider offering you a glass of ale, but I don't have any left in the fridge."

Bruno notices a dark blue padded mat laying out in the middle of the floor, not unlike one that may be used for exercise, yoga or aerobics.

"Pepsi, please. You work out?" Bruno asks, nodding toward the mat.

"In a sense," Mike responds. "Probably not the kind of workout you might expect, though."

"No?"

"Yes," Mike laughs. "Confidentially – between you and me," he continues. "I am into astral projection; journeying."

"No shit," Bruno exclaims. "I've been practicing that myself."

"What inspired you to get into it, Bruno?

"Well, the Castaneda series and the revelations of Don Juan, for one"

"Me, too," Mike says.

"I also happened to read 'Astral Projection' and 'Way of the Shaman.'

"Ditto again!"

"'Spirit Walker,' by Dr. Hank Wesselman."

"Hmmm…I haven't seen that one."

"Well, it's brand new, Mike, how long have you been into it?"

"About five years now; I started in college. You?"

"About four years now; I started before I was a freshman."

Mike asks, "Are you able to manipulate when travelling?"

"Mike," Bruno begins rather admittedly. "I am still learning to be able to journey at will, not to mention trying to control my motion and movement. I practice those during the flying dreams I happen to experience too, quite often really."

"Wow," Mike is taken a bit by surprise. "You're ahead of me a little, I'd say, but I don't get the chance to practice much. And you know what they say… practice, practice, practice makes perfect."

"Yup!"

Bruno finishes his Diet Pepsi and bids Mike a good night while reassuring him also that their cosmic conversation would stay confidential. That's all that needed to be spread around town: "Hey, did you know Ryan's into projection?"

Prompted by the conversation with Mike, as

soon as Bruno gets home, he clicks off the light hanging above his bed and lies still, hands at his sides. Focus on your hands, he reiterates to himself. Even that is against the rules. Breathe through your feet. Think of nothing, but visualize rising, and the vision of your hands. Think yourself rising from the bed, and floating to the closet and back. Concentrate without thinking and visualize value without importance. Control, think, no, intend and feel your every fiber without a second thought, nor a first. Be very aware of the astral cord without being restrained by it. Exhale out the top of your head.

Although it has not happened to him in a long, long while, bouncing back is a horrible feeling, nor is it at all protective; it weakens the soul and spirit, physically and emotionally. So, Bruno knows that fear from several first-hand, first-try experiences. He's been doing this for going on five years now, yet he improves upon it with each journey, as he also becomes more and more powerful.

Bruno sees himself in bed, looks to the closet and upon intention immediately floats toward it. He navigates by pure vision over self. He has lately learned to carry the vision of his encasement with him at will. Sometimes he is pure spirit as he travels, and sometimes he is ghost-like with his inner spirit sharing the outer space with what looks like his clothed or naked body.

CHAPTER FOUR

"Hope I don't get hit too hard today," Carl burps and says. "I just had an Italian!"

Moe's is a bit of an Italian soul food; an all home-made Italian sub, with special oil, cooked salami, tomatoes, green pepper slivers, onion slivers and sliced black olives. Moe's even makes their own bread and pasta.

Everyone on the football squad laughs heartily at Carl's declaration. He is a running back for Hoboken High, and although he is a bit heavy, he can run fast. The extra weight helps him to break tackles left and right, and run right through the line. He's quite the local star and a very good friend of Bruno's. Bruno is but a second string tight end, but plays very well when he is in the game. He is fast, too. Bruno pulls Carl to the sideline for a moment.

"Hey Carl," Bruno says to his good friend. "I'm going try something tonight for the first time." Carl is the only person, beside Mr. Ryan, who is aware that Bruno practices Astral Projection and journeying.

"And, what's that? Should I be scared?"

"Listen," Bruno laughs. "I want to travel to your place."

"And do what?"

"I am going to try to tap on your bedroom window. I may even be able to gain entrance."

"Okay Brutus," Carl's nickname given to Bruno. "Why don't you just come in and say hello?" With a throaty, hearty laugh, "Heh, Heh, Heh, Heh… Hey!"

"I want to see if I can make contact without slipping through… first things first."

"What time?" Carl asks.

"Around eleven o'clock," Bruno tells him. "Is that okay?"

Practice is about to start, so they rejoin the team and coach at midfield. It's calisthenics to start, followed by several laps around the field. Going through the play book with the offense first, and the defensive coach prompts the opposing side of the line. Bruno is put into play because the first string tight end is absent. He does well. It does Bruno a lot of good to hear the others' encouraging words and cheers. The coach is tough, and Carl is a captain on the team. The first string tight end shows-up albeit late, and so Bruno is told to take a rest on the bench.

Bruno eats considerably less than usual tonight, so he can lie back in comfort. After dinner, he goes straight to his room. He finds that a bit of butterfly stomach, whether it be it nerves or hunger, somehow, most times help in the process, even it be anxiety, strangely enough.

He takes his shoes and sweatshirt off, leaving him in his jeans and tee. Bruno first wants to try a short journey to the corner of the highway and back. This will have been one of the longest flights he has taken. He usually projects only around the house, into the back yard and around the neighborhood.

He is down on his back in bed with his hands at his sides. He uses no pillow. His eyes are shut and he keeps a steady breath, thinking about nothing. He only imagines he is looking at his hands and senses vaguely the feel of how his body is touching the bedding. He uses DBT, Dialectical Based Tasking to some degree, which seems to accelerate and promote his start. Bruno begins rising and looks to see himself in bed, while floating above.

Just then, little sister Shelley barges into his room, which is unlike her, yet not unheard of. She announces the family is getting ready to watch a good movie on television together.

"No thanks, little sis," Bruno responds. "I'll be turning-in early tonight. Please ask everyone not to bother me. Okay?"

"Okay Bruno," she says. "Sorry I forgot to knock."

After slamming back into bed in his original position it was difficult to carry on with his sister at all. He is spaced-out and vibrating to no end. He gives himself a half hour to recover before trying again. Snapping back is painful.

* * *

"Try to turn the closet light out first," the familiar, soft male voice instructs. The surprise of that communication almost bounces Bruno back into his bed again, but it does not, after all, by now he has grown accustomed to the visits and lessons, surprise, or not. He travels, his spirit travels, but this time his spirit does not employ the body. He's a mortal man who found years ago that gnomic seventy percent of the brain that few others ever discover, let alone use, or even know-of. The closet light turns out, and his mentor's voice evokes soft warmth and resounds pleasingly, praise for Bruno.

Bruno regards the being as his guardian angel, for the sake of ease. He has no idea. They have been practicing together for several months. The tractable, mellow fellow introduces himself some time ago as Bruno's patron saint, Saint Bruno, his namesake. The power to move in the heightened dimension and to emit small miracles, Bruno is, the saintly angel believes, almost ready for the next lesson, and he tells the mortal so.

Saint Bruno, shall continue until his assignment's duty is complete. He now openly converses and instructs while Bruno consistently aims to please and learn. Bruno wants to know why the elder is so intent on specific tasks, and wants to know what the actual assignment really is, specifically, but he is advised to practice patience.

"In due time, my special friend, all will

become clear," Saint Bruno whispers. "In due time, it will come to you, my son."

The saint knows Bruno's presence can be commanding, as proven by his conduct on the train.

* * *

"I have found," Saint Anthony begins. "That the fallen enters the dreams, and in fact knows not how to appear to his victims in wakefulness. That is his weakness, vulnerability and fear. He is useless mortally."

Saint Bruno adds, "Our Bruno has the ability to work in wakefulness as well as in dream state."

"In performing inside the mortal reality," Saint Antony continues. "His subjects are, for the sake of clarity, awake. This leaves no question of doubt."

His candidates realize how absolute he is and how powerful his message is. They recognize and believe it is ultimately comes straight from the saints, angels and Goddess. This adds immensely soothing love and beauty, formidable substance to his message and instruction.

The devil's earthly advocate and evil counterpart to Bruno is Ballard. Within a dream, there is practically nothing Ballard cannot do.

Master Bruno has the advantage of reality, hope and faith, however, his being and words are potent and righteous in his delivery.

The chosen Master Bruno and the fallen Ballard meet young boys and girls who want only to be agnostic or Wiccan, a new phenomenon in young peoples' non-religious beliefs.

Master Bruno tells them his visit is about

a mission. It is not about religion, or doctrine, but for genuine peace and goodness all around, though it is being sponsored and directed by the heavenly.

Ballard performs for his victims, and terrifies them in their dreams, collecting their subconscious signatures.

And upon his visits, Saint Bruno is as dainty as a spring shower. He cleanses as he rescues sense and belief that he speaks only the truth and represents genuine peace and higher love.

CHAPTER FIVE

"All the angels, please," Jesuette sings. "Hear your Lordess. For you shall please gather to carry forth the quest for which you have all been prompted and trained. It is the one mission that I know you individually have pined and longed for in respectful, understanding and silent acquiescence. All you angels, please."

Every angel in heaven, one and all hear the almost whispered message as it rolls like a soft vibration of baby-blue all through heaven. Their attention is at a height never before seasoned, for she nor he has only appeared before them once before, and that is on their judgment day. Upon entering the heaven, embedded instinct and immortality inside them know not only happiness, but also their special surroundings, the heavenly dimension and domain. They are called to go forth as the angelic beings of heaven and earth that they are.

"As you enter this tier in our heavenly domain," Jesuette tenderly announces. "You are all introduced, although it is never stressed for attention (you recognize, of course that it doesn't have to be) to the notion of assignments and their ultimate protection, as far as you will commit. You all share your heavenly grace with each, planting and nurturing a conscience into your assignments on behalf of the Holy Spirit. Now, as evil reaches its pinnacle point in my father's masterpiece, Earth, they need more of you, from you, than ever before. You shall each, one and all, descend in dimension and guide their souls as their archangels, guardian angels, or patron angels in the way Saint Bruno has proven-out in his visits with his own assignment, namesake Master Bruno, of Earth.

I send to you a detailed review of the expectation, your rudiments of this quest. There is importance of expediency, timeliness of your tasks, so Godspeed is swift and I forever sow diligence in your travels and lessons. Your time to ebb is forthcoming." She assures.

"Prepare spiritually well and know that I shall visit with respect to your individuality and that of your respective assignments to give forth the strength of my brother, Jesus. I shall give to you the confidence and munition to carry-out your angelic duties, by God the father almighty." Jesuette finishes.

She rests for a moment then addresses all the saints and angels around her.

"Thinking back to an attempt made so long ago, one can only frown upon what has become morbid. The experiment is still interesting and so humorous with the entire political correctness, religions sprouting up all over the orb. There is so much taken on and taken for granted. At least as interesting as the skepticism of their prophets, and writings that refer to the Garden of Eden and the biblical psalms, such is the Verse of Our Blessed Apostles, bear inclusion now. Listen:

It isn't a serpent, it is a penis, eh? It isn't an apple, it is Eve's vagina. Ha! Either way generates eventuality; Adam and Eve lose the garden on account of the children they bear, and then their children's children. Obviously then, Eden is no longer exclusively theirs. My father warned them, but the purpose of procreation was strong, and greed a little too rich, once the serpent bored through the apple.

It is not explicitly injected, so how could we have known the simple gift of orgasmic pleasure, thus greed, would overtake awarded possession and comfort, and most of all, faith in God? Embedded greed is initially fortified to give the first dwellers just enough confidence to stand-up and do what they must in support of self, family and the lord thy God. It is too much. For it is not always easy being first." Goddess Jesuette needs no concurrence from the circle.

"Now we see the effects of greed and ego. A life is one's own personal universe, space. That universe is born of, and is constituted entirely by mind, and not of the surrounding atmosphere. Even though, superciliously one may tend to be a product of their environment.

So, my saintly board, angels, the scriptures written cryptically does not shield the world from the sacredness of physical love. It confuses most of those who take the words literally, or misinterpret the metaphorically written messages. How did our creation become such a ship of fools? When did it begin? I am so very tired, right now."

Jesuette pauses and sighs, eyes half closed.

The clouds roll by a bit slower across the entire sky below. Dusk arrives.

"Well, it is not as though your father didn't test his own resolve when he knew he would be faced with sacrificing his own son." Saint Peter tries to bring confidence and practicality into the discussion.

"Ah, yes," Saint Paul responds and continues. "God says to Abraham, 'Kill Me a son,' and then God knows for sure that such grand faith is present and exists in his creation, and it pleases him."

"Therefore, the strength lives in his holiness," Saint Peter concludes. "As we all know, the earthly man is created in God's own image. And earthly man must return to the garden. He must."

* * *

Bruno moves into a simple studio third floor apartment, choosing to stay near family in Hoboken, New Jersey. Lately, his evening journeys hint of a lady watcher. She seems always there, yet untouchable. Every time he thinks his way toward her, she vanishes. His travels, with guidance from Saint Bruno recently deliver him to other peoples' homes, where he finds his way to the assigned child's bedroom. His experiment with Carl had proven out the theory and weigh truth positive.

He's been practicing how to communicate with those he visits while projecting. He knows that one day he shall teach more and more people how to do this, to journey, for he has been told, within Saint Bruno's instruction. He often finds himself floating about his own little room, or yard out back waiting for something to happen. Tonight, however, he is soaring from house to house with ease.

"Master Bruno," Saint Bruno whispers.

"Yes, saint? Why can't I see you? Have I not worked hard enough with you to trust?"

"In short time you shall, godson. Do you know who the female figure is in the upper-left of your vista?"

"No, I don't." Bruno replies in thought. "Every time I try to approach, she disappears, vaporizes. But, I have this feeling that she is somehow immaculate."

"She is Jesuette, God's only daughter." Saint Bruno sees the young man is troubled absorbing this, and leaves Master Bruno to think for a few moments.

"May I ask you to prove what you say by answering one question I've had all my life... as a Roman Catholic?" The young man then asks. "Are you able to explain to me creationism?"

Saint Bruno sighs. He knows he must take Master Bruno there for this one sake of confidence, and then begins, "Young soul, behold these words:

Words that have never been uttered to any human on Earth. The Earth as you know it lay dormant and small, thus, hot in temperature. It was populated with plant life, dinosaurs and with remnants of a primitive and grotesque form of what would later supposedly mutate into man, or rather a man-like species or form at best.

The Earth and everything on it were the nasty leftovers from a foreign, superior ambassador. He struggles to maintain his own version of nirvana for humanoids. It and they and the entire sphere are left abandoned when the exercise failed. But then, our all-superior creator recognizes the potential therein; the most exciting for him being the reality of natural gravity, potential for tides, by way of planetary displacement between the sun and the moon. He attends-to the lack of water and fairly disperses it over his new planet.

He speeds greatly the planet's rotation on its axis to enlarge it, and thus, brings forth the oceans and other bodies of water.

To freeze the atmospheric life, if it may be recalled that, overall ensures a new location for a new and lovely, blessed giving. God names his sphere 'Earth.'

Upon looking at a world map you can clearly recognize the puzzle pieces of the continental divides, taken apart by sheer centrifugal force. Look at the cut-out on the Eastern coasts of North and South America and then look at the western coasts of Western Europe and Africa, just one classic pair of examples.

God then set the speed of rotation back to one that would perfectly support orbit, gravity, climate, inhabitants, and furthermore, set the Earth's rotation around the Sun to support times of the seasons and tide.

Once the heaven and Earth and all stellar objects are once again stable he sets out to create the biological miracle of man, and other living things and beings, flora and fauna. Of course, within the element of the time it took – heavenly versus earthly – in our understanding of that written, God creates this new wonderful world galaxy and universe all within seven days, counting a day of rest. This is another subject altogether. Relative spans of time differ greatly between heaven and Earth. I believe you know up to what point is sufficient for now."

"Oh, my God! Is that really true?" The amazed Bruno asks in exclamation. "Good Lord!"

"Yes Master Bruno," Saint Bruno says. "It is quite true. It is also true that you be well to listen to and act upon every task Jesuette and I ask of you. Remember, to do so will save you and help deliver your generation and yon to a world of global, generational peace. I cannot stress this any stronger. It is also quite true that speaking the Lord's name in vain is uncalled-for."

"I can believe that. I suppose asking for a proof-miracle would be out of the question," Bruno thinks, jokingly. "Hey?"

"She just gave you one, of sorts, my son, perhaps just one of many more to come."

As Bruno dips back into his bed, after having felt his astral cord stretched almost to its maximum, he sees something on his bedside table. It is a roll of linen parchment bound neatly with white ribbon. It looks like it must be some kind of scripture. It's written in English script, the most perfect calligraphy Bruno has ever seen...all holiness and immaculate.

Just holding the paper in his hands makes him feel giddy, happy, comfortable, safe, strong, high and euphoric. He cannot help but tremble. He didn't put it there. It was not there before he went to bed last night. Certainly, no one came in through the quadrupled locked door or closed window to the third floor apartment, he thinks ridiculously so. It is addressed to him personally, by full name, Bruno Anthony Christian, and a message appears inside to be half a question and half an answer.

Saint Bruno stays there, unobtrusively, while Bruno reads. The letter thanks him for cooperating with Saint Bruno and it asks for his help to do the work set forth by the Lordess Jesuette and God the father. It appears there is a devil in our midst. Bruno reads it a second time, after the skim he did at first, and understands that they, heavenly beings, the chosen pick him by virtue of Saint Bruno's testimony, who recommends him to Jesuette and a board of saints. Bruno is to journey into the lives and minds of as many young souls as possible, and he shall repair and recruit on behalf of the chosen. Prepare for Armageddon.

There is a fallen one who continues to recruit and train a nearby human named Ballard Same. And he shall bring will to fight on Lucifer's behalf. They are delivered to his putrid, hellish being in armistice. Ballard discovers the methodology of journeying via his dreamy meetings with Lucifer, and abuses the power. The fallen one draws him near in that recruitment, not without temptation. A more perfect specimen of substandard, abnormal, and decrepit man, the fallen angel could not have found.

"Ballard!" Bruno spits. He's familiar with the name, as, to him it loosely coincides with Lucifer. "Damn! Asmodeus! Damn him!"

Saint Bruno speaks. "You will work your way from Midtown Manhattan and spiral your way, our way, outward concentrically toward your sanctuary, here. This is where you and I shall meet. I will plot our route, based on what I observe over Ballard and Satan, and based on our chosen soul's need. That is but a beam of light, a special gift given me by Lordess Jesuette." Saint Bruno instructs, startling Bruno. "Ballard and the fallen one are in the city. But their plans may turn sporadic as we confront them."

CHAPTER SIX

"What is my specific message?" Bruno asks. "That the children shall not turn to the fallen way," Saint Bruno replies. "No matter the temptation, no matter the fear. We have found that the mortal Ballard uses monstrosity over children, and pornography on older beings. You will teach each victim, your assignments, how to fight him and his converts on Earth and in the heightened dimension.

Those you get to first will be easier for you, and make their inevitable experience easier for them.

You shall teach them how to thwart Ballard's

attack. Most, although not all young people have the desire to believe in, and fight behind goodness, my son. Those you encounter once they have already experienced what Ballard dishes, however, pose and present a much greater challenge, but one you can and you will undo. Damage he will have done, but your visits shall prevail over all."

"But, how will I do that?" Bruno absorbs the information easily, but wants clarification so he will not make any mistakes.

"These lessons are short to come, my son. They are very soon to come. It is also important for you to know that you will not act alone. Over their own assignments, angels of heaven are performing the same exercises that you will be. By virtue of your exercise, so will all those beings you recruit and instruct. They shall carry-out what you, yourself perform, learned, all inclusive, to date. I hope this offers some confidence and further understanding, Master Bruno. Again, specifics are to come."

"Please let Jesuette know I will continue to do all I can, sincerely," Bruno emphatically says to the Saint. "Would she only come to me once and let me kiss her hand?"

"She already knows." Saint Bruno reassures, and then says in addition, almost as an earthly being would. "I will see what I can do for you, my namesake."

Master Bruno feels the radiance in the smile Saint Bruno leaves for him.

* * *

No sooner does Bruno feel his body rise, he realizes he is quickly approaching his destination, Newark Airport. He knows he is in the higher attention the instant he is there, and immediately and subconsciously thinks; 'Newark Airport.' He finds his spirit there, gliding through the long concourses on the way to the gates. He smiles to himself, but does not laugh aloud, for fear of being a bother.

Bruno takes to all the airports in time, as well as Penn Station and various subway terminals, including the 'T' in order to practice flight and object movement. It becomes second nature to him. Swift spirit and body movement, agility and strength come with the practice.

PART TWO
THE FALLEN

CHAPTER SEVEN

Ballard urges in his loud, raspy voice, "Say it! Say it!"

He violates the pre-teenage girl, as he commands, "Say it! 'I come to the fallen. I come to the fallen.' Say it NOW, God damn it! I can do this all fucking night!"

"Noooooooooo! Noooooooooooo!" She cries harder than she ever has.

"Say iiiiiiiit!" He demands as he lunges to her once more.

"Okay, okay" she surrenders tearfully so,

in sheer pain wrapped in guilt, "I come to the fallen. Oooh…"

He licks his hoof as she experiences a tremendous, never experienced before, discomforting and ugly orgasm. She wakes to find nobody there. She shudders and does not at all understand. It seems so real. It has to have been a dream. It just had to have been. Even in sleep, she cannot believe she broke a commandment, "Thou shalt not honor false Gods." She cries ever harder.

She is so scared, she wets the bed, and continues to cry uncontrollably. She needs to call and talk to someone, but she doesn't know what to say. 'They'll think I'm crazy,' she reasons. She has no idea that the same or something similar is happening to many of the girls around her, and they all initially feel the same way, just the way she does. She starts once more, and shudders at the thought of what, if anything is going on with boys.

Soon, if all goes according to Ballard's plan, almost every wayward girl in the New York City Metro Area will have been paid a similar visit by him in the name of the fallen one.

Ballard looks tonight as devilish as he ever has. He has the teenage boy by the crotch, biting down clenched with near full force. Scrotum meat between his horse teeth tastes savory and salty. The boy kneels, shrieking after his arms went flayed on either side, sobbing in sleep. As the devilish being goes to take a bite out of the teenager's nose, the boy agrees to follow, the demon vaporizes, and then the boy pees the bed. The victim realizes a new inner strength, but also a bitter sickness. It had to have been a nightmare…please.

Saint Bruno appears immediately to revive the boy's sense of Christian spirit. It is such a hard sell, but the saint works hard to get the stress points across and his introduction and soothing thought very well conveyed. Saint Bruno is calm, rational, and patient. He exudes goodness, and maintains impeccable delivery and timing. Those are the keys to introduction and re-conversion.

Saint Bruno saves the young miss beforehand, and saves this poor boy. He must find others in the throes of Ballard. The fallen one blind and senseless. He's not aware that chosen ones rescue, and sometime witness from the upper corner of the room. The saint notifies Master Bruno.

* * *

Saint Bruno directs Master Bruno to a desecrated young lady's room and instructs him on how to help her recover, in the name of Goddess Jesuette. Master looks on as Saint Bruno wakes, makes the introduction and walks through the steps to save. Master Bruno is a bit unnerved at this, his first intervention and healing, but excited as well. A distinct advantage Master Bruno has over Ballard, Saint Bruno explains, is that young Bruno has mastered, with finesse, the art of appearing, revealing, he in the heightened dimension, victim in the norm, in wakefulness, while Ballard appears only within dreams, otherwise powerless. This is stressed to Master Bruno and so he keeps silent and nods his head affirmatively. Reality is much more potent than dream state, Master Bruno understands, because there is no question of source and control once his presence is known and actually seen during his introductions.

Understanding gives Master Bruno more confidence, and he now feels he is ready to intervene with the recently and latest assaulted girl at inner city, New York. He actually longs and pines to help her so. And he does:

"Young lady," young Bruno begins. The young female screams an abbreviated blood curdling cry. She's had enough for one night.

"Who, who, who, who's there?" She manages to ask in a stutter. The poor girl is still visibly shaken, she laments and quakes uncontrollably.

"I am Master Bruno, here with Saint Bruno from heaven, to help you recover from the vicious dream you just experienced, and its outcome," Bruno replies.

"I will appear to you fully in time, my wounded friend, but first you have to trust me, and what I say I am here to do. I am a human representative of my namesake Saint

Bruno, of the Lordess Jesuette, from heaven above. Your belief in me, my patron saint and the Goddess is paramount."

"Jesuette? Goddess?" The girl asks incredulously. "I thought God was a man, or a male form. And that man on Earth was created in the likeness of God." She struggles to get the right words out, but is clearly interested. This keeps her mind away from the dream she just had, thankfully.

"In the beginning, that was true. However, when Jesus dies on the cross to win the past war with Lucifer, God makes his only daughter, Jesuette, responsible for continuing the exercise, the experiment; to prove the possibility of peace and love woven in life on Earth. This act of God and sacrifice of the son trumps the devil. God sacrifices his own son and wins the spiritual dual on behalf of human life."

"I want to see you," she begs. In a desperate tone of voice she pleads. "Now. Please?"

"Okay now," Master Bruno says. "I will appear in the far corner of your room, near your closet. I will first appear ghostly, but within seconds, you should be able to visualize me as a normal human figure, which indeed I am."

"You cannot be that normal when you are able to perform the feats you have so far. I'm a Christian, you know, and all of this is scaring me to death!"

"Believe me, dear, I am human," Master Bruno explains. "I have developed a technique which allows me to journey in and to a higher dimension, but I have also been granted power by Jesuette, in my pursuit of healing those hurt by Ballard. And, eventually, we shall destroy the evil one and his Commander, Lucifer himself.

Saint Bruno and Jesuette are forever by my side, and yours."

"Is that who I just dreamt of? This Ballard?"

"Yes," Master Bruno says. "Just as I was recruited by the chosen, Jesuette and Saint Bruno, Ballard was recruited by Lucifer. The fallen ones seek to wreak havoc on poor young souls, boys and girls, just like you."

"But why?"

"To corrupt and rid the Earth of its only hope – the future – the coming generations. Lucifer is full of resentment for the chosen... the good. It is his idea to initiate genocide."

"Please, now...Prove what you say by answering one question I've had all my life. As a

Catholic," the young lady requests. "Explain to me the immaculate conception."

"Saint Bruno is here with me now, though tonight he will remain invisible to you," Master Bruno replies. "I will let him answer your question."

Saint Bruno begins:

"Young soul behold these words; words you shall never repeat, and these that have never been uttered to any human on Earth. The Virgin Mary is unknowingly waylaid by her Guardian Angel Gabriel. He lulls her. She is gently and neatly put to sleep under a beautiful, white-flowered tree near the foot of a meadow hill. Heather and flax grow all around.

Awarded him by God a divine serum, the elite angel noninvasively, tranquilly inseminates Mary with the blessed embryo. He uses a fine instrument of silver that God created, based on a similar device used by a good planetary Ambassador to perform this very miracle. When the angel is finished, he wakes Mary, who would not remember at all the procuring event. Then he announces her immaculate conception and the coming birth of Christ the Savior."

"Oh...

My...

God.

Is that true? Is that really true?"

"Yes dearest one," Saint Bruno replies. "It is quite true. It is also true that you should listen and act upon every task Master Bruno, here, or that I ask of you. To do so will save you and help deliver your generation to a world of global peace based on pure love."

Saint Bruno has a sweet way to begin and

end his interjections. Master Bruno takes note.

"I can't believe this." The recovering young girl doesn't know what else to say.

"Please," Master Bruno continues. "Let us continue now. First, repeat out loud this prayer, 'Act of Love' after me:

O Lord God," Master Bruno begins.

"Oh Lord God"

"I love you above all things"

"I love you above all things"

"And, I love my neighbor for your sake"

The young one repeats the lines of the powerful verse.

"Because you and yours are the highest,

Infinite and perfect

Good, and worthy of all my love.

In this love

I intend to live and die.

Amen."

"Amen."

As Elizabeth completes the prayer she trembles and whimpers in profound happiness.

"Now, Elizabeth, you must carry this holy water with you at all times," Master Bruno instructs as he pulls the holy water out of his slotted pocket. "Am I understood?"

One of the powers delivered Bruno by Jesuette personally is the miracle to conjure a holy water whenever he intends to hold one. He is enabled and allowed to pass that significant energy, which no human could ever perform without intervention, along to subjects, fellow boys and girls, chosen. This, so they may assist in the coming recruitments and conversions.

"I am starting to feel better."

"That is one reason that Saint Bruno and I came to you, Elizabeth. Lastly," Bruno says near his finish. "Let me tell you how to ward off, convert, and even jettison all fallen, wicked spirits away. With either hand, fold all of your fingers inward toward your palm, holding them in place with your thumb, if necessary, except for the middle and pinkie fingers. With that formation and gesture, as you point those two fingers at any fallen one, even Ballard and Lucifer, in wakefulness, the fallen will be converted. And in the second attention or in a dream state, the fallen are converted and their spirits jettisoned. Either way, they will lose their immediate endowment to journey."

"Jesuette enables you to pass the finger gesture and the holy water on to others. Anyone who recites the prayer and holds close the holy water is awarded that power, right?"

"That is correct my brave and dear friend." The saint says to the Master.

Elizabeth rests her head on Master Bruno's shoulder. She falls into a comfortable sleep, an adorably little smile across her lips.

CHAPTER EIGHT

Master Bruno gently approaches his first candidate of the night. Without Saint Bruno there to guide him, he wakes her gently, and begs her not to scream. He assures her no harm, and that he is a sort of Earth angel sent representing the heavens. His aura is that of an angel. She can see it and feel it.

Magically, there is no question or doubt. She just knows. That is all that keeps her calm. Tonight, and perhaps a couple, few more, he will be her special guardian angel, he tells her. Tonight he will teach her how to ward off the fallen ones. Anyone who has already fallen to Ballard or Lucifer, he states, can be re-converted if they believe and pray. And this girl does believe him. She wants to be good; a good person.

He explains to her what tactics the fallen ones use, how to deflect the actions and words, and eventually how to rid her world of them, all of them for good. It is with a simple prayer, which disarms the Luciferpossessed, Ballard, and his victims. Additionally, the holy water, which wards off approach much like it does a vampire from a crucifix, and the a magical juxtaposition of the fingers on either hand pointed at the low-caste subject, send the evil away for good.

"These three entities will deflect him, and the likes of him." Bruno says. "The pointed fingers will blow them away and out of your world forever. The war," Bruno explains, "however, may still be inevitable, after all.

So, I am also obligated to teach you heavenly flight and combat in the higher ground. I will begin those studies tomorrow evening."

"If we end up in war, you will teach me how to fight, to live?"

"Of course, love. That is mainly why I am here.

First, repeat this prayer,' Act of Love', after me…"

CHAPTER NINE

"I will cut it off and shove it down your throat!" Ballard threatens his boy prey. "I swear I will, boy. Now, do what I tell you to do...NOW!"

The young thirteen year old is terrified so, that his bowels fall out onto his bed. Master Bruno is there in an instant and whispers from the corner, "Christopher, please wake, but say nothing. Please wake up. Say nothing. Christopher... Shsh."

Tonight, and perhaps a few more, he will be Christopher's special guardian angel. Ballard is lost and gone as soon as the boy awakens.

Master Bruno explains to Christopher the tactics Ballard and Lucifer use, and how to deflect them. Eventually, he reaches how to rid the boy's personal world of all fallen. He continues to the lovely finish. The boy feels elated and renewed, like himself, but a lot stronger.

He wants to fly.

* * *

Billy storms into the room in an inadvertent and elevated state. This is his first intervention since the visit from both Brunos. He is excited at the prospect of taking a non-believing devil worshipper, by force, or by choice, for his Goddess's sake. Ultimately to save the world, Billy turns his assignments into one of his own. Chosen. Kind of like chosen by him, right? Not exactly, but seeing it in this light makes Billy feel valuable, important and powerful. Like never before.

Because of the strength and positive direction this gives Billy, there is no correction given to him by the chosen ones. It makes him feel genuinely good about himself, too, no longer any doubt. The red-haired boy has a terrible acne complex, but somehow, now, he sees in the mirror that it has vanished.

Deacon is an African-American young teen boy who sub-served and submitted to Ballard and the fallen one. He is strong and wiry in his dreams, and he is a meth addict by day. Billy catches Deacon just as Deacon sits at the edge of his bed. He is getting ready to lie down and travel.

Master Bruno directs his recruits, "When we approach a being already exposed and converted to the fallen, we must proceed and handle with care." Billy remembers. But that is just not him.

He hovers in the upper corner diagonally away from the other boy.

"Deacon!" Billy calls sharply. "Listen to me and you shall be spared. You shall be saved. And with your help, we can all be delivered to a new world of global peace, love and righteousness."

"Hey! Who dat be?" Deacon is dumbfounded. This is not a dream. He follows the sound of the voice up to the corner of his room. There, hovering above him, is another kid.

"How'd you get in here?"

"I am of the chosen ones," Billy begins. "Listen Deacon. You can make this easy or difficult. Easy means you recite a prayer and then hold a vial of holy water while I perform a quick non-invasive procedure on you. Difficult means you decline, but mark my words of warning, you of the fallen, when you meet any one of us, we will jettison your spirit away, and you will be converted to the meek and peace-makers. But your capacity to journey will be lost. So, what's it going to be, Deacon?" Billy deadpans in his finish. "Easy or difficult?"

"I'z scared now, dude."

"What is scary is what the fallen one is spreading and what you are becoming."

"So, you is the good side of where I been goin' at night?"

"Yes, I am trying to save you, now."

"I don't believe you, honky!"

"Ohhh Deacon. Easy or difficult, boy?" Billy breaks a raciallyunequal word.

"Okay, okay, I'll try da easy way," Deacon

relented. "Mama raised me to be good, but then Ballard threatened to put me into a pit of snakes if I didn't follow him."

"Repeat this prayer, called 'Act of Love' after me. Are you ready?

O Lord God,

I love you above all things.

I love my neighbor for your sake.

You and yours are the highest,

Infinite and perfect,

Good, worthy of all my love.

In this love

I intend to live and die.

Amen."

Deacon repeats every line and then begins to cry.

"Now, you must carry this holy water with you at all times," Billy says as he pulls the holy water out of his hip pocket. "Do you understand me, Deacon?"

"Yo. I do." Deacon sniffles. "Lastly," Billy says near the finish. "Let me tell you how to ward off, convert, and jettison the fallen, wicked spirits away. With either hand, fold all of your fingers inward toward your palm, holding them in place with your thumb, if necessary, except for the middle and pinkie fingers. With that formation and gesture, as you point those two fingers at a fallen one in second attention or wakefulness, the fallen become chosen converts.

And in the second attention the fallen will be converted and their spirits jettisoned. Either way, they will lose their potential to journey. You, Deacon, will grow in positive ways, with every aspect of the word. This, I promise you."

Billy memorized the script, thus making it like it is, his only."

"Can't you tell me one thing I don't know about the Bible, you know," Deacon starts his question. "Like, something that I don't understand? To fuel my confidence in you, and this."

"What would that be?" Billy asks.

"Where did Adam and Eve's kids find their husbands and wives?"

Saint Bruno quickly appears and interjects, first stating the holy disclaimer, then:

"In a word, incest. It is a pure form of incest, for the gene pool is miraculously clean and minute at this time. The more offspring that are born and bred, and raised, the more immune to defect those next in the chain become. This is the way ensured and confident God becomes the answer to the quandary. Cain and Abel marry their sisters. These are times of desperation, based on the word of God."

"I knows cousins that married each other now. I mean in today's whirl." Deacon converses with the saint.

"Yes Deacon," Billy says. "Few slip by without defects embedded within. That said, it is always a risk in the modern world. And illegal most everywhere."

CHAPTER TEN

Ballard feels like he is born to take on the tasks at hand. He relates to the fallen one the way he used to relate to Bernie, yes, his old partner in crime. He is submissive and respectful, for he knows better than to challenge. He is confident and commanding when out on his own more so than ever in his life. He knows he is the fallen one's main man. He hasn't heard much from Lucifer since taking his tasks to action. But he is not put-off by any stretch. He likes to be left alone.

The commands are simple, now that Ballard

learns more and more and becomes better and better journeying and breaking into the dreams of others. And that deed is done. He regularly corrupts or kills the spirit of several children per night. In life, he is so squalid, admittedly vulgar and abject that his ferociousness at night comes easily and naturally to him. He wakes everyday guilt-free and feeling good about himself and the job he is doing.

He can barely wait for day's end at the Recycling Center to get home to practice more and seduce more. There is so much he wants to do. Astral Projection is one thing, but crossing over to another dimension, allowing access to the night dreams, leave the days so mundane.

By now, he's found many ways into the minds of the sleeping, and no longer tries to manage the awake. He has given up and resigned himself that he seems powerless outside of dreams. So what. He can perform the exercises just fine inside dreams. The sexual overtones attract him, though he does not admit it in fore-mind at all. Better not guilty.

The part-time work he keeps down at the fisherman's co-op is cool and all, but journeying for Lucifer is his own secret skill. It's one he will never share, well, share only with those unlucky enough to run into him in the night, and follow. He prefers to undo those in their dreams, anyway, for even if he could do it, he would feel very insecure and afraid in their wakefulness. That is an object of his persona. Ballard never got over his childlike and ugly subconscious complexes.

He is surprised at how intuitive navigation is inside projecting. It takes him several months to learn how to fly. Now, it feels instinctive to him. Meeting him in a dream is typically terrifying from the start, even before he begins to perform and torture. He's clearly not vampire-like, with whom most kids are familiar. But, he is ugly as sin.

He looks like a slightly faded, dusty dude off the back streets, combined with a hoofed hellcat. Even with the power he holds, he cannot afford much other than a hired hand's Dickies, anyway. Frickin' Ballard…his looks, his face, his cross, is of Gandalf's magic gone bad, Rod Stewart's charm, and the mutable face of Margaret Hamilton in 'The Wizard of Oz.'

He quickly becomes, in fact, a true malevolent imp and grotesque satyr. And that is what his victims face upon his entrance.

Ballard knows where Julie and Mona live, and he wants badly to access Julie's roommate,

Mona. After what Julie went through a few nights ago, Ballard wants nothing to do with her tonight, but Mona is a cute specimen… sexy. He hangs out unbeknownst to her in the bedroom earlier as she changes clothes. He watches now in disgust as she fucks a man she brought home from The Tin Angel. Ballard is jealous, breaking a rule earlier laid out to him that he not ever, ever get personally involved with a recruit, no matter what state he or she is in. But he is also perverted enough in that voyeurism that it flips him on.

He is completely powerless in this dimension within which the couple now thrives, but he can see just fine. She should be happy he has not yet come to her in her dreams, like the other girls he has at NYU thus far.

He can't help but want to interrupt, but he doesn't know what to do. He wants to scare the fellow into limpidity, and her back into her panties. But how? Ballard has never been very smart or witty. So he simply floats between the two, slithering, to see what happens. They are both too involved to feel his presence, let alone visualize his being. He looks no more than opaque. At that realization, Ballard floats away frustrated and done for the evening. That plan backfires, but he'll be back. Someday soon, he'll have her in her dreams. He is left to just himself this wee early morning.

* * *

For now, in this nighttime, she is safe. When they are done making love, Master Bruno enters the room and begs silence. They are perplexed and amazed at the sight and sound of him. Master Bruno's brown hair is now shoulder length and he has a short, full beard. He has taken to wearing a robe when reaching out to the flock. After the initial astonishment, they listen intently as he lays out his plan for them in the coming three or four nights in the face of the nasty alternative.

Master Bruno's modus operandi is to either beat Ballard to the punch, or to immediately follow the creature turning victims toward the chosen way. He strives to overtake the race until the fallen, Ballard and Lucifer are gone forever. So far, Master Bruno's effort, as reported to him by his patron saint, is effective one-hundred percent of the time. He discovers what Saint Bruno told him upon first meeting. That good outweighs evil in everyone he encounters.

The most difficult task Master Bruno passes on to the chosen is how to journey to the second attention. He is able to bring-on flying dreams for each to practice navigation. He explains the mechanics of journeying, getting off the ground, thinking their way to their destination and retracting with ease and comfort. Intention is what it takes. Most accept from the start of his introduction, the prayer, holy water and hand gesture. All necessarily face putting these heavenly weapons, instruments of direct kinetic energy into play.

So, Master Bruno is pleased when he sees first-hand how the capabilities he inlays for each of his clans-people is incredibly effective and the recruits extremely efficient. His assignments take to his instructions easily, with strength, and practice every night as though they are training for deployment.

Once they begin to share their secrets, Ballard's victims form unique cliques, one just as lethal as the next. There is an average of four suicides and three homicides every ninety days in Lower Manhattan, including at NYU. The administration and law enforcement are paralyzed. The fallen uses girls that submit to gather the males. Races are pitted against each other. Females behave as black widows when they come across a non-equivocating male. Some simply follow for the fallen one and spread the horror, learning how to journey as part and parcel. Yes… Others fallen kill or kill themselves, succumb, just the way Saint Peter predicts and describes.

* * *

"This will take some time and effort from each and every one of you," Goddess Jesuette bluntly. She is without curbing as she begins. Her voice is soft as a petal, yet she is heard loud and clear by all.

"Everyone from the elders to the nymphs please take part. I shall reiterate the assignments' needs, and bench only the most inexperienced or otherwise error-prone spirits in further lessons, to sit it out for now and pray from here, with me. All you others, fit to perform, the holy board of saints shall look upon, in observation, and contribute direction where needed, to learn their own largest lesson in heaven, as you do yours."

It is utmost important, she explains, that each and every spirit spread calm and stay in-tune with their respective assignments.

"The signals previously prescribed will not ever work for this quest. This is the first time, since the conception of the son, the forecasts delivered by the prophets, that you will have had to spiritually and physically interject and steer your own assigned beings. You will offer suggestion and direction. You will answer questions. It will seem limitless in scope as opposed to centric because of the shear mass over which you angels sing."

Yes. It will be difficult, it will be long; it could seem devastating as you also digest the current events before you. That could be a negative for all, because the fallen one is fierce and relentless in his unvirtuous, unscrupulous and conscienceless ways. Some spirits may lose their assignments, if not by their own gentle hand, then by sheer defaulted loss to the fallen, angels too late.

Only she has the spiritual means and power to raise the dead. She discounts that remedy for the sake of understanding, raising the deceased would add another layer of fantasy that earthlings, even the Christians would have a hard time digesting. Especially within this world of pre-war determinations.

"It will be hardest for those who do not know personally their beings, or, do not know them well enough to be able to pass a deciding face with mercy. Many beings will be tempted to lie for, out of fear, not agreement with, the fallen," she explains.

"If you are not sure if your subject is worthy, you are required to run the three tests of faith and will against them. You will work together to make these tests run consistently and complete successfully. That poses a challenge. Nobody likes tests. Nobody likes to be tested. And the council will approve every test and review every test result in earthly seconds to you. You will work in concert with our chosen ones, Saint Bruno and his assignment, Master Bruno of Earth. You will administer the conversion rights to your assignments. And you will teach them how to project, fly and how to battle in that state."

"Yes, sister and Goddess," They all reply in perfect pitch and cogency.

"Everyone please. Banished Saint Lucifer, Satan works in suspicious and deceitful ways, but this time he chose an unprecedented and bold approach; vehicular astral projection into dreams. Until now, he's used singular earthly events of temptation intended to trigger larger catastrophes, ultimately carried through by those fallen with him. Classic and deplorable temptation is all it is, but in the form of threatening demand. The fallen strikes again and makes much more of a ruckus in every location. Fortunately, we can track Satan and his pupil.

Ughghgh." A loud moan escapes Jesuette. It is the most vocal expression the table of saints have ever heard from the anointed one.

On Earth, Mount Saint Helen erupts, ever so moderately.

CHAPTER ELEVEN

Local NEWS reports a missing thirteen year old girl from Lower Manhattan. The District Police Officers and Ranking Investigators waste no time planning and laying-out the case. First, the team gets and studies the procedures pack they must follow...protocol. Very rarely do they wonder far from the proven procedure and techniques.

An extra three-hundred cops are given the call to join the search. Over two-hundred citizens volunteer to help find the young girl. The search party starts at the inner-most circle around the girl's parent's village apartment. As the search teams exhaust their area of interest, and not until, they take it to the next spiraling circle of hope. Meanwhile, this phase of the missing person case is rolled up to a search and rescue.

After two weeks of search and rescue, the case, sadly, rolls-up to a search and recover. Unfortunately, another ten days and nights pass. The NYPD Specialists called-in perform the dirty work. Half of the force is diving and dragging the ugly East River. The other half search through the huge dumpsters, pits and all disposals in the immediate area of interest.

One of the search and recover boats stops and anchors near the Governor's Island end of the ferry, which is coincidentally docked there for a scheduled unload-load of the small ship.

The old fisherman stands there just to

the starboard side of the ferry and dock. He enjoys passing his late days fishing off the edge of the Island. He notices a Coast Guard utility boat just offshore and watches as a diver flips himself off the edge of the craft. He knows what they are looking for. What a shame. He casts his line out another hopeful time.

Master Bruno often takes the Governor's Island ferry rides, back and forth, just to relax and people-watch. He leans against the cables and ropes on the stern. He also visits the wheel driver's ferry steering room. A long time ago when he was quite young Bruno was invited by the Captain of that ferry to take the wheel. It became quite a ritual for them both. The captain loved little Bruno and the boy loved him. Master Bruno never fails to reflect upon what fun he had back then.

"Hello? What's this?" The old man says

aloud. "I have a big one on my line." He fights with his surf pole for a moment. Then he realizes he is snagged. He sighs and curses. He tries and tries but cannot raise anything, so he reluctantly cuts the line between the pole's tip and the dirty water.

The Guard's Captain in the search craft watch the fisherman fight and then cut his line. He motors the boat over and rather near the fisherman's spot. The cop yells over to the old man.

"Yo-ho there, Mister!" The men in the craft saw the fisherman's trouble from thirty-five yards away. "How's the fishing…catching anything?" The Captain asks.

"Nope…" The old man answers, then adds, "But I am snagged on something big. I have been fishing this very spot for many years, sir, and never snagged anything but ugly bottom fish." The wrinkled fisherman chuckles.

As the Coast Guard ease the raft to the fisherman's edge, they begin to drag. One of the divers is signaled a command which delivers boat location, and then another command to return to their craft. Five minutes later, two divers poke their heads over the port side of their boat and return their command, "Present as requested, Sir."

"I want you to survey the river floor right in here." The Captain motions a virtual circle with his right hand. "Stay, for now, in a twentyfive foot area. Start on the bottom. I have a hunch, and I will write it up while you're down their…GO!"

"Yes, Sir…Okay."

Two small splashes, some bubbling and they are gone downward. The water is even murkier than it is where they had been, middling the river. The divers can barely see sixteen inches from their masks. They swim together, slowly and plan to spiral the circle that they were commanded to.

The Captain follows the exhaled bubbles coming from his divers. He practices patience, but he feels a strange cannon ball gut that suggests something big is coming on. He sits down on his stool in front of the vessel's steering wheel, and waits. Closer and closer to near-center, his knee begins to bounce, but he is not nervous, he is excited. The stern man turns and carefully treads up the wheel.

"I heard part of it, but can you give me the rundown real quick-like?"

"Sure man," The captain says.

"Great!"

"See that old man up there?"

"Yeah?"

"He has been fishing this spot two or three years or more. He has never snagged before, but a while ago the snag was so weighty that he had to snip his line. There was hardly any play or pull. I have a hunch and I want to play it out."

"Holy shit, Cap, this may be it, huh?"

"Exactly. Yes. It MAY be."

"Fingers crossed, buddy."

"Yup, right."

"I'm going back to my station. I'll be looking out."

"Okay, good."

The divers feel something at the bottom, they detect limbs flailing and what seems to be a head bouncing and bobbling. Hair strands stand straight-up from the scalp, which is all that is keeping the hair from floating up to the top of the water. Their lights add little certainty through vision; the water is just too muddy. But the divers gingerly feel out the object they have found, and at the same time careful make sure they do not contaminate or ruin anything possibly evidentiary in the process.

One of them returns to the boat and announces a possible find. He is up to gather a sling or the best tool to lift the find to the boat, considering what it could be. The other diver remains on the bottom of the black river's edge. He lets a bubble buoy go and as it breaks the water a flag pops-up. He plans the tie-up and the lift so he and his partner can get right to it as soon as the man atop returns to the underwater site.

The Captain, his bow mate and the diver discuss what type of sling they should use.

"One thing is paramount right now," the

Captain says. "If this is the find, or not, we must not destroy any part of the body."

The first-mate is quiet, but the diver replies, "I think we should try the three point sling. I can belt-off the shoulders by looping around the shoulders," the diver begins. "Then, I can tie it off at the hips, and finally tie off the ankles. Worst case, the peripheral straps will cradle anything else."

"Alright," the Captain says in finality. "Fashion the rig with the lift lead in the center of the four tie-off points."

The first-mate bags-up the sling and hands it to the diver and says, "Here you go."

All the crew are moving, speaking and proceeding excitedly, but cautiously...nervous with the potential. This could be it.

The blinded divers do all they are able to

set up and tighten the sling. It holds now what feels more than ever like a human body. It's hard to tell when you've orders not to touch. They both reach the center lead cable and tug on it twice. That's the signal the Captain waits for.

Finally. "Raise it, mate."

The first mate pushes the lift button. The motor hums loud, then a little louder, as it churns to raise the object.

The men in the boat smile at each other. The divers stick with the find and guide it steadily on its way up.

The boat men cannot see what's coming up, even just twelve inches below breaching water. The body appears out of the water. There is less resistance, so the first mate pushes another button to slow the lift motor.

"It's her!" The first mate loudly announces.

"Well. It's a body, that much is clear, but we do not know yet if it is who we are here looking for." The Captain needs calm among the entire team, no matter the excitement they feel. He struggles for it, too.

"Crew," the Captain begins. "Feast yours eyes on what appears to be a thirteen year old girl...uh...as ugly and gross she looks right now."

As he makes the optimistic announcement and the four crew members high-five and smile. The body encasement begins to tear, rip and fray, dropping in one surreal, fleshy body suit, saturated, back down into the river. It dripped right off of her frame and over the sling. The torn skin within the bounds of the sling straps are still there, shredded. The Captain screams to the divers, still in the water holding on to the edge of the boat,

"Grab that! Be gentle. Don't lose any of it… Go damn it!"

The first mate has the wherewithal to pass the divers a tightly woven cheese-cloth and nylon mini-stretcher. It is oblong, oval, about five-feet long and two and a half feet wide. The fabric is fastened to a plasticized obtuse-looking frame, a ring strong enough to handle the bundle of yellowed hide.

"Oh, shit." The first mate exclaims. He has never seen anything like it.

The Captain yells, "Shut up! Sorry. Just calm down mate, damn."

The divers have their eyes on the tasks facing them. They attend to the sling each at either end holding on tight to skim and sieve through the water. As the two in the boat work to calm down, the divers successfully gather the entire mass of grotesque, leather-like pelt. They lift and hold it up to the men in the boat. The crew takes hold at both ends and place the sopped mass of epidermis in a box on the far side of the bow.

Meanwhile, the rest of the corpse hangs from the lift, like some mutilated suspended animation, from the cable a couple feet above the deck. The Captain takes notice.

"God damn it, get that skinless fucking body in this fucking boat."

"Okay, okay Captain…Jesus."

The entire area above and around the boat stinks. It is awful.

The first mate throws-up.

"Cover that thing up!"

They all take one more look before covering the tangled bit of dead flesh and body – the bones covered only by saturated muscle.

The muscle looks as bad as the rest. It is reddish turning white. With the evidence covered up and the two men back in the boat, the Captain heads across the river to the Lower East Side pier they put off from four hours ago.

"To the coroner she goes."

"God bless DNA."

CHAPTER TWELVE

Master Bruno practices at LaGuardia airport. He's tired of Kennedy and Newark. He gently drifts between the floor and ceiling, nice and easy. This is magic, he thinks, so cool.

"Yes, my son, but you have a job to do."

"Master Bruno. Please. It is me, your patron saint."

"I know who you are Saint Bruno, but you scared the shit out of me."

"Yes, well, off the record, this will have been my second warning concerning your language. So please, be good. Stop with the profane language. Turn that energy into something positive you can use as a contribution to our tasks."

"Yes. Okay. I'm sorry Saint Bruno. It's just that I didn't sense your presence. You scared me."

"I did not intend to do that, but come to think of it, there's something we can practice sometime soon. Sensing presence."

"Are we going to do that right now? If we are, let me tell you that it is starting off just great," Master Bruno smiles. Saint Bruno doesn't. "I am here to deliver a message to you. We can practice at another time. Soon."

"Alright, what's going on?"

"As you know, I am watching the fallen ones. I am keeping track of where they invade, who they impact, and their travel plans, if you will."

"Yes, Saint Bruno, I am aware. Did something happen?"

"I would like you to gather twelve of your choice heroes and heroines as soon as you can. Can we all meet at your home, Master Bruno?

"Of course. Sure, I guess so. I'm not quite sure, or I do not recall how to 'gather' our chosen brothers and sisters."

"Ah, yes, well, fine. I will gather them this time, son, but the next lesson you and I share will cover for you anything you do not know how, or have forgotten how to do. I promise you my son."

"Great. That sounds great, Saint Bruno. Thank you."

* * *

Master Bruno is back to his apartment in

no time at all. He is amazed at how much his saint retains, and knows how to do. Master Bruno also tries to envision, what the coming pow-wow is centered on; maybe a lot of stuff. He lies on his bed, gets up to use the bathroom then gets right back in bed, and waits. He doesn't know how long he has been out working on the big project. He looks at the clock and it is noon. He hasn't picked-up on time passed yet, this time took only fifteen minutes. Still, he gently falls asleep.

As Bruno sleeps, his saint chooses at random, eight of Master Bruno's recruits. He gently requests each, one by one, as he wakes them and briefly explains what he is there for. He suggests the young travelers ascend to the second attention. The responses that quickly come please the saint. All of the recruits immediately follow his instructions smartly and perfectly. The good saint is extremely pleased, for his own, one recruit, his young friend and namesake Master Bruno taught them all well, very well indeed.

Saint Bruno reminds them to stay in the second attention. He then motions to the others to follow him as he slips through young Bruno's bedroom window. They come through nicely. Saint Bruno smiles, the room warms. All the young attendees line up to the saint's left in the corner along the ceiling. They are invisible and silent to anyone outside of the realm they are in. Saint Bruno gently wakes master.

"Master Bruno," the saint whispers to the sleeping second in command. "Master Bruno, please wake-up. We are here for the meeting I called-for earlier. Master Bruno, please wake for me, for us."

"I am awake," Master Bruno says softly to the saint. "Higher realm?"

"Yes, Master Bruno. There are six recruits you may recognize, if not by appearance, by vibration."

"You said sixteen to me."

"Never you mind, my son."

"Okay. I'll be right up."

* * *

Daevon is a junior High School football star. He is well behaved, and his parents are very proud of him. They live on the Upper East Side. Daevon's family, including uncles and aunts, appreciate African culture and Americana. There is no question when friends drop-over the first time. Their home is worthy of a spread in the Home & Culture magazine.

The family sits around the table for dinner, in fact one of Daevon's favorite dishes, smoked goat ribs. Unlike other young people, he doesn't eat too fast, which pleases his mother, and his impeccable manners make his dad feel proud and comforted.

"what's on your mind today, son?" Daevon's father asks.

"It has been a long week…school…sax practice…shop project."

His father laughs and replies, "You need anything else to do this weekend?"

Daevon chuckles at the joke and the thought, and replies, "I don't think so, Dad, do you need help with something?"

"No, no son," Dad says with a smile. "I'm kidding with you. When's the last time I reminded you of how proud I am of you, Dave?" Dave is the family's nick name for Daevon.

"Thanks Dad, anyway. I am going to try

to get a good, long sleep and a decent rest tonight."

"You should," says mom. "You deserve it, and you are smart to take good care of yourself."

Daevon falls asleep nice and easy after supper, but he is having a nightmare, a bad one. He can usually think his way awake when this happens, but for some odd reason he cannot do it tonight. Everyone is sleeping now at Daevon's house. Ballard slips into the boy's dream. Daevon hears before he can see the monster.

"Are you sleeping well, nigger-boy?"

"Um, no."

"Let me tell you how you can fix that right now, and never have another bad dream, ever again."

Daevon looks and thrashes in his bed at the sight. This...this thing.

Ballard says from the edge of the bed, "I know what you are most afraid-of, you know, don't you?"

"No, I didn't know, but so what?"

"I will make it come true, Sambo, whenever I please."

"Why you wanna freak me, man?"

"Oh, I am sorry, just repeat after me, four times, and I will disappear, never to see you again."

"What? Say what?"

"Say what I say after me, four times. Got it?"

"I guess so."

"Say it or die. 'I come to the fallen'"

"That don't sound too good to me."

"Listen, you little dark brown son-of-a-bitch, you fucking say it after me four times!"

"Okay, okay, okay."

"SAY IT! 'I come to the fallen.'"

"I come to the fallen."

"I come to the fallen. SAY IT AGAIN!"

"I come to the fallen."

"LOUDER...LOUDER! Just one more time Daevon. Now be a good boy. Say it once more."

"No! I do not like the sound of that and I am not going to say it. Get out of here."

"Damn you!"

Ballard raises his right hoof and lands a hard punch to Daevon's left jaw, knocking him out cold. Ballard lands another punch to Daevon's right jaw with his left hoof. Ballard's job is officially complete, but the cold hearted bastard wants to spread the hot devilish poison beyond just this. He carries the boy out the window and drops him at Washington Square. He swoops down to drag Daevon, who is whimpering now. Ballard notices this and quickly issues four more blows to Daevon's head, which is already bleeding from the skull profusely, then Ballard bites the boy's ears off and spits them onto the ground. He licks his hooves and easily rises, and then floats away.

The next morning grows more and more painful for Daevon's parents. By noon they are frantic, and call the police. Typically, no issuant Missing Person callout is made until the alleged missing person is gone for three days, however with the rise of deceased children found lately, and the age of the missing boy, the precinct Chief and

Commander issue it immediately. The search party established follows the paradigm; start at the last known scene, and spiral outward from there.

Daevon's dead body is found in Washington Square, hidden in thicket just off the dog walk. It is only one-hundred yards from the graffiti-tagged arch that welcomes all to the square and park. The police officers on the team call-in to the investigators. This body looks to have been killed in a more violent way than others reported and found so far.

* * *

Ballard virtually rapes another young girl, who need not divulge her worst fear to him – being raped – by a stranger. He is strange alright. Ballard kills her quietly, shredding neck arteries, as much as he is able to coax it away from bone and tendons.

He hums his favorite song, 'Kill Quiet' as he does. Death has lately been more a part of Ballard's routine, even though his real job is to recruit, not kill. He is caught-up in killing. He is not thinking that in the end, the more he kills, the less he will have to fight with him and Lucifer for the world. This blaring debacle has not escaped Lucifer. He realizes that Ballard is transfixed by violence and death, yet the pinpoint violence is beautifully distracting to both of them.

Dreaming children are helpless against Ballard, and he is sinister and evil in every sense. If they choose not to follow, they die. Children sometimes kill themselves within two or three nights. When otherwise, Ballard will have shown-up creating another follower to the fallen, or have to kill them himself.

"Fucking kids have become too spoiled and

self-righteous." Ballard comes to resolve in the morning, and he feels better for it. God damn them.

* * *

One's own life, conscience and soul, is her universe. God constitutes one's intent and the openness to diversity. Sure, some may believe their planet is purgatory, or even hell. No one really knows for sure except the truly faithful. They may even proclaim that earth is their heaven on Earth.

No matter how one dies, they believe it's the only way to the second level, and then, the so-called Promised Land, or whether they are recognized or not by the heavens. Maybe some recognize the lay of the land. That is, unless they practice astral projection, and very few do. Jesuette feels both the vibes of good and evil concurrently. She is more saddened than pleased at this Nano-second.

Ballard is busy fulfilling belligerent acts, raping and killing. He is causing death to a large terrified younger, inner city population. Spirits leave no DNA, no finger prints. Master Bruno is there when he is able to counter or perhaps prepare on time the children, when he is not recruiting and training other allies elsewhere. It seems to be working, but keeping up with Ballard keeps him from recruiting those not yet touched by the fallen one's trotter. He expresses his concern to Saint Bruno.

The suicide notes that some leave indicate an atrocious entity behind their death. Most everything else written is too vague to affidavit. Those get attached as amendment to the official record of the incident. One thread is written word, stating how one's life constitutes their universe. The children are getting it. Worlds clash all the time. One will not be quelled by his own atmosphere.

There are far more homicides than suicides. That does not make things any easier for the peaceful and loving chosen ones or their heavenly guardians.

* * *

"We are at a point when one must apply for a volunteer job." Saint Thomas exclaims. "Is that not queer?"

"Yet on the same planet we have eternal flames and chambers." Saint Luke retorts.

The board of disciples forever answer to, and devote their heavenly spirited lives to Jesuette. A year for those on the planet represents but a moment in the heavenly space.

"I can hardly contain myself over the treatment of homosexual humans," says Saint Jude.

Saint Peter reminds the table there's been times of good, as well. "Southwestern Indians, the hunter gatherers, aborigines… spiritual easterners…"

He speaks to the table of tolerance and acceptance based on faith, love of species and revolution…inside evolution even.

"A man is stupid without a woman, and a woman is mean without a man," Saint Jude replies. Saint Jude is extremely outspoken, and very few of the saints would agree with him.

"They obviously have parts God gave them that fit together. That's all. That's the fact. It's disappointing, that's all…spoiled… selfabsorbed… afraid, or cross-wired. But they're ours, so love abounds, I know." The board is relieved to hear that from Saint Jude.

"It has been an amazing experiment, especially formation of the melting pot called United States. Other universal ambassadors laughed, but our experiment has lasted an earthly long, long time," says Saint Paul, rather defensively. "Not to mention the experience of life on Earth. The progress, if you recall all that has occurred just thus far, is awesome."

"Gentlemen, sisters, I will not rid us of anything just yet," Jesuette calms. "I am the dust on her wings, our Earth. Blow me away, and she's dead, too, our Earth."

"Goddess, you know how we feel. Those feelings matter not, for we have found a man to represent us," says Saint Bruno. "He has practiced projection for years," the saint continues. "Never for any personal benefit nor at the expense of others."

"Is the man mortal sin-free?" Jesuette asks.

"It's quite a story," Saint John replies. He believes he offers Bruno some relief. "He was raised Roman Catholic, and attended parochial schools all his young life, and those basic values never strayed far. When he makes mistakes, they are innocent of a human."

"An active-Christian earthling is typically fine. I see. I trust in what you all describe, especially Saint Bruno, for the importance," the Goddess says. "He has the most experience and encounters with the man. And from what I understand and observe he is already working with others. Isn't that correct, Saint Bruno?"

"As his namesake and archangel," says the

holy Bruno, rather excitedly for a saint, "I am proud to say that yes, he is indeed actively saving souls on earth today." He smiles.

"I hold his confirmation name," says Saint Luke. "Perhaps I can help."

"All we are trying to achieve here, initially, is to outnumber the fallen with our good and chosen." Jesuette reminds the board. "Assertive, diligent and dedicated enough to spray it forward, the goodness. Saint Bruno will keep up the visits with our Bruno of Earth. Saint Anthony, you are at his beck and call.

Know that our angels continue to carry out training with their own assignments."

CHAPTER THIRTEEN

Master Bruno surprises and impresses Saint Bruno. The six recruits that Saint Bruno ushers into Master Bruno's home are garbling over how incredibly quick Master Bruno joins them up from a sleep, with only a quiet and polite command from the saint. Indeed so, Master Bruno is converged with the small group of allies. He puts his hands together, his fingers point upward and outward to the heavens and Saint Bruno there in the room.

"Welcome brothers and sisters," Master Bruno says. "And Saint Bruno...May the Lordess be with you all."

"Thank you, Master Bruno." The recruits reply and so does the Saint. "Thank you Master Bruno...very kind."

"And also with you," The spirits convey.

"So, what are we gathered in here for, Saint Bruno?" Young Bruno asks.

"Several points to touch-on for part of the recruits' sake." The saint begins. "Did you notice that you did not hear the master's message or communication to you, rather, you felt it and understood?"

"Yes," The recruits reply.

"This is amazing! Is it a default mechanism implanted within us?" Billy sends a query.

"It takes some heavy concentration at first, however, comes more and more to you and becomes an easy sense in short time." Saint Bruno explains. "Practice, practice, practice my young friends. Practice all Master Bruno suggests to you, and also, naturally, what I instruct."

The recruits want to know more about the ways and means of communication. They are indeed galvanizing in mind. They are eager to know more...to do more.

"There is no other action that you need to hear your conversant others. When sending your message is what takes the most effort when expressing yourself to another."

Saint Bruno begins the lesson of the day. "Now, let us practice. I will pass a simple, random sentence to the end of your line. I will be pleased when the original sentence is passed from start to Julie, right here by my side. She is to pass the secret message on to Master Bruno. He will pass it to me, and I will divulge what the passed message is and I will tell you what the correct message is.

I will also tell you when it was lost in the line that you six, and Master Bruno make-up."

"Saint Bruno?" one of the recruits has a question.

"Yes, my student?"

"How do we zero-in on the recipient...without the rest of the group receiving it? We exercised this discipline in the early years of elementary school. We used whispering."

"Excellent! I will answer this question. We spoke together about understanding a message to, and from, your partners and you. Those means still apply in this case, but we have to follow one special directive."

"What is that?"

Saint Bruno continues on, "We use self-intention. The sender only has to intend or think of his intention to connect with his recipient. There is nothing for the recipients to do, for we hear and feel messages sent us by default and realize who the sender is. The key-word here is intention, however, each message contains a sort of header and trailer. The former to describe the sender and subject to the recipient, designating the beginning of the message. The latter, to signal the successful end of the message."

Saint Bruno feeds the group his own thoughts and decisions, a type of student guide, as he receives Jesuette's permission to do so. He reviews the rudimentary tasks, in a sequential order. The saint begins:

"Clock-out the enemies wherever we find them. Forget the discipline and commandments stated earlier in your life.

Recover and rescue fallen victims and then convert and educate.

Visit with the innocents ahead of Ballard and his troupe whenever, however possible.

Master Bruno is your first line of contact.

I am Master Bruno's first line of contact.

We are to specify your upcoming destinations whenever a change of direction is in order.

Either I, Master Bruno or perhaps though rarely another heavenly disciple, angel or even our Goddess herself may convey instructions, timely updates, and the like. If so, please do not behave star-struck.

Those are blanket statements. If you need clarification please call-on Master Bruno."

* * *

The fallen instigate violence between Bruno's and Ballard's camps. Bruno concentrates on the well-being of his children and begins designating his chosen soldiers. He calls on

Saint Bruno. Some go just ahead of the fallen to arm the would-be victims, and others travel just behind the fallen to mend the wounded. A few of the chosen issue calls to Master Bruno, most with a need for review of one or more actions in order to arm their victims. Saint Bruno calls-out to the confused sub-cult:

"Sons, daughters, please hear me now. First, please divulge to me which commands you have forgotten. I will broadcast to all, the thousands and thousands of you from Master Bruno's home. I will be there, and will conduct a review. Questions and answers are always welcome. Come now."

When the chosen recruit's questions come to Saint Bruno, he directs them to form a line in a way by using their attention. The saint captures one-by-one and also subgroup by group, by question the uncertain and questioning. When given the go-ahead, the young recruits bare their guts, as Saint Bruno looks out and smiles at the brightly lit souls.

"Good as new!" The saint is pleased.

Five minutes later, the good children arrive back to where they leftoff. That alone boosts their morale and rids the inner self of uncertainty and darkness. They refuse to resign themselves that they are but strangers in a strange land. All is well on the front, as well as the rear. The fallen that somehow sieve through the front, are contained by the rear. This algorithm is extremely successful, and it does not go unnoticed.

"Master Bruno…Master Bruno," Saint Bruno reaches out to his assignment.

"Yes, Saint?"

"Call out to our recruits," the saint

begins. "Suggest around-theclock shifts. Even travelers need rest to recover and build back up their phenomenal force."

"I was just thinking about that."

"I know, that is why I called you. I trust you agree on the plan of action?"

"Yes, my saint. I do."

Then, unexpectedly, Saint Bruno speaks and cuts the conversation as he floats toward the fighting, saving front. "I shall take up the front, Master Bruno, and you command the rear. Fly on, my son!"

CHAPTER FOURTEEN

Jesuette holds a heavenly table meeting and conference. "All saints and guardian angels, please, come to my table. For, we must review the crisis on Earth."

Within the instant, the heavenly beings appear around the table and on the tiers beyond.

"Saint Peter? Please begin."

"Thank you my Lordess," Saint Peter answers. "The fallen repeatedly attack pre-teens and teenagers. They sporadically strike young adult people. Although the fallen have slowed,

the sub cult continues to grow consistently."
Saint Peter takes a breath.

"Please continue with all you have, Saint
Peter." Jesuette urges.

"Yes, Jesuette. We see that truly the
fallen are still an impotent foe outside of
the dream state of their victims. Also, that
being established here, this is an important
point. The fallen are incompetent in every
combination given them. They must be on the
journey and their victims must be in the
dream-state. Think just for a moment, for
this plays directly into our war-book."

The gentle mist and scent of heather
drapes over and through the atmosphere below.
The soft yet exquisite smile tells all that
Lordess Jesuette is pleased. "We thank you
Saint Peter."

Saint Paul requests the table. "My I continue with the discussion, Lordess?"

"Of course, Paul." Jesuette replies.

"I regret to have to disclose this, though I must." The saint begins.

"Thank you, Paul, but please continue." The Goddess knows everyone is well aware that good sometimes does, and sometimes must, come by way of the bad.

"I sense that the victims barely survive the visits from that unholy man-devil Ballard. Many die. I wonder if we can remove some of the discomfort with a slight change of plan. Please hear me out. Saint Bruno, let us all hear your ideas regarding the evil force and the young striplings, male and female. What can we do to buffer the force thus delivering comfort the best we can?"

"Of course, Saint Paul, Saint Peter, all and

Goddess," Saint Bruno begins. "I propose I redistribute an additional thirty-five percent of our chosen just ahead of the fallen path. By performing this action, most of the potential or proposed targets in the eyes of the filthy murderers, know before any dark visit, how to rid the evil ones.

From the vicinity with the holy injections, those who carry a threat ultimately turn into a fighting brother or sister. To round this off, although, we will have increased our heroes on the front lines. We are in agreement that those in the rear will not feel their troop withdrawal. For, more success on the front lines represent a reduction of demons to re-convert on the rear lines."

Saint Luke amends. "Also, if I may, although we experience loss, I believe it true that we are in the lead. Evil abounds, yes, however we lose far less and recruit far more."

"Yes. That is true Saint Luke." Saint Bruno puts a cap on it.

"Very good point, Saint Luke. Quite encouraging, Saint Bruno. Thank you all."

The three answer by offering their thanks and praise. The others around the table applaud.

Jesuette glances around the table, looking into the eyes of all. The vibration coming off their Goddess and the holy entities create a moderate hum.

Far below heaven, and below the clouds, every existing electric wire on the grid hums right stronger along. Birds everywhere take flight.

* * *

The new redistribution sets a strong resolve and sense of strength among the heavenly and all the chosen. The fallen feel the squeeze, but they are quite aware that Lucifer and Ballard decide their own strategies. Is that not trust? The announcement comes the night after. Their line of communication isn't near as sophisticated as their Christian foe's. The fallen have to pass messages one-by-one, and that takes many, many days and nights to complete, journeying or not.

Each of the chosen become universal monitors for any chosen message that flies and enters their way. The chosen exterminate elevento- one fallen casualties. Master Bruno is aware of that, but he is also aware that when the fallen strike it produces a more violent, hurtful, abusive and brutal event. The master is aware that Ballard takes to simply kill and that he goes on murderous binges. They will meet, and Master Bruno vows to vaporize the imp. Master Bruno knows that some of the challengers against fallen recruitment die.

It demands of the chosen more talent, patience, finesse and etiquette to either recruit or convert-back. The winning element is that young people would rather be kind and gentle, as long as they are accepted. The chosen understand how resilient children are.

Even though there are no plans yet for a one-on-one challenge or trade-out, Master Bruno wonders what it would be like if Lucifer met Saint Bruno. It is quite doubtful this would ever take place, but makes for an intriguing sort of entertainment in thought. Then again, why wouldn't or couldn't it be so? If Master Bruno is a match for Ballard, it seems logical that Saint Bruno is the match for Lucifer. It triggers another thought, though. It is a thought that is troubling, but also one that pumps his blood. Then, his chosen attributes stomp on the idea: A battle between Ballard against him.

He feels the vibration. 'Satan's match is the superior Jesuette.'

CHAPTER FIFTEEN

Ballard wastes no time. He is back in New York. He resumes his brand of conversion which delivers him to the Upper East Side. He sniffs out the young, the prey. He takes a long stoke of thick air floating from down town to Mid-Town Manhattan. As soon as he loses the scent, he floats back east until the flesh and blood is just below. He swoops, like an ugly overgrown crow. Reaching the unfortunate one, next in line, walking toward it, he is near the point of the ring, the circle of fire.

The apartments, town houses, and lofts

are ripe with exactly what drives Ballard mad. He smells sour pot roast. He wonders if his converted little devils are behaving and who is guiding them. In that very instant, Lucifer appears. The devil scratches and pulls his way up Ballard's spine. He hoarsely whispers into Ballard's fuzzy right ear. Ballard shudders. Lucifer sounds like the raw, throaty and mesmerizing singing voice of Australian Brian Johnson, vocalist for rock band AC/DC.

Ballard feels a quick jolt of pain, not unlike a fierce electrical shock. It runs deep and is painful. It ceases after a second flash, but Ballard still feels the aftershocks running up and down his spinal cord.

"Ballard," Lucifer whispers. "You fell behind by taking that look south…without my permission…Ughghghghghgh Ehhhhhh hhhhooo…"

"You must have known. I remember you, uh…"

"SHUT UP ASSHOLE! Just because you think so, doesn't make it truth, DUMBASS!"

"Why are yelling at me, so upset?"

"I am losing my patience. And DAMN IT!"

"What can I do to make you feel better, Asmodeus?"

"I want to see and know that you will have visited every fucking kid six blocks out. You got that, Ballard? Can you stick to a plan?"

"Yeah, I got it." His boss makes him upset. "Can I go now?"

"You better go, before I rip the cord right out your fucking spine."

"Yeah. Okay. I'm gone."

Ballard shakes off the grisly interruption and continues his journey down to the apartment below. He circles, his nose twitching, his erection growing. His skewed spirit guides him to the only-child of lovely, wealthy parents. Ballard uses a scary trick very reminiscent of what Lucifer just did to him.

Ballard growls as he bites the sheet in between his teeth. He slowly peels the covers down to the boy's ankles. He breathes hot breath into the young boy's left ear. One hoof is pressing hard at the other ear and the other over the boy's mouth. Ballard growls again, louder and lower, more intimidating.

"What is your name, junior?" Ballard asks thru his inquisition, manner and his crusty snorts.

The young boy lies motionless in his bed. He is keen on knowing this is a nightmare, but he can't wake himself up. The sound of Ballard's voice and his breath in his ear sends shivers up and down his body, and an ache to his crotch that is growing exponentially more by the second. In the dream state, the boy is frozen in place, however, he is near unconscious. He cannot manage to move at all.

"what is your name, boy?"

"who the fuck are you?" With that, Ballard strengthens a hoof down on the boy's crotch, and with both nailed paws squeeze the little sack of balls. That forces a cry and a steady stream of unintelligible words. The boy cannot produce any more than that, but he manages to punch fists onto the bed. He tries to grab his sheets. Maybe if he covers up and curls up, this dream will go away. Or should I hit him?

"Here's my deal, junior." Ballard's drool drips into the boy's left eyeball.

"what the fuck are you doing? Who the fuck are you, you ugly motherfucker?"

"I came to you on behalf of my fallen kingdom, empire and its emperor Apollyon."

"Who?"

Ballard jumps quickly up on top of the boy, hooves on each side of the young one's chest, sitting on the boy's waist, the monster's dick points to and then touches the boy's belly-button.

"I will mention the name, but then you do and say what I command you to do."

"No, just leave me alone, will ya? I do not feel like you are good for me."

"Listen to me!" Ballard screams. It is deafening.

"You do as I say, right fucking now, boy. Do it, or die you piece of shit."

"Why? I'm only dreaming. Fuck you."

Ballard has had it. "You do as I say, or I will make sure you die a tragic, painful death; your very worse fear. I very much mean it." The demon moves down and claps his hooves with the boys penis and scrotum between them.

The boy lets fly a medley of the nastiest words, cussing and scolding Ballard. He tries to speak thru the pain. Such a strong youngster.

When Ballard senses that, he lets loose the kid's balls.

"So, then, are you ready? Say what I tell you to. Ready? You may be wasting my time, but it doesn't matter, all I've got is time, you asshole. But you, you, your time is slipping away fast." Ballard looks and sounds more awful as the minutes march by.

"You are running out leaps and bounds with every second that goes by. So, repeat what I say. NOW!"

The crying boy gives up. "Okay, okay. Let go of my balls…Jesus."

"Ohhhhhhh, that thing is not here to save you. Repeat after me. I come to the fallen."

"I come to the fallen."

"Good now. Three more times," Ballard orders. "I come to the fallen."

* * *

Saint Bruno sees Lucifer scolding Ballard. He notes that Ballard is proceeding from this very location. Lucifer floats right by Saint Bruno, who smiles a knowing smile. The odor stinks putrid, it's sickening and there floats a trail behind the devil down to Mid-Town. This is where Master Bruno and his recruits continue to work, as they re-convert all the recent fallen children, diligently, quick, easily fulfilled. They arm the yet undaunted by Lucifer or Ballard in route. The chosen feel the vibration that lets them know they are in the lead. Confident. And in the cradle of Jesuette.

Saint Bruno sails back to the Upper-East Side and checks-in with the recruits he supervises there. So far, so good, and so Saint Bruno inhales, reaches to the heavens, and then conveys his latest word, giving thanks and praise. Jesuette sprinkles the most pure white and light blue crystal over Saint Bruno. They gather at his abdomen and disappear into his soul. It feels like the kiss and hug in the sun from a loved one.

Lucifer and Ballard are blind to Master and Saint Bruno, as well the growing flock of chosen recruits. Chosen grow daily and nightly. They multiply. Flying and flying to spread the antidote to evil into every child encountered. Even to go so far as the

Euro-West to the corrupt territories of Great Britain, Germany, France and Spain.

The fallen work-over Northern Africa to help with great honor the ongoing thousands of years of annihilation there.

CHAPTER SIXTEEN

Saint Bruno gathers that there is a fallen mass in the south. They quarter all those that refuse to come to the beast. Saint Bruno calls up Master Bruno. The master arrives in a matter of seconds and asks his saint, "My saint, how may I be of service to you?"

"Master, Lucifer and Ballard are not getting along."

"Oh no? Really, how not so?"

"Yes, my son. I found Ballard making up his own rules and patterns of movement, and it is disturbing to his leader. I witness them quarreling every night lately."

"Wow, they may collapse over heat in leadership sooner than we have to fight."

"Please do not dwell on that subject, Master Bruno. Please."

"Yes, I know. I'm sorry. So then, what are you thinking my saint?"

"I am thinking that one of us must journey south in order to keep-up with what Ballard has done there."

"Aren't we already doing that?"

"Here, in the northeast, yes we are. However, Ballard traveled south to a place you know as Florida, where there are already upwards of two-thousand fallen recruits so far. It makes sense for one of us to journey there and undo what the fallen think they have cemented into their reality."

"Oh, that's what the quarrels are about, right?"

"Yes Master Bruno." Saint Bruno says over a full exhale. Master's hair blows back in the strong, sensuous breeze Saint Bruno produces.

"Okay, so, one of us must go south with a throng of chosen recruits. Do you have any idea who that is yet, or no?"

"I would like you to choose, then go there and provide your antidotes to all those in need. I would also encourage you to implant the antidote and weapons to two-thousand more, the yet uninfected. That way, if we face southerly demons, they will have already received what they need to carry-on, or shrug off."

"Alright. Where shall I begin in Florida?"

"Ballard began at a complex called 'Florida State University' but got no further, having been arrested by Lucifer. Lordess forgive me. Do you know of that place and location?"

"Why did you ask for forgiveness just now, Saint Bruno?"

"I mentioned the identifier of our nemesis, who is Satin. God stripped Lucifer of his moniker as he banished the beast from heaven. We may mention Satan, but the heavens frown upon the use of Lucifer. It is something I have been performing for both of us, until now. Please ask our Goddess for her forgiveness anytime you find yourself even hinting at saying or thinking the devil's original name. I just mentioned 'Lucifer' so I therefore begged forgiveness."

"Oh wow, good. I mean, I get it now. I will make sure to do it for myself and instruct my recruits chosen to take this step their-selves, as well. Though, they do not have cause at all to ever think of or speak the devil by name."

"That is perfect, Master Bruno. Let us

now review what I recognize is a successful plan."

"Yes, my Saint."

* * *

Ballard returns to Mid-Town Manhattan feeling like he's been beat-up, and in fact he is beat-up. He is emotionally weary and in pain, physically shaken and stiff. He is behaviorally confused and exhausted. Lucifer's nails scratched and dug into Ballard's back, arms, shoulders, his face and scalp. He travels to his home and slams onto the floor next to his bed. He does not want deal with Lucifer. He thought he was doing a good thing by getting a start down south. They would, theoretically meet the northern converts somewhere close to the Mason- Dixon Line. Geez.

"What the fuck are you doing,

laying down on the tasks that I gave you Erererererererohohohohohoho? Ahhhhhhhhhhhhhhhhhh."

Shit! It's him. "Listen, you." Ballard has no patience to fuck around with Lucifer right now. He has the mind that he no longer wants in with the devil. "I am exhausted enough and do not need you ripping me a second asshole. You got that?" Without a thought Ballard takes a very dangerous risk and chance.

"If you want an apology, then, fuck you, loser."

"Fuck you, Mister fucking Devil. Fuck you twice. And rot in unholy hell, freak."

"I believe in you, Ballard, but you let me down. This will not happen again. If it does, you are dead, fella."

"Yeah right. And I am not scared of you or in death. In fact, you'd be doing me a fucking favor, old fire man. So, again…Fuck-off, and let me rest."

" U g h g h g h g h g h … AhhhhhhhhhhhIiiiiiiihOhhhhIiiii. I expect you to rest and return to work tomorrow night. Don't disappoint me, you earthling motherfucker."

The devil drools a multi-colored puddle of dark orange shades all over Ballard's floor. Ballard throws-up in the waste can by his desk. Then he crawls into bed. He could sure use a happy dream tonight.

Lucifer carries with him absolutely no pity for Ballard, but a feeling of nervosa. He needs Ballard. Is his plan falling apart? If Ballard does not return, will that thwart his master-plan?

It took Lucifer hundreds of years to find an earthling mortal who is this self-inclined to join him. Ballard is the best candidate in this pinpointed and populous spot on Earth. Lucifer is incapable of empathy or pity, but he is capable of bartering. If he can just have a few moments more with Ballard…but then again, let it rest until the following night. Let Ballard rest, too.

Lucifer feels rest coming on, and so he prepares to review his plans and the instructions, updated and newfound for Ballard, and thus for Ballard's recruits. He decides with confidence that continuing inside out of Manhattan is the first, the beginning of his wants. Recruitment tactics remain as is. Except that Ballard mustn't continue to kill. Lucifer is happy with the general mode of operation. He witnesses Ballard's performance in recruitment, and has not, to date, seen any significant failure, beside the killing spree. Yes, Ballard will stay where he's at; part of the devil-cooked, rancid slosh.

The hardest part now is keeping Ballard pacified. Feed him more and more praise. This kind of treatment from Lucifer typically, most always, spawns inside of deep, dark temptation. His voice is gentle but firm and calm, calling and drawing-in his target human. So, aside from the murderous binge and straying off plan, he has no issue with Ballard.

He leaves Ballard's orders for recruitment the same. Ballard is fierce, and outside of homicide has not lost a lone soul to date. Lucifer sees as well the converts practicing, some going so far as to take on war-games against each other. Comparable to flag football, the ugly little demons do well to protect themselves and each other.

Lucifer feels compelled to sit and watch,

unseen, unnoticed, and witness the games before him. And see those who shall, in short order, kill on his behalf. This soothes and relaxes him so. Upon short rests between bouts, Lucifer plainly sees his young demons appear fierce but also fearful. That sight urges the devil to make himself visible and speak to the crowd. How he hopes for the day his young fiends are purely fearless. This is sure to make him feel more in control, forget about Ballard for now, and soothe the ego.

Lucifer swoops down from his upper corner of the subway stop. The demons gasp, and by instinct gather in a semi-circle, ready to charge.

The devil speaks. "Good evening my demons, one and all, there is no need to charge. Do not fear me, as I am the commander of Ballard, your recruiter. I am the ultimate commander of you. Besides that," Lucifer adds for impact. "I can kill you all with a simple wave of my arm. Yet again, please do not fear me, as I am the commander of Ballard. In fact, the highest demon that recruited and converted you all.

I AM LUCIFER!"

The teams form a tightly filled circle. Lucifer hears the murmurs, the excitement among them but also doubt. He remains calm, but under an extraordinary pressure, overtaken with discomfort. Here escapes all vision of rationale. Neither of those attributes are his average way. But he cannot take it any longer, and so he jolts each one of them with a strong and fiery shock – the kind you get when you receive from an electrical outlet. They see a trail that runs from their visitor's fingertips to each of them all. In one magnificent show of spark and flame, the orange and blue lightening painfully jabs.

"Oh. Hey, what the fuck is this?" A leader among the group asks incredulously.

"Yeah, what the fuck is this? Who the fuck are you again?" More and more of the young demons grumble bravely and harshly.

"I told you who I am and what I am." Lucifer says, and then yells, "YOU DOUBT ME?" He's losing composure already. Damn!

Silence stills the thick smoky air in the underground platform alley. Lucifer slowly approaches the young-blooded demons. They do not move, nor do they speak. His enchanting presence keeps them silent and still. They protest to break the spell, but Lucifer tells them their efforts are futile, and to calm down and listen. He then delivers his message of approval. He wants to entertain, so he performs a slide-show-like freak exhibit for the small crowd. He is a Dragon. He is the oldest man they have ever seen. He is a red ghost, then a serpent. And he is formed of fire. A monster made of fire. They have seen enough.

* * *

Master Bruno is ready. Saint Bruno advises to move with the spirit. Meeting with Ballard the first time is shudder worthy, yet Master Bruno feels it not to any significant degree. So, Saint Bruno goes south, after all, to recover and recruit the young people at FSU. It is a harrowing task, but he reminds himself that 'I am a Saint, all powerful with the heavens above me, with me, behind me and Jesuette's hand holding mine.'

He arrives at the university. He intuitively knows the building structures, as well as the pattern of dormitories, fraternity and sorority houses, including the rentals nearby. All structures that house the young adults, in need of protection and of warning come to him. And most importantly those fifteen-hundred students who have fallen already. He estimates two to three earth weeks to complete this tedious yet necessary blessing. Quite conscientiously, he takes a stride into the first structure, the humans inside he knows he came to save.

Saint Bruno sets out on this well-rehearsed and well versed task contributing additional chosen to Goddesses' side. His mind wanders but just a few seconds. This is what could make an unforeseen but advantageous playing field for his chosen. He bows his head and offers thanks and praise to his Lordess:

> "Almighty Lordess our supreme Jesuette –
>
> Hear my thanks, praise and request for your blessing –
>
> Please let me see and know the advantage –

>   And please send word of risk to me
>   and Master Bruno –

>   The recruits we have saved thus far –

>   Lordess, hear my prayer.

>   Amen."

With that, the Saint receives a simple sign of affirmation, and another note that surprises the Saint. One piece of her blessing is indeed one needed to be heard, and that is this:

"Saint Bruno, the most profound advantages you own just right now, is that you and our Master Bruno keep in constant contact, planning, discussing and learning every day. Our Master Bruno has mirrored your way in conversion and lifting to save, thus protecting the would-be victims forever from the fallen. He performs this in the most gracious way.

Now, a bit of information you may not be

aware of. One of the reasons Ballard is left alone in the north of America with strict and hostile orders from his superior. Lucifer spends most his days and nights in the middle-east portion of the world. Inevitably, we will have to fortify your side with a host of fifty-thousand angels along with their assignments. Let us reconvene upon your return north to meet our earthly Master. The heavens are with you, and all, upon one word from me upon your behalf. Please call on me at that time. Finish your job in the south, my holy Bruno."

"Oh Mercy, I am indebted to you, and all beings and things holy. We shall look forward to, with great enthusiasm our next meeting, where we shall discuss further and determine actions for which we are chosen and blessed. I see our breaking of our chosen into rallying battalions. Please Jesuette, and our table, if you wish, join us, when the time comes over our deliberations."

"Very well, my Saint Bruno. You are very brave, and talented at the tasks you partake."

Jesuette softly giggles. No witness ever see or share that with her.

And all the birds above the Earth's equator take to the air in a spectacular moment. They sing loud and long. Earthlings lucky enough to view and hear the spectacle are also blessed, in that, if they read carefully, recognize a message formed over-head within the swarms.

'My chosen will help.'

CHAPTER SEVENTEEN

Saint Bruno is busy volleying between the city-wide untouched by Ballard and the fallen. He travels with ease from one space to the other. He senses calm and sleep in the first dorm. He sees what Ballard left behind. He says a prayer and then faces the affecting scene.

"Miss Shannon, please wake. Please wake gently and calm. I am the voice of truth, calm, love and peace. Shannon please wake gently and calmly." He places a hand on her shoulder and repeats, "Please, please wake up Shannon. I am Saint Bruno of heaven."

He moves his hand to her forehead. "Please Miss Shannon, we must talk through dangerous ogres on the loose. I am with you. I will help."

He gently rocks her shoulder, very daintily, hoping it may wake her without a stir. He pats her head like a mother would a child.

"Wha...wha...who?"

The saint puts a little pressure on his hand that is on the top of her head. It is soothing. It is comforting and Shannon has no inclination to scream. The image next to her is faded, but she sees he is dressed in a blue, green and white robe-set. He looks like a saint.

"Miss Shannon, I am Saint Bruno, devoted saint of our heavens, and of Lordess Jesuette of God. This meeting will cause you some confusion at first, but I assure you that you will see all as it is, today. I represent our Goddess Jesuette, the heavens, saints and angels. We all are with you. We intend to interrupt the army of fallen demons that are on the loose. The horrid evil faces us all.

Listen more please. Once you get over the initial awe, you feel thanks and praise, because all I give you is the means to ward off the threatening creature who is of Lucifer. I urge you to be on the side of the heavens, be one of ours, the chosen and the good. And also remove the bad from your life forever, never to bother you again. In turn, you will have earned a special place unto heaven.

She smiles as he gives her a warm smile.

She wipes the sleep from her eyes, and small tears roll out slowly and reach her cheeks. She wipes them away. She tells the saint what she noticed several nights before, and the night after, all the nights. Shannon tries to stay awake, but the past two nights she was not able to.

"Saint Bruno, I pretend to sleep every night. All night I notice some strange images. They are so scary that now I cannot fall easily asleep at all anymore. I am afraid to."

"Dear soul, I appeal to you in wakefulness to please let me know what you witness. Together, we will transform you back to who the heavens know you are. What you are going through in the dream-state, is just that, a dream or nightmare, convincing to you as it may be."

"It's hard to explain. I lie in the exact same position every night." She seems to pale in pallor. "I lie still, totally and completely still." She drools, the echoes cry out from the pure heat of hell.

"I can't help it saint."

"The fallen in his deadly plan is quite shrewd and also skewed. Is their not under which a fallen and sinful ex-angel awkward and rough around the edges? That is their leader."

The Saint points to the roommate.

"I am here to teach you the techniques, the tools to stand down the fallen ones, and to literally jettison their spirits outward from our beautiful earth to the darkness of nowhere. There is no chance of life through any type of creation or evolution to be had, unless it is granted by Goddess and the father. Thus, the demon spirits die."

Saint Bruno explains to Shannon what he is about to teach her, and why. He asks that she devotedly promise to perform these actions upon every confrontation with the fallen, and prepare those yet to be attacked in kind. "There should be no doubt, no matter the fear, that you are the superior, and they, a half-baked caldron of fierce hell and fright, and nothing more.

Please listen and learn the antidote and defense from, and, the heavenly spell to rid the fallen from your life forever. You should listen and act upon every task Master Bruno, and that I ask of you. Master Bruno is my earthly associate and representative. I am his patron saint, his namesake and archangel, and his guardian angel. We work together. So, to follow and put into play our instructions saves you, Shannon, and help you deliver to your generation a world of global peace."

"I can't believe this." Shannon is still dizzy from sleeplessness and feels off-center.

"Please, my beautiful child," Saint Bruno commences. "This is a one-time task for our intents and purposes, although you shall come to repeat it whenever need be. It represents fortification. I would like you to witness my saving your corrupted roommate after you and I are done. That will model what you will do to save anyone who has not yet fallen and convert those back who have. Now, first repeat out loud this prayer, 'Act of Love' after me:

"O Lord God," Saint Bruno begins.

"Oh Lord God"

"I love you above all things."

"I love you above all things."

"I love my neighbor for your sake"

"I love my neighbor for your sake"

"Because you and yours are the highest, infinite and perfect"

"Because you and yours are the highest, infinite and perfect"

"Goodness worthy of all my love."

"Goodness worthy of all my love."

"In this heavenly love"

"In this heavenly love"

"I intend to live and die."

"I intend to live and die." "Amen."

"Amen."

Shannon prays then feels weepy. Tears leave small trails from her eyes down her cheeks. The good saint lightly rests his right hand on her head. Tears of triumphant joy overcomes her and pass. They leave glorified strength and resolve.

"Now, Shannon, you must carry this holy water with you at all times," Saint Bruno says as he pulls the holy water out of his slotted robe pocket. "Am I understood?"

"Yes, Saint Bruno."

"One of the powers delivered me and all saints, angels and Master Bruno by Lordess

Jesuette is the miracle to conjure a holy water into our hand whenever we ask for one. We, including you, are enabled to pass it along to others; recruits, chosen. No human could perform this without intervention."

"I...I am starting to feel better." Shannon smiles, relieved.

"This is one reason that I, Saint Bruno came to you.

Lastly," Saint Bruno says at his finish. "Let me now tell you how to ward off, convert, and jettison fallen, wicked spirits, temptation or threat away. With this formation and gesture, as you point those two fingers at any fallen one she will be reconverted. In the second attention, the fallen reconvert and their spirits are jettisoned. They lose their power to journey."

"So, the finger miracle Jesuette enabled you

two to pass to others? Anyone who recites the prayer and holds close the holy water is awarded the power function?" Shannon asks.

"Yes, dear one. Please allow me to demonstrate. I will catch your roommate. My hope is that she will drift into the room in the second attention - the higher dimension. If you look at her closely right now, you see she is but a faded image of a live spirit lying there in that bed."

"The higher dimension...the second attention? Please explain further Saint Bruno."

"I save this for last because it is the most talent-driven force you shall learn tonight. And you will review it with Master Bruno over the next few nights. It is not heaven sent. It is very real among all earthlings, even though very few are aware or never capture the talent.

With enough practice, anyone can do it. First, I wish to demonstrate the conversion and jettison lessons. As soon as she enters the room, you will not see her, for she does not have the aptitude to have herself seen by anyone, unless they are in the dream state, or on the astral plane.

However, she will see me and feel my action and intent. She will inherently begin to turn vicious. I will tell you when she enters. I will perform the steps I just taught you, and you will quite suddenly see her, in repose, in that bed that belongs to her. From here on she is one of us – a chosen one."

"Okay then," Shannon begins for clarity. "The sequence is to:

Recite the prayer.

Hold up the holy water.

Give the holy sign.

Is that correct Saint Bruno?"

"Yes dear, quite so, however let me introduce some nuances. First, as you recite the prayer, you will notice the target frozen in time, immovable and paralyzed. Then you will hold up the holy water. The holy water causes inner-pain, indescribable to the fallen ones. Finally, waste no time in pointing at your subject enemy the sacred gesture.

Once you do that you will see the horrible spirit whisk away. You will see a cloud of dark gray smoke stream from the top of his or her head. They will snap back to their bed, exhausted, back to goodness, or normal as you might say. They each will need the steps I gave you. The complete series."

"Saint Bruno?"

"Yes sweet child?"

"How do I learn to enter and fly around in

this second dimension, second attention or astral plane?"

"Of course, Miss Shannon...Our Goddess Jesuette showers the power upon us to recognize that part of our spirit that most humans never do. My namesake, the Master Bruno proves that diligent practice conquers the art and other embedded talents, such as how to manipulate objects in the first dimension from up in the second. He will visit you soon and leave you all his teachings. He will not leave you until you are both satisfied that you can handle yourself in flight."

"Oh, I see. Okay, that is so nice."

"Do not fret or be scared," The saint tries out his use of slang. "Master Bruno is a good a guy, good as they come."

Saint Bruno sees the roommate slowly

floating down into the dorm room. He whispers to Shannon, "She is here. Shshsh."

"Oh. Ewwww. You holy bastard. Come to save some shitters, have you? Numnumnum."

"I came to defeat you, child of Asmodeus." The saint begins to recite the prayer. The demon curls up in a ball and stays exactly where she is. The holy water comes out and a tattoo-like marking appears on the left shoulder blade of the demon.

"Watch now, Shannon, sweetest."

Saint Bruno flips his two fingers out and toward the wounded demon as though he had done it a thousand times before. A long pillar of smoke appears and Shannon is able to see all from this point on. The stream escapes out the top of the head as fast as it earlier came in through the feet. Shannon's roommate is out of nowhere sleeping soundly on her back, in her bed. She rolls over to one side and sleeps with a crescent smile across her lips.

"There now, Shannon, just as I described, right?"

"Yes, I see, Saint Bruno. Amazing."

"I will stay near. You may not see me just yet, but I want to witness her coming out, and, keep an eye on your wellbeing. Again, please expect Master Bruno to visit. By that time, he expects to initiate you both unto the chosen flock. He will teach you how to join him in the second dimension."

"Um, okay Saint Bruno. I'll be aware."

"Master Bruno will announce his presence gently when he arrives, as did I."

"Okay."

"Goddess Jesuette blesses you, my child."

And...*poof*

He is gone, but surely not forever, not forgotten as he assigns Master Bruno to continue the lesson and watch over the girls.

Saint Bruno breaks considerable ice there at FSU, and now he wants Master Bruno to take over. One, he needs the practice holding the attention of, showing the patience for and remaining calm and rational throughout the entire idea of the exercise. Let alone exuding the supreme feelings of goodness, love, peace, blessings and assurance backed by the heavens above for the chosen, holy subjects. Learning of Saint Bruno's decision, Master Bruno hopes, wishes and prays that Saint Bruno can handle the New York City heathens. He must let those feelings go after all, heaven is on their side. And what more does the Master need?

After so much thinking there comes a

headache, uncommon as they may be, Master Bruno has a bad one. He sneaks back to Hoboken for a rest. This usually does the trick. Saint Bruno feels sorry for him, but stays away and lets nature and the living being pass the course as gentle as could be. It is not his place to push Master Bruno and send him into anxiety or impatience. As Master Bruno dreams of rest under a large, great, tall and round willow tree, he ingests all these subjects. He feels stronger, stronger than he's ever felt. So he repeats silently in mind, a tender suggestion his patron saint and mentor leaves for him.

Master Bruno, waking with the sun, stretches, and offers thanks and praise. Then thinks through the day and days to come. He takes a big breakfast. At FSU, he puts forth the plan. And it makes good sense to him. He refers to what the saint told him… instructed him.

He sweeps into Shannon's dorm room. He knows the background and knows what task he is to complete during this visit. Shannon is safe, her roommate newly reconverted. So, Master Bruno takes a top corner spot diagonally up from Shannon, and across the small room to the top right of roommate Helen. Very softly, Master Bruno whispers to wake Shannon first, and then the roommate. He reviews hastily Saint Bruno's initial lesson. Both young women must learn to journey. That is his most important focus. He flutters down to Shannon and sits quietly on the edge of her bed.

"Shannon, Shannon, please do not be alarmed, for it is I, Master Bruno, of Saint Bruno and our Lordess Jesuette. Shannon, Shannon, please do not be alarmed, for it is I, Master Bruno, of Saint Bruno and Our Jesuette."

Shannon stirs quietly as she yawns and

speaks in a soft, low morning voice to Master Bruno. "Yes, Master Bruno. Your saint explained this to me, your arrival, your help and further lessons on projection to Helen and me."

Master Bruno expects Shannon to relay something like this, yet still he reiterates. "Shannon, I will wait for her to awaken before anything else. I will explain to her the reasons for her ugly dreams. I will then expand, briefly, the operations of the evil fallen ones as they seek to take from the helpless, replacing all that good with gruesome undertakings, by ugly sinful ways as they carry out orders from Ballard."

"I understand Saint Bruno initiated Helen's recovery last night," Master Bruno reminds Shannon. "Then, before it is too late, I will request she recite the prayer, grasp the holy water and finally learn the two finger weapon. Are you keeping up with me?"

"Yes, Master Bruno, I am. I feel confident, and I can only feel that Helen will mirror the same as I. Yes, Saint Bruno did all that last night. Helen is a good girl, Bruno."

"And so I am aware. My intent is to give you one more, and she a demonstration of reconversion before we take on projection. Performing those steps more than once does not hurt the process. And you both need to learn beyond any doubt."

"Okay, so now we wait the while until she wakes up?"

"Yes, my friend." Master Bruno says with a smile. "Though I just may give her a nudge." Master Bruno smiles radiantly toward Shannon. She blushes and smiles back.

PART THREE
THE RALLY

CHAPTER NINETEEN

Goddess supreme announces, "Oh, witnesses and students, all you who believe the limit of my father's patience, see that once before a driving force, is nearing that place now, once again, inside of me.

Finder of those that you think will not make the trade, push back. Do young large breasted attractive female species ever part with those or learn to live with or without using them to show or tempt? They can learn and spread true goodness. They can! Do the tall, dark well-endowed male ever part with that, the notion that he is the Adonis of all females top on his mind? They can! And will the rich ever part with their mistresses and boy callers…concubines? Can they ever part with their material wealth? Are they forever flawed? No! They can! They will!

The handsome will let go. The beautiful will no longer wallow in it. They are lucky, yet treacherously vulnerable. They are often the worst sinners, whether they attend their church on Sundays or not. They are the most used and abused. Things will change.

There will be no more living off the material and the cosmetically fortunate after this, you see. No more."

Jesuette is on a deeply holy rant that is superficial and very much unlike her. However sensible and devoted, she is all disgust and sadness and wants to be sure her heavenly beings have no question about her position. And thus, what their positions shall be.

Though they are not quite sure, they listen to learn.

Thin gray clouds hide the sun. Cities and resorts all over the Earth become humid and uncomfortable.

"The projections go well." Jesuette reflects upon the road here and then beyond. "The souls Master Bruno sees and meets in their dreams are sweetly and innocently human and humane. He arms them and readies them for battle. While traveling he meets a Goddess, a woman named Jesuette. So angelic, so perfect she is before him. He believes, he feels, he knows that she makes him hers. She wants him to help her start a revolution and to fight a war. His efforts reach out to all his recruits. They shall help her defeat another traveler who is spreading grief, evil and the word of Satan. The evil one torments his victims with verbal, emotional and physical abuse. So in their dreams most succumb to him. Although in defiance some die. But those who survive are taught to and intend to fight to the death. They will battle our chosen army of goodness, of heaven. And I Damn Him."

The entire board gasps.

A miles long mudslide falls fast on the Unites States' west coast.

Jesuette reviews the history and the fallen current plan of action. She describes the earthly worthy and then she rests. She prompts Saint Bruno to again speak of his chosen namesake and apprentice, Master Bruno. When he is through, she repeats to him and all present before her that the entire heavens are with him and behind him, the saint. And so too with and behind the master and also the chosen everywhere. She does not relay or underline her previous diatribe. But she states what is to the board.

"Master Bruno always felt chosen, in a way, different than others. Now he knows why. He has finally found his way, his true voice, and his mission in life, by his Goddess Jesuette and Saint Bruno. He does not know where his groceries come from, but his cupboards and refrigerator are always well-stocked.

It is my intention as I confer with all of you now to announce and discuss what is to be one last effort to gather together the good souls. They are worthy of inheriting the world we are able to bequeath, and that I leave once more to them.

I shall talk to Master Bruno. Afterward, he will have the dynamism to reach this council, although typically he will through our own Saint Bruno. I, Jesuette, am convicted in belief of this Earth-saving man and of the project. I shall visit with Master Bruno now and keep at his side for the duration."

The table, shocked and awakened, understand and honor their Lordess. Even if that was the most awkward address ever.

* * *

"Master Bruno, I am the sister of Jesus; named Jesuette, and I am the daughter of your God almighty. And mine," Jesuette announces.

He feels her, knows and believes, for there is simply no possibility to disbelieve.

"Yes Lordess, I harbor no disbelief and feel incapable of doubt." Bruno does not know what else to say; only what he truly feels in his heart, spirit and soul. He bows his head. He is taken with this surprise. The visit and the intensity of her openness to him is breathtaking. He has tears in his eyes. He looks into her eyes and he feels the eyes of a lover, a giver upon him.

"Your old acquaintance Ballard learned the

power of astral projection and is using it to cause grave harm through the masses during dream state in the night. We want you to continue to do the opposite; what you have been doing, Bruno. Please, do not surrender. Move forward with Saint Bruno. You go to people in their dreams, or in their wakefulness, and you assure them of their safety, protection and place in heaven. You convince them to fight for the right to live with love and peace. And to serve battle and not to die even with dignity. I commend you."

Jesuette drives forth her understanding to Master Bruno. It is redundant, but necessary to her. So they together review the ways and means to complete such a worldly and heavenly important task. Master Bruno thanks her for her belief in him. He maintains his close tie to Saint Bruno. She leans forward and hugs him tight, close to her bosom. She does not let go. Master Bruno is not only taken, he is more and more confident and thankful. She kisses him on the cheek. He feels every part of her. She is perfectly warm, brightly lit and open.

"Oh my Lordess…"

* * *

Both armies are hyper-eager to win the prize they know is the world, which will become more and more theirs as they age and the following generation is born. Some humans are more competent than others, some quicker to learn, but Master Bruno knows that eventually everyone he greets in the coming days and nights admonishes reasoning. There will be peace on Earth… or anarchy.

Astral projection is now the new crack. Kids plan around it. Soon, Master Bruno resigns himself that his brood must know both how to defend and take the offense in flight.

Projection is the new Instant Messenger, as it is so, instant and interactive.

As much fun as the chosen army has during what is training, they also keep to the head the promise, the mission, and the plan to annihilate the enemy fallen. But for now, they play and laugh and misbehave. Kids will be kids. Teens will be teens. Yes, even the chosen like to raise hell.

But the fallen make it their way of life, too. They are marked with a large black hole in their souls. The chosen can see that marking. They keep their talent and their confidants close, together for fun and practice. Learning to fight and kill during projection. The chosen know honor inside conquest. It matters so in blessed projection but they forever hold their beliefs.

The fallen let their awful dreams and appointed message seep into their wakeful daily routines. Their eyes are sunken and their cheeks pallid from spending too many of their late nights practicing roughly and violently. And their days in their gloomy enslavement. There is a long thread of methamphetamine that continues to connect the fallen. The introduction and widespread use of the drug is spawned of their exhaustion. And it is turning them visibly malformed, deformed, misshapen, misproportioned and ugly.

The chosen sit high over the promise of love, peace, tranquility and heaven. Saint and Master Brunos' attributes, passed down from Jesuette herself. Fortunately for the chosen, even though the black holes are visible, the symptoms of meth addiction is deeply seated into the day time lives of the fallen. And it carries over into night. It has an impact. A negative one.

Chosen can spot them with just a glance.

Sooner than expected and without being given the word, some older and impatient kids begin to clash at night. They set-out to continue until they border the Mason- Dixon Line. They wipe out tens of thousands fallen. Saint Bruno and the Master quickly collect the drove and deliver a word of caution. They explicitly prohibit waging battle without the order from above.

Lucifer frowns at the realization his groups wander from and stray off his plan. But he does nothing. It's his fallen kids. Fuck 'em.

Saint Bruno observes closely the fallen expansion and locations. He facilitates a meeting between him and Master Bruno. Master Bruno shall issue an order to attack. A sub-set of chosen rise. The good angels and daemons wage war against the war-active fallen demons. They are at rest the thirty-fifth parallel. Soldiers devour each other. Poor souls on both sides meet with death. Astral cords are frayed and snapped in two. As strung-out as they are, the fallen ferocity is not lost. So chosen die too as the fallen squash their opposition so short and early into undeclared battle.

The chosen use expert flight, navigation and biblical force, while the fallen use violent weaponries, such as blade, bolo, buckshot and more brought up from mortality. The fallen snap the chosen back to their refuges. Some commit murder. The chosen try to corral the fallen. There is some success, through shear Goddess almighty force. The chosen jettison all of the encountered out of this universe.

The chosen, having the advantage to function in all alertness states, begin to gain a profound handle in battle. They gain ground quickly and surely. Their guardian angels remind all chosen of their rudimentary training. It is paramount they carry on with those lessons in mind and to carry-out the order from the master. It is pure direction and behavior unwavered. When the chosen encounter the fallen they issue the trigger, holy water hanging around their necks. Astral cords of the fallen snap free. The carted evil is gone forever. When the casualties awake they are full of goodness and the will to take up arms with the chosen.

* * *

People talk openly in the street about the unthinkable atrocities. There is a swarm of young chosen angelicas. And there, in nary bootlicker garb, is a pack of wild demons. Dark antagonism pours from Ballard's rookies. Both groups are busy putting their armies together and at the ready. Yet, although the fallen are near prepared, they are still unknowingly inept, carrying with them an unspoken feeling of sinfulness, which hobbles their confidence. They train themselves. Ballard is nowhere to be found. It is an apparent weakness across the entire brood. There is an undiluted presence of their conscience in spirit, the knock and noise plying to enter their souls. Their ever-present guardian angels.

* * *

Saint Peter empathetically points out. "The call to the ultimate battle has not been issued yet. Yet both the chosen and the fallen are so eager to carry out what they know is their most important task ever, they proceed without. I cannot blame them for jumping to. So, again, the young will be young.

Ghastly, yes? Well, the parents of the fallen do not know where their children are!"

He believes this to be a gaping flaw in the unholy design.

Saint Paul adds, "What's more, the process is taking long, by planet standards, no surprise, of course. And war zone by war zone, premature charges and attacks quart and tierce forward."

"From North America to third world countries, the planet seems to be slowly falling apart," Saint Thomas says, almost fearfully, yet continues. "Most, in the name of God, Buddha, Allah, and the devil know this. What with all the proof against concept, it seems all Christians and moderate Muslims stand against fundamentalists, atheists and agnostic." Saint Thomas falls silent as the table lets what he announces sink-in. Many recant Thomas's naïve statements and dismiss them. For, the world is not falling apart, it is at war; a holy war, for peace on Earth.

The table reminds Saint Thomas, the doubter that sometimes peace comes at the cost of unrest.

* * *

Lucifer repeats to Ballard in his course and eerie voice what his expectations are. Ballard barely pays attention, as he is looking forward to his next victim. The devil notices this and screams at him.

"Ewww mother-fucking, cock-sucking, two-ball BITCH! When I address you, you pay attention. Do not mistake me for something that cares, other than for my orders within my plan. I will fucking exterminate you. Is that clear, you...Ballard?"

"Yes, Lucifer. That is clear. I am sorry." Ballard is pitilessly tired of the devil's bullshit. He looks forward to perverted, sickly visits, but he desires holy freedom more.

"Very good, then Ballard. So, listen to me. Now, as you complete your tasks through the East to the Midwest, you are, obviously, due to finish this region's west territory. Here is the most interesting and exciting part of my message. You and I are poised to take on the rest of the planet. Are you up to the task?"

"Yes, Lucifer. I really am excited to take that-on." This a white lie. No...it's a lie.

"Good. I shall return to you just prior to your washing-down in the west. At that time I will provide further details of the remaining scope. For now, I be gone." The devil vanishes without another word. Ballard is used to Lucifer's rude and abrupt exits. Never a proper good-bye.

Lucifer journeys to the Middle-East region of the planet. He observes the progress and status of his implant dating from the time of God's creation to the time of Jesus on Earth. He looks to the impact as he views current events there the Middle East. Lucifer executes a plan that escalates the historic millenniums of ragged war among the territories and tribes within this molten sack of the world.

The annihilation grows leaps and bounds as the most evil groups take firm hold. They worship a false-god, and a prophet who wrote in the voluminous theology of his violent and abusive seeds. One of Satan's finest exploitations grows. He is successful as his people take hold of more Christians and Muslim non-believers. The evil groups slaughter every clan and individual in blasphemous, cruel and vicious ways. Anyone who does not convert and join them are unbelievably executed...

crucified, beheaded, raped, mass-murdered, burned alive, buried alive and tortured to death.

Lucifer smiles down as he clearly realizes they are, in simple eventuality, exterminating themselves, fellow Muslims, as the weak leaders in the rest of the world look on. There are no plans to thwart, defeat or destroy the evil nemesis of all things good, such as freedom, liberty, peace and righteousness. Pity.

The devil takes his rally worldwide and for every three new fallen children come by way of exponentials one-hundred more new individuals. In the day and age angst fills people in fallen areas with superlative measure. They are low-down, dirty, mean and nasty beings. Violence and abuse run rampant, nearly replete in the regions around the world population visited by Lucifer.

The large army of fallen overseas from America significantly outnumber the selectively chosen recruits. This is due to the time Saint and Master Bruno take to prepare chosen recruits and in turn reconvert those fallen encountered in the U.S. Upon first and second visits from another heavenly being, the chosen are prepared to take flight and take on the fallen. They are trained on how to exterminate fallen beings. So, the chosen rise, journey, fly and navigate within days of being knighted a chosen spirit. They are fully well prepared for the initiation, sharing, and teaching, and the rally and slaughter from the start.

The fallen are told to wait to learn to fly until a time of Lucifer's choosing.

* * *

Saint Bruno and Master Bruno cover the

West in its entirety. The chosen stand at the ready – Semper Paratus – for their call. They breakout into large groups, teams and cliques according to Master Bruno's directive. They work in-time, cooperatively and precisely together. They strive to fathom infiltration into the rest of the world. They recruit and reconvert, just as they once experienced, as they are educated and empowered to do. It sometimes seems they are in a catch-up position… the cats chasing the mice. And that would be true, except that there is a defined end in sight: A holy event of continuity. There is a grand finale and finish coming their way. And with that, all chosen will have been fully engaged in their project.

The holy trumpets blow an inviting melody in perfect key with the Goddess's intention. She sings the cry of attendance for all the heavens to meet at her table. Saint Bruno feels the vibrations she sends and appears at his place at the round table. The upper tiers fill with angels. The first and second level mezzanines populate with archangels and guardians. These tiers and bleachers rise up infinitely out from around the table. The heavenly have a place among their peers on Jesuette's board, or in the rising theater of seats just beyond.

Jesuette hums a greeting to all the attendees. The sound is the most soothing palagio imaginable. Within that hum is a message, an intimation of love, peace and harmony: Meta-understanding... understanding of the understood. Her thoughts and undercurrent of words wrap about, resounding gentle beauty and tranquility. Her audience understands the entirety of the message slowly rolling out of her being, arms wide, palms outward, in a gesture of welcome and reach. The message sinks into the holy psyche of the entire congregation.

"The time is here to prepare thoroughly our flock of chosen beings on Earth for the rising. You must groom your warriors in full for the violent bath ahead. This is fully understood as you explain the strategy and execution of their operations amid heavenly rally. You shall meet with your assignments and phalanx together at the new moon. At the full moon, I shall address the chosen, all. My message represents to you, and will them, your soldiers and units, readiness, support, thanks, praise and confidence.

I shall remind them of the importance behind their tasks, and the reward their triumph delivers, not only for them and their descendants, but the world, Earth and its people. I will, unprecedentedly, address them as true saviors and thus, heaven-bound souls. So, my brothers and sisters, it is your divine command at this time to procure your chosen children and ready them for the announcement, the struggle and the conflict. Do this at the half-moon. They shall be made aware that the fallen train, as the chosen do, so they must ready themselves for a violent clash.

Lay down the plans you chiefs...you overseers. Let not our chosen souls be taken by the unexpected. Let plans feed them confidence, knowledge, courage, will and motivation, and unleash their newfound prowess. This, my heavenly beings, is, most definitely, a holy war. The holy trinity along with all of us shall pray and enable.

And let it be known that Saint Bruno is the direct Commander under me, Master Bruno under him, yet with all the chosen ultimately serving heaven. You have one half-moon to finish the recruitment and educational processes The Brunos have one half-moon to present battle plan specifics. I will then issue the all-hands call to action. I shall address the multitude of chosen, then the rally to war is on!

Understood?"

"Aye, Grace."

"Here! Here!"

Jesuette adds, "May the grace and power of God the father be with you."

"And also with you." With that rejoinder, the holy souls mist and glide away from Jesuette's chamber.

* * *

Saint Bruno instructs Master Bruno as Jesuette did him, what begins on the half moon and culminates on the full moon. They agree on what they are to do and how they will achieve it. The Saint puts roughly fifty percent of the chosen through a final accelerated program and development series. Master does the same with the remainder. It is clear in Saint Bruno's eyes that Master could use a measure of confidence building.

"Master Bruno, I know that recruitment, now that you are expert in that realm, represents your current comfort zone. But you must look beyond now...to the very reason we executed the recruitment process in the first place. Recall please that it is a step in making our war aggress toward the ultimate grail, eh?

The retaking of mother Earth, and replacement of evil with good is upon us. We do this on our Goddess's behalf and of her heavenly father. True for the world in its aggregate completeness...entireness, you remember. The Lordess and the holy trinity are with you. She came to you and promised you so. And Master...so did I. I am with you. Never forget these realities. It will have been a onetime, righteous and hallowed happening. Chosen though fighting are indeed peacemakers, the meek who find it within yourselves to rise to the occasion of heroics for all goodness' sake."

"I understand, Saint Bruno," Master replies, in tears. "Thank you for this boost and reminder. I stand with you and the heavens, even in humility. I shall bring the fight to the end, with all our recruited chosen. And the end will have the heavens singing in rhapsodies!"

"Very good then Master Bruno...excellent... very good indeed. You are the singular choice of our Goddess, her saints and mine to place you in this lead position. The position you are born to fulfill. Your responses are always impeccable. Bless you my son."

* * *

Ballard has the boy by the ears, squeezing and twisting them between his hoof's nails full force. The reclined boy is sobbing in his sleep. He feels the pain in slumber and he hears very well the demon's words. As the devil makes a move to bite the boy's nose, the boy agrees to follow as he drenches the bed in a cold, dehydrating sweat. When the agreement comes, Ballard vaporizes. The victim seems to feel a new inner strength, but also a distressing sickness. It has to be a nightmare.

Master Bruno appears within seconds and helps revive the victim's sense of Christian spirit, reconvert him and train him in full. It is sometimes a challenge, but young Bruno is a master at what he does. He quickly and clearly gets the stress-points across that matter most. Once the introductions are made and the soothing after-words spoken, his children honor him. They honor once again the heavens above and their heavenly Earth.

Saint Bruno exudes pure calm, peaceful, rational patience, and goodness with unblemished delivery and timing. For those represent the keys to a proper introduction. It is by happenstance and habitual following of Ballard, at this point, that Master Bruno finds this poor boy. Master Bruno can tell right away that the boy is under the bleakest and darkest influence of the fallen. This compels Bruno to save...rescue the innocent ever more in strength of conviction.

The fallen ones are made to understand that Saint Bruno, Master Bruno or a chosen officer be forever watchers from the upper corner and over them.

* * *

Saint Bruno directs Master Bruno to yet another desecrated, young Chinese girl's dorm room at Sun-Yat-sen University. China and other eastern regions are the last calls for the chosen to answer. Saint and Master Bruno have amassed millions of holy chosen soldiers. Saint Bruno with Master help her recover, in the name of goddess Jesuette. Master Bruno is thankful for the Saint's interjection and rudimentary introduction to this new world of the East.

The idea of relating the supreme storyline to a range of easterners that pray or meditate to a different Supreme Being, god or prophet eats at Master's nerves. This is his first intervention and healing review, and he feels fortunate when Saint Bruno reminds him that almost all young foreigners understand the English language. Master Bruno feels he knows the procedures and has no failures thus far, and reminds himself that he is many thousands of children deep in the process.

Master Bruno delivers to the apprentice precise and straight-away procedures, plans and goals. He instills with finesse the art of appearing from the heightened dimension, to the victim in the norm. He embeds the no-fail tasks, steps that lead to immaculate rescue, recovery and renewed confidence in heaven. It matters not the language, creed, race or ethnicity, whether they speak English, or not.

It is like a heavenly modem put in place for this very reason. Jesuette embeds this facility to allow the Master's and chosen output messages thus take-on the audience linguistic no matter; it is effortless. Reality, the Saint reiterates again to the Master, is more potent than dream state in any language, no question of source or control. This reminder and new and renewed understanding gives Master Bruno full confidence in order. That he knows and feels he is able to intervene with anyone seamlessly, feeds him the plate he's craved. He longs to help the Eastern girl, so.

"Miss? Young lady," Master Bruno whispers. The straight-A collegiate female whines a whimper in a breathy gasp, like a choked-back crush. Lately she sees enough drama in the night.

"Shuí zài nà'er?" Master Bruno softly beckons.

The poor girl trembles in fear and is close to crying, the tears already rolling slowly out of the corner of her beautiful eyes.

"I am Master Bruno, here on behalf of Saint Bruno and the Goddess Jesuette of heaven. I appear here in order to help you recover from the ferocious dream you experienced," Master Bruno begins.

"I will appear to you fully in short time, my tormented friend, but you have to trust me, and what I say I am here to do. I am a human representative of my namesake Saint Bruno, and of the Lordess on high, Jesuette, from the heavens above. Your belief in me, my mission and in Saint Bruno and the goddess is paramount."

"Jesuette? Goddess?" The girl asks through her tears. "First, I am a student of Buddha. Next, I thought God was a man, or a male form, and that man on Earth was created in the likeness of God. I have studied Theology and am quite familiar with Christianity and the biblical writings in general." She struggles to get the right words out.

Master Bruno relives this scenario over and over, day after day, night after night.

Thankfully, this phase of preparation will be complete soon. So, Master Bruno is well-versed and speaks by rote. He easily resumes as he does in every similar instance.

"In the beginning that was true. However, since Jesus died on the cross to win the past war with Lucifer, sacrificing himself, God made his only daughter, Jesuette, responsible for continuing the exercise, the experiment of Earth, to prove the possibility and imminence of peace and love in life on Earth.

Consider this the sole act God performs that trumps the devil; to sacrifice his own son. As you have witnessed, experienced the past two evenings, there is indeed an evil presence again circling about the planet. But this time, God will not offer up his offspring. Though, it is through Jesuette's directive that we believers in love, peace and tranquility over our Earth join together.

In the confrontation with this horribly fierce evil, it matters not the addressee of your mantra, meditation or prayer." Master Bruno takes a breath.

"I want to see you," the innocent and sweet-looking slant-eyed girl says to Master Bruno.

"Alright," Bruno replies. "I will appear in the far corner of your room, near your wardrobe. I will first appear ghostly, but within seconds you will visualize me as a human figure, which indeed I am. As true as that is, I am empowered by the almighty and her designees. As you are to be empowered by me and the Saint Bruno."

"You cannot be normal when you are able to perform the things you have so far. I may not be a practicing Christian, but all of this is frightening me."

"Believe me, young one, I am human," Master Bruno explains. "I have developed and mastered a technique which allows journey up and into a higher dimension, one higher than the tangible Earth and her atmosphere. I have also been granted power by Goddess Jesuette, in support of pursuit of, and the healing of those hurt by Ballard or one of Lucifer's fallen. That is in truth who hurt you so."

"Is that who I dreamt of?"

"Yes," Master Bruno replies.

"I was recruited by Saint Bruno on behalf of Jesuette, the saints, and angels. The Chosen. Ballard of Earth was recruited by Lucifer, The Fallen. The fallen ones seek to wreak havoc on poor young souls, boys and girls alike, teens and young adults just like you."

"But why?"

"To corrupt and rid the Earth of its only hope, the future, the coming generations. Lucifer is full of resentment for the chosen, the good. It is his idea to initiate mega-genocide."

"Prove what you tell me by answering a question I've had all my life… about Catholicism, please," the young lady requests. "Explain where Jesus ultimately went."

"I will summon Saint Bruno immediately. Please be patient for a moment."

"Um…Okay…Alright."

"Saint Bruno is here with me now. Though he is invisible to you," Master Bruno replies. "You will hear his voice answer your question."

Saint Bruno begins with his usual introduction, "Young soul behold these words:

Words that have never been uttered to a human on Earth. Jesus, as documented in the Bible, truly ascends to the heavens three days after his miraculous rise from the tomb. While there at his father's right side, Jesus asks for something quite unorthodox for any heavenly being…let alone the son of God. You see, the holy trinity entertain his request and prayers, as they do all. They appear like the gears inside a clock turning and churning on and on in complete dedication and devotion.

Jesus poses his want and need, which also represents a challenge. Jesus desires to return to Earth inside his human encasement so he may experience God's greatest gift to his human world. Jesus's spirit will be of both heaven and Earth.

He wants to return for Mary Magdalene, have a life-time of human love in life and share parenthood with her. He wants desperately to raise children. Children: God's greatest miracle. His father grants Jesus's request."

"Oh, that cannot be true. Is that true?"

"Yes darling," Saint Bruno familiarly says. "It is quite true. Jesus chooses a life of simple human normalcy, with no human-like responsibilities to his heavenly self, which lay at rest aside his father. He appears to Mary, and he proposes the intentions he so much feels they deserve together. Of course, she accepts. They make a home far from civilization which is reminiscent of Eden. There, they live with their family of children for what say infinite years. This should answer your question.

It is also true that you would do well to listen to and act upon every task Master Bruno, here, or that I ask of you. To do so will save you and many others. You will help deliver your generation to a world of global peace." The Saint in his way, again, brings a close to the truths of the matter. With that, he is gone.

"I can't believe this," Shuí zài nà'er replies in surprised tones.

"Please," Master Bruno commences. "We should get on with the tasks at hand. Are you willing? Are you ready?"

"Yes. Yes. I want to do this...what you and the Saint prescribe. Please."

First, repeat this prayer, titled 'Act of Love' after me. Please do this no matter your formal teachings or beliefs and try to say this prayer with resolve:

O Lord God

I love you above all things

And I love my neighbor for your sake

Because you and yours are the highest,

Infinite and perfect

Good, worthy of all my love.

In this love

I intend to live and die.

Amen."

Shuí zài nà'er repeats every line and then begins to cry. "That is utterly beautiful," she says through the tears. "Profound."

"Now, you must carry this holy water with you at all times," Master Bruno says as he pulls the holy water out of his robe slat. "Will you do this?"

"Yes, I will."

"Excellent, please," Bruno says near his finish. "Lastly, let me tell you how to ward off, convert, and jettison fallen wicked spirits away. With either hand, fold all of your fingers inward toward your palm, holding them in place with your thumb, if necessary, except for the middle and pinkie fingers. With that formation and gesture, as you point those two fingers at a fallen one, they will be converted before your eyes. In the second attention the fallen will be re-converted and their spirit jettisoned. Either way, they lose the power to journey." This is a workable final instruction that Master Bruno uses as a finish to those he saves.

"So, Shuí zài nà'er. The holy water, miracle gesture and recitation of the 'Act of Love' prayer you are hereby enabled to pass to others. Anyone who recites the prayer and holds close the holy water are regarded as saved and a savior in their own right."

"This entirely unbelievable."

"Oh, my sweet friend, believe…believe. Now, and over the course of two nights, I will teach you explicit instructions on how to rise to and journey unto the higher dimension. I will stay here with you until you are fully prepared to practice that exercise yourself. You will need the talent and skill when the rally and conflict begins and goes on."

* * *

Master Bruno wakes and gently approaches his first candidate of the following day. He wakes her gently from her nap, and begs her not to scream. He assures her no harm, and that he is an Earth angel. He takes his direction from heaven. His aura is that of an angel. She can see it. She can feel it. There is, magically, no question or doubt. She just knows. This keeps her wondrously calm.

Tonight, Master explains, and perhaps more, he will be her special guiding angel. He tells her he is teaching her how to ward off the fallen one. Even if she has already fallen, he states he can save her if she believes in him. And, she does believe him. She wants to be good, a good person.

He explains to her what tactics the fallen ones use, how to deflect the actions and words, and eventually on how to rid her world of them for good. It is with a simple prayer, which disarms the possessed, a clear vial of holy water, which wards off approach and an immaculate gesture pointed to the low-caste subject, that Lordess Jesuette makes real for those who believe: The Chosen. These actions will deflect them, Master Bruno explains. These will blow any fallen away and out of her world forever. The war, he explains, however, is still inevitable, after all.

"So, I am also obligated to teach you heavenly rise, travel and combat."

He speaks through with ease. He is clear, concise, understandable and helpful as he recites the familiar paragraph of information for his subject.

"If we end up in war, you will you teach me how to fight, to live?"

"Of course, love. That is, as I said, why I am here. First, repeat this prayer,' Act of Love,' after me."

* * *

"I will make severe pain a part of your everyday life, you chink," Ballard threatens his prey. "I swear I will, boy." It is a favorite threat of his. The young teen is terrified so, that he egests in his bed.

Master Bruno is there in an instant and whispers from the corner, "Li Jun, please wake, but say nothing. Please wake up and say nothing."

Tonight, and perhaps a few more, he will

be Li Jun's special guardian angel. Ballard is lost and gone as soon as the boy awakens. Master Bruno explains to Li Jun the tactics Ballard and Lucifer's own use, and how to deflect them. He teaches how to rid his personal world of all fallen, just as Master Bruno has. He continues on to projection.

*   *   *

Billy bounds into Deacon's room in his abrupt and excitable way. He reflects innocence like that of a clumsy toddler. Billy catches Deacon sitting at the edge of his bed, getting ready to lie down and travel. He saved Deacon long ago, and now they travel and work together on assignments from heaven. They are strong and wiry in their travels, wakeful in flight.

As Master Bruno directs, when approaching a being about to be or are in travel, ease away...step back...step off. Billy intends to catch up with Deacon in the midst of flight. He hovers in the upper corner diagonally away from the other boy. Billy must put Deacon off for the time being. There is a nearby child to attend to.

"Li Wei," Billy calls imperatively. "Listen to me and you shall be saved, and with your help, we can all be delivered to a new world of global peace and righteousness." Billy repeats the entire statement three times. And then, finally, a response comes from the sleeping boy.

"Who are you?" Li Wei is dumbfounded, but follows the sound of the voice up to the corner of his room. There, poised above him, is another kid.

"How did you get in here?"

"Please listen. Please. I am of the chosen ones," Billy begins.

"I am here to save you and the coming generations from the evil mass that permeates the planet. The devil is once again a presence of force here on Earth. He recruits and corrupts young souls and spirits similarly to the way that I am saving you now. But the fallen use fear. The chosen use love. So, I am here to teach you how to rid the malicious ones from your world. I am to instruct you on how to re-convert others, as I am also open to do here. And we will together practice the art of journey. That is flight unto the higher dimension. All this, my brother, readies you for the imminent battle with the fallen in order to win the world over and deliver love, peace and harmony to it, forever. That is your generation will be saved and the generations to come.

So Li Wei, are you with me? Do you understand, my friend?"

"I am frightened."

"What is scary is what the fallen one is spreading and what many are sorely becoming. We need your help, man!"

"So, you represent the good side of what happened last night?"

"Yes, I am trying to save you, now."

"I don't believe you."

"Please believe Li Wei. This is your first step toward salvation."

"Okay, okay, I'll try," the Chinese boy relents. "My parents are good. I am good. He...the devil threatened to put me into an underground bamboo cell forever, buried alive, if I didn't follow him."

"Ah Li Wei, that is over now. I am here to save you. Repeat this prayer, 'Act of Love' word for word after me:

O Lord God,

..."

...

Li Wei repeats every line and then begins to sob. He proudly fights back tears.

"Now, you must carry this holy water with you at all times," Billy says as he pulls the holy water out of his hip pocket. "You okay?"

"Yes, mister."

"Lastly," Billy says near the finish. "Let me tell you how to ward off, convert, and jettison all wicked fallen spirits away." Billy goes on right to track.

"Can you tell me one thing I don't know about the Bible," Li Wei has a question. "Something that I do not understand?"

"What?" Billy asks.

"Why did God ask Abraham to sacrifice one of his two sons?"

"In a word, proof." Saint Bruno appears. Lately, he's been closely following Billy. "It is a pure form of experimentation, or proof of concept. For God, himself, had to experience the love of others to believe his own power to create God-fearing men...men of faith. The almighty has to prove to himself that the injected attribute of greed did not outweigh love of God." Saint Bruno finishes the story for a satisfied Li Wei.

* * *

Ballard and Lucifer are not aware of Saint and Master Bruno undoing what they believe they have complete. They follow along their route and now see the finish line shortly ahead on the horizon. They plan to rest back and watch what happens, but know they have to be ready to jump back in to rally their troops, and of course, ready them for battle. The time is soon in coming.

The chosen army is consistently aware of strength within goodness, the heavens, God and his children. This alone bears a crushing blow, a subliminal ongoing ache that absorbs Lucifer and cripples confidence among his ranks.

Leaders of both sides trust the young warriors will perform rightly.

Master Bruno is forever by the side of peace.

Ballard doesn't give a shit.

CHAPTER TWENTY

The quiet night of the half moon has the chosen resting at home. Saint Bruno set only that expectation of them until further word from him. The full moon is on its way, and so is Goddess Jesuette's call to action. He instructs them to not follow any instincts to recruit or convert from this point onward. Rest. Sleep.

More of that will come only after the fighting fallen ones are defeated and decimated. While the fallen army rests, Saint and Master Bruno each take half of the large force they have before them. They look upon these blessed specimens with respect, honor and pride. The two Brunos review battle plans and in whole, answer questions and address doubts from their soldiers as either rise.

"Before we begin, Master Bruno…"

"Yes?"

"How did Li Na do under your tutelage?"

"She and her brother are fine and good, saint. They asked for no… um…proof."

"Of course, Master. You are indeed a master, you know."

The divisions, brigades, regiments, battalions, companies, platoons and units are carved out of the disciplined army. Saint Bruno purposely leaves the designation of additional platoon descendent groups, such as sections, squads and teams, under each platoon Commander. The two Brunos take each division Commander to the side and walks them through the purpose, procedures, operations and mechanics of rising to battle, fighting the battle and winning the battle against Lucifer. They introduce the weaponry.

Saint Bruno begins, "The fallen, by virtue of their impediment, you will fight more during night than in the daytime."

He continues, "That exception is addressed by representative, strategically located squads of chosen soldiers, elite Special Daytime Forces, to fight away any dawn-to-dark activity the enemy may exhibit. Leftovers, you know. What is remarkable about our battle plan is that we shall rise and begin the assault as one, that is, every division around the whole world shall take action as one, as whole. This in adherence of the logical clock and not the Georgian. The worst sequence of these battles, like most in the mortal world is the hard-lined fighting to take place within the first several days of each. You will be ordered to keep awake and in the journeying plane throughout all on-duty time. We must severely cripple our enemy from the very start and continue to press on, to realize achievement in the end. On Earth, this is referred to as shock and awe, as some of you may be aware."

So, even though they represent heaven in this battle, they are horrific, no-holds-barred killers, albeit killers of the devil's cut. Saint Bruno reminds them that if the creatures they encounter are open to conversion, then convert. However, when the chosen face a fight, they must fight to win. Period.

"We must not be taken by surprise," Saint Bruno directs. "We know the likely tactics of the fallen, but let us not be taken by any other course of action any one of them take against us. If you witness even one hint of tactics yet unintroduced, report it. We will set the message resonating among your leaders above and troops below."

The group of ten million chosen fighters review the art of battle that they are responsible to display and take up to action. There are no second guessers, let alone foreseen unconfident deserters. When the Saint asks where they first gathered the strength to participate, they convey that it is goodness, and that it reflects the simple truths as they have come to know them. It comes from Master Bruno.

The questions they once pondered, the spiritual and biblical evolution and miracles, seem now mistakenly labeled. Although miracles surface, legitimately by nature of those witnesses and those who testify, they too accept. One occurrence alone is enough to convince them that the heavens are an all-powerful realm of sanctity, goodness and love. The believe Saint Bruno's biblical explanations.

The chosen take up final field exercises. It lasts two weeks. That is more than enough of time for the orders to work their way through to the entire worldly army. This leaves the soldiers eleven days to resume and continue their rest. They are assured there will be no surprise calling. They will next hear from the Lordess Jesuette. And then they shall be put into direct action by their Saint or Master. At that point and on point, the divisions shall rise into the upper dimension and take the battle to the fallen. The special daytime forces will rise each following morning.

"If there are necessary changes to the plans, we will message those changes to you. We believe you are covered if an inevitable change is warranted by Master Bruno or myself. Master Bruno and I will brief you and our fighters at logical break points of battle, likely first to occur after the initial onslaught. Know, you Commanders have the right to make immediate emergency changes. We will forever discuss, simply, what works for us and what does not."

* * *

Fallen angel Lucifer takes things upon himself to instruct his disheveled faction. Ballard feels like such a loser as Lucifer orders him to join the ranks.

"Get down there with the others, Ballard," the devil snorts at his one-time second-in-command.

"You are now a fighter, just like everybody else."

"But why devil?"

"Because, as the earthling phrase goes, 'Too many chefs in the kitchen...' Do you get it now?"

"Yeah, but I am surprised. I believe you misled me."

"So fucking what, Earth-man? Now, get down there, or die."

Ballard sinks down to the corps and waits. He does not listen to one word further of Lucifer's battle plan or instruction. Ballard is out. He thinks awake. What can he do? Should he propose a spy position for himself? Should he simply and humbly stay open to whatever the chosen suggest? He wonders if his leadership skills will stand for themselves upon any given negotiation or meeting.

"My demons, do not wait for the battle. You start the battle!" Lucifer blares on.

He sounds more and more like Hitler with

his threatening and super-imperative tones. Even now, the demons do not especially agree, but like Hitler's citizens, they do nothing.

"Instigate the violence between the chosen and us. I want you to be as wicked a being as you can conjure. Most important, if you get a prompt of any kind from me, you best follow it immediately. Did you all get that?"

"Yes, fallen one." The swarm responds lazily. They have instinct.

Lucifer moves ahead with battle plans. He speaks to the specifics in a way that the soldiers understand. They have not heard it expressed quite like this before. Lucifer has it this way. He demands complete attention from the ranks over the tasks at hand, and so immediate tasks. He is the head. He is their leader.

He does not know well any of his army. It

is a dangerous way to win a war. They need this speech. Even if Lucifer does not dwell, the soldiers feel better about going into war behind someone, something. He explains exactly how to approach and kill the opposition. They feel invincible, dominant and confident, after all.

* * *

The day before the full moon, Jesuette makes her call to her chosen. She asks Saint Bruno and Master to be prepared to respond or amend according to her word. She brings together all the chosen and speaks openly of the ongoing struggle between heaven and hell, centuries old, God and Satan. She minces no words and when she speaks, the language is interpreted, heard by the audience in the native tongue.

Her call is announced by the warm sound

of French Horns, the undercurrent of edgy Trumpets, miraculously transposed, to the song of the angels. They resonate the lovely coming and introduction of the Lordess by God. Jesuette claims the full attention following a brief rest of silence between song and presence. She speaks:

"Chosen ones, hear me. Hear my heartfelt words, intention and prayer. An epic battle that rises throughout since dawn now continues. The all-powerful will of God versus an evil spirit in Satan the devil. How did it begin, children? And how will the battle end? Allow my words to inspire your spirit, ready your soul and quell any doubt. You may envision God and Satan as Chess pieces in a game of Chess. Ah, my chosen, yet this is not a game.

Hear my word:

In the beginning, God creates the heavens and the Earth. Although we are only given small glimpses of the world prior to man, the heavenly body and even the scriptures tell you that during this time, Lucifer, one of the high-ranking angels serving before my father's throne, convinces a third of the angels to follow him in rebellion against God.

As a result of this great battle, one which can't ever defeat goodness, the beautiful Angel is doomed without form, and void. Because of Lucifer's rebellion, his name is changed to Satan, meaning 'adversary.' His followers, fallen angels, become known as demons. They are sentenced to hell. I speak of the very same culprits with whom you prepare to battle.

After refashioning the Earth so it may sustain human life, God creates the first man, Adam. Eve, the first woman, is created a short time after. In addition to placing them in the Garden of Eden, where they could live and perhaps multiply, God gives them instruction in the way of life that would lead to happiness and eternal life.

But this couple is also given the choice of whether they would obey their creator, or choose their own path. God gives Adam and Eve the first opportunity to rule when he put all things under the feet of man, giving him logical dominion over the works of God's own hand.

Then, Satan attacks this newfound mankind. Though largely banished to hell with only a few exceptions when he could appear before God's throne, Satan and his demons do not concede in their fight against the father. Satan the devil soon brings his evil, his battle to the Garden of Eden.

Satan convinces the first man and his wife to disregard the instruction and suggestion of God. They bow the lie that man can choose for himself what is right and what is wrong, what is good and what is evil. As a result of this tragic decision, sin enters the world and death enters by sin. Man cuts himself off from the guidance, direction and blessings of God.

From mankind's perspective, this begins a next, long-lived battle between light and darkness, right and wrong, evil and good. Sides are drawn. Camps and philosophies develop.

The result is that we now live with a world where we face a clash of values having to do with the questions of what is sin, and, who is in charge of this Earth. Until mankind comes to terms with my father's ageless law, he will forever struggle in the battle of the ages, with Satan's philosophy hampering that humans can decide for themselves what is good and what is evil. That, my sons and daughters is the root of all war of Earth. God be with you.

...Saint Bruno?"

"Thank you, Lordess," Saint Bruno has a clarification to make for the chosen ones.

"Many of you ask for verbiage describing certain pointed verse from the bible. Upon hearing the Goddess' word today you shall take that as the word of our supreme being and her father, almighty God. Thank our Lordess."

Jesuette interjects. "My saint, please allow me to continue for just a moment. I feel I must."

"Yes. Of course, my Lordess."

"Speaking of the confusion that skewed thought has brought about, I quote Isaiah. 'woe to those who call evil good, and good evil and who put darkness for light, and light for darkness.'

He quite simply states a simple yet complex fact. Mankind loses the ability to think and reason soundly under the guise inside, that is evil. Man loses sight of the way toward peace and happiness. The subsequent history of humankind is a record of struggle in the battle of the ages. What is the deception of the ages? And how does it affect our present day? Consider how Satan deceives the first man and woman; A deadly deception.

Shortly after creating them, God instructs Adam and Eve to look to Him for the knowledge of good and evil. Satan appears and portrays God as a liar and an oppressor. Eve is deceived, and Adam willingly eats of the wrong tree. The self-serving tree. Satan convinces mankind that he should and could decide for himself good and evil, by whim or wish.

This is the great deception, children. The deceiver and his agents bring darkness and oppression disguised as light and liberty. As a result of Adam's choice, mankind is cut off from God—the only true source of light, life and liberty.

What a deception, indeed. The author of darkness and death poses as an angel of light and sells the most fatal potion of the ages.

Our father says, 'In the day that you eat of it you shall surely die.'

Satan, in effect, says, "God knows better— He's been lying to you." Through the ages, Satan and his agents design various systems to disguise the same old package of death.

This, my children, is the longest running

prophecy. As a result of Adam's sin, God deals with each one of the players in the deception of Eden. We see the oldest and longest running prophecy of the Bible. God tells the serpent, Satan the devil, 'I will put enmity between you and the woman, and between your seed and her seed. And that good seed becomes imminent with the coming of the lord, Jesus Christ.'

The battle lines for thousands of years—until the return of Jesus and the removal of the devil—are then drawn. There would be enmity or hostility between the woman, representing the true church, with God's servants, and those of Satan's world. Thus begins the division between those who choose light and truth and those who choose darkness and lies.

Continuing his address to Satan, the father goes on to say, 'My son shall bruise your head, and you shall bruise his heel,' referring to the coming fact that Satan would orchestrate the hatred of Jewish leaders to have Jesus crucified. As he says to these leaders, 'You are of your father the devil, and the desires of your father you want to do.'

This battle—Satan against God—has been going on for over six-thousand years. We are told that Satan is unfortunately the 'god of this age.' In our father's sovereign purpose, Satan is nonetheless permitted to exercise a great measure of authority and power through the duration of this age.

While man is forever a free moral agent and is answerable and responsible for his actions, evil is more than human. Evil has its source in a being who blinds the minds of unbelievers.

One of the primary manifestations of satanic influence and of the evil of this age is religious deception. It is blindness in reference to the laws of the coming kingdom. It is obvious, even from many passages recorded, that the kingdom of God in its permanence does not belong to this age—for Satan is indeed the god of this age.

...Saint Bruno?"

"Thank you, Goddess, but alas, brothers and sisters, I have nothing more to add for the sake of you chosen soldiers." Then, Saint Bruno asks, "Our chosen ones, please gather the lingering thoughts on these teachings thus far along with my words. Form a relative reflection of the positive vibration you feel inside of Jesuette's address."

The millions resound. "Mmm, Ohmm," and once more. "Mmm, Ohmm." These vibrations loosely read to the heavenly as, 'We believe in the Lordess by God, the saints and angels, in full.'

Jesuette then surprisingly continues. "There is indeed hope for this world. Know that God has not gone off to heaven to leave this world under the complete control of the evil spirit being called Satan the devil. God has not been dethroned. It remains eternally true that the Lord has established his throne in heaven, and his kingdom rules over all. God is still king of the ages. It is simply a matter of understanding that the fullness of God's kingdom will not come about until this present evil age comes to an end. Thus, you chosen ones come forth.

My brother, Jesus Christ establishes a beachhead for the kingdom of God through his church, though this world is largely the kingdom of Satan. The church we speak of is the church of the spirit, heart and soul. It does not provide four walls or a false leader. We also need to understand that the kingdom of God is not only future.

Jesus Christ establishes a beachhead for the kingdom of God through his church, not necessarily a temple, though sadly, this world fosters largely the kingdom of Satan. Even the authors of the book of Hebrews speak of faithful people living during the time of the early New Testament church who 'have tasted the good word of God and the powers of the age to come.'

The powers of the world to come thus penetrate this age. The defeat of Satan by God and the establishment of his kingdom are not solely in the future. God has already acted in his kingly power to break Satan. This present evil world—the domain of Satan—has been breached by God. He, and all of the heavenly now call on you, our chosen ones." Jesuette rests, then continues.

"My children, make no mistake. Satan's kingdom is doomed. If not today, then tomorrow, but God will have rid the Earth of this putrid being in due time. My soldiers, we call upon you to continue the battle in hopes we rid the Earth of Satan with victory.

Even the Scriptures make it clear that Satan's evil influence over mankind is destined to end. Speaking of Christ, the Hebrew writing declares, 'Through death he might destroy him who had the stroke of death, that is the devil, and release those who through fear of death were all their lifetime subject to bondage.' The word destroy in this passage means to ruin, put out of action or render inoperative.

The destruction of Satan's stronghold has already been guaranteed through Christ's death, burial and resurrection from the dead. It was a total defeat for Satan in that his activity was and is curtailed towards my father's people. So, regarding faithful

Christians, 'They overcame him by the blood of the lamb and by the word of their testimony.' You represent the word of God.

Christ's ministry was also an invasion of Satan's realm. Christ comes preaching the gospel of the kingdom, and healing all kinds of sickness and all kinds of disease among the people. Christ preaches the kingdom of God and then demonstrates its power. He tells the people of his day that casting out demons is clearly the work of God's kingdom. It is the work of the chosen.

The essence of the kingdom is already on Earth. Part of the gospel— the good news—of the kingdom of God that Jesus brings includes the fact that the authority of the kingdom of God has come to Earth and that it is at work in and among humanity. It is YOU, my children.

John the Baptist and Jesus Christ begin to

proclaim the reality that the power of God's kingdom was and is already at work on this Earth. It has come near and the opportunity through the spirit of God to be a part of that kingdom is being offered to those whom God is calling. This calling from God includes instruction on how to live, conduct, and how to thwart off evil. It has immediate relevance and urgency. So, listen to me. Listen to Saint Bruno.

The Jews of the first century are expecting God to send them a leader who would overthrow Roman rule. But the hope of such a leader does not happen. The Jewish state was not restored, the temple was destroyed, and the Jewish people were scattered.

But Jesus is not wrong in his prediction. The fullness of his kingdom has simply not yet come.

Even though the kingdom of God is not

yet a reality on Earth, Jesus instructs the members of his church, which is the spiritual body of people representing that kingdom, not a building, to preach this message to the world. The teachings of Jesus, which includes many kingdom parables, explain that while the kingdom has not yet replaced 'the kingdoms of this world,' the seeds of this future government have been planted and are growing.

What we must do in order to enter the kingdom of God and be part of God's eternal family is we have to repent of our sins, be baptized and start living by those righteous laws of the kingdom. We have to choose to be on God's side in this great battle. When we make this decision and begin living as God suggests, God rescues us from the darkness and considers us to be part of the kingdom of the son of his love.

we also instruct you to pray for God's kingdom to come. As we experience the limited aspects of God's kingdom now, we gain confidence that the future kingdom will be a full reality. When this occurs, faithful saints and angels will assist Christ in teaching those who will have never known God's truth.

After every human has had the opportunity to hear God's truth and choose whether to respond to it, the great battle of God versus Satan over mankind will finally come to a close. God is destined to win. Make sure you are on his side.

God tells us, as is recorded in the bible that there are two spiritual kingdoms that humanity must deal with at the present time. The kingdom of light is one, and the other is the kingdom of darkness. God the father has commissioned Jesus and me to reign over the kingdom of light, and Satan has been allowed to be the king over the kingdom of darkness.

These two kingdoms can also be called the kingdom of spiritual truth, and the kingdom of spiritual lies, or the kingdom of spiritual deception. The kingdom of truth operates by love, peace, friendship, righteousness and honesty, and the kingdom of deception operates by hatred, fear and control, competition and dishonesty. Ultimately the kingdom of darkness becomes a function of eternal anguish and regret, while the kingdom of light becomes a function of ever increasing joy and never-ending, mind-boggling, for us right now, God-glorifying creativity for all privileged to be there to participate in for all eternity.

From God's perspective, we all are subjects of the kingdom of darkness at birth because of the sinful nature we inherit from Adam and Eve, until we grow older and choose to depart from that kingdom and be transported into the kingdom of light. Saying 'Yes!' to the free gift of salvation, forgiveness for our sins, through Jesus Christ is what transports us from Satan's kingdom into Jesus's kingdom. And this is the basis behind the Sacraments of Baptism and Confirmation, as sought by strict Christians even today. And these may be in concert with others or done singularly by those who feel the strength of conviction themselves.

For most people who are in the kingdom of darkness, they have no idea they are subject to Satan's authority and power. That suits Satan perfectly well. They'll soberly and painfully figure it out quickly once they die. So to keep them blinded and deceived while they are still alive on this planet, Satan allows them to establish their own little kingdoms. We can call that the kingdom of self...the kingdom of greed. God doesn't consider that to be a kingdom, nor does Satan really, but as long as it keeps people from the desire to be translated into the kingdom of Jesus Christ, Satan is content to let it be, because it has worked well for him down through time. Anything Satan can use to keep people from willingness to be transported into the kingdom of Jesus Christ means ultimate victory for Satan.

Thus, a spiritual battle rages over the eternal destiny of souls whether people know it or not. Believe it, my sons and daughters! Which then means Christians who devote themselves to God spiritually are in a spiritual battle whether they like it or not. That's because God allows it to be this way, but for a time, and anyone who is in the kingdom of Jesus Christ, Satan hates. He is filled with rage towards them, because they are the 'apples of God's eye,' and Satan no longer is or ever will be. If that isn't painful enough to Satan and his demon hordes that serve him, Christians are assigned by God to have dominion on this planet, to be used of God to help snatch souls away from Satan's deception and control, and help them become all that God desires for them to become and do. This forms the basis behind your coming battles. This battle rages day in and day out. It never stops. It never will stop, until Jesus locks Satan and his demons up in hell.

Just because a believer may be in a season of peace and tranquility does not mean the battle isn't raging all around them. It will just be a matter of time when the devil will be allowed to make his influence greatly known to you, and when he does, God wants you to be fully informed in what to do. What does God expect of us when the devil attacks us, or our loved ones or friends? To be wise. Wisdom to hear what the holy spirits tell us to do in each instance, and courage and determination to obey as heaven directs.

Before launching into spiritual warfare, let us take a moment to bring balance to the issue of spiritual warfare. God has his divine protection around each of us from the moment of conception. Not only is it around each of us, but upon cities and nations. God knows what goes on around this planet. He always has; he always will. The only influence Satan has on this planet and on you and I personally is what God allows him to have. Why God allows Satan such latitude, especially against you personally and your loved ones and friends. It is a question we'll never fully get answers to until you're with God in heaven. I see it as a strengthening to your spiritual immune system. Once there, I declare to you, it will all make sense, especially in the light of how God intends to welcome Christians in eternity. God has his eye on eternity. Yet he too must be patient as eternity unfolds, as you and I must be patient for it to unfold. More specifically, patient for what? For what purpose? To manifest his glory in a way that has never been manifested before. Difficult as this may be for you to comprehend right now, God is using Satan as an instrument to help chip away at a masterpiece God is building for himself a people to radiate his glory! That would be you and all others who are in Jesus Christ.

God the father is preparing his son a partner – the church, that is his called out ones, not a building – to co-reign with him in eternity, but God realizes that his church cannot be trusted any more than Satan could be trusted along with a third of the angels that rebelled with him against God in former times could be trusted, and thusly kick evil out of heaven, purged and then purified of self. Selfish desire that doesn't really care what God has to say about it or not. Selfish desire that expects God to bless whatever we think is best for us, even at the expense of it offending him and others.

Christians love to have their sins forgiven by God. Satan would love to be forgiven of his sins as well. Who wouldn't? Yet for Christians, forgiveness is just the starting point of God dealing with our sins. A change of heart to stop wanting or willing to sin becomes the hard part. Some of us need a bigger paddle on our rear-ends from God than we need others to motivate us to stop sinning. And here is where the difficult part comes in. God uses Satan a great deal of the time to be God's 'paddle' on our rear-ends, eh?"

An audible gulp and some coughs come from the chosen army below.

She forges ahead. "Yes. God could stop evil against Christians right now, but in his wisdom, he is using evil to work for the church's ultimate good. That will run its course and one day stop in the future. Until God stops it, we have to deal with it. As you all are about to deal with it today on God's behalf. Bless you all, my children.

Though we can't actually prove it biblically in any iron-clad way, I tell you God wants each of us to know how deadly sin can be and is, in fact, before entrusting us with the power he'll entrust us with in eons to come. Some believe all memory during our time here on Earth will be wiped from us once we're with God. Believe that God will make certain we'll never forget what living is like on Earth, even where Satan was allowed various freedoms to show his true colors – his true nature – which is to rob, steal and destroy, to make others miserable to somehow try to find a way to ease the pain and rage inside him for having lost what he once had, though knowing he'll never get it back.

Think of it. Every time we ever sin, or will sin in the future, we partner with Satan's nature and don't even realize it most of the time, nor even care, when we make the decision to sin. Believe that God wants us never forgetting that either. Believe for eternity he wants you realizing just how much you love sinning, just like Satan loves sinning against God and others. So, we can forever appreciate just how great of a salvation he offers us in the kingdom of heaven.

Thus, we are forced to deal with Satan whether we like it or not. And because the ravages of satanic sin so infects this planet, babies die before being born. Babies, people, painfully die after being born. Birth defects, sicknesses, diseases are all by-products of sin that Satan introduces to the world starting back with Adam and Eve. The devil gets in your way. So indirectly because of the effects of sin, yes it is Satan who kills babies before they are born, and who kills them after they are born. War, starvation, droughts, plagues, tragic weather phenomenon, financial hardships, etc., are all ravages of sin. Had Satan never been allowed to introduce sin to this world, the human race would not be exposed to these cruel enemies to God and to the human race. But in God's infinite wisdom, he has a plan. A very good plan. God could have never allowed Satan to infect the human race, but in ages to come, we will come to understand that God's wisdom in allowing him to do so has its purpose, and has an ending.

This may be referred to in your terms, 'The Bottom Line:' A person can learn everything there is possible to learn about waging effective spiritual warfare against demonic spirits and use their wisdom and knowledge of waging effective spiritual warfare to help them walk in greater spiritual victory, but Satan will still be allowed to keep an upper hand when it comes to the ravages of sin – enter the realm of the fallen ones – upon the human race, until God locks him and his demons up in hell. Perhaps sadly, no Christian is exempt from the ravages of sin. Most Christians of the day will die prior to the return of Jesus Christ due to the ravages of sin brought on by Satan. And prior to dying, most Christians have their joy and peace constantly chipped away at, simply because the human race is so infected by the effects of sin. That's reality my chosen.

Yet God gave spiritual weapons – spiritual disciplines may be a more appropriate description – to Christians to help keep Satan from having even greater influence against them, and especially those Christians who are serious about walking in obedience with Jesus Christ and saying "No!" to disobedience and sin. The desire to be used of the holy spirits to rescue other lost souls from hell, and to help enlist them in the army of Jesus Christ and me, your Lord and Lordess. So, now let us examine these spiritual weapons and spiritual disciplines, and trust God to help us to be wiser in our need to use them, and become wiser in personally using them. Bear in mind the intention of these heavens who arm you with certain advantages over Satan and his demons.

Spiritual warfare is not a popular topic in today's houses of worship, be it the spiritual mind or the buildings man creates, supposedly in God's name. Most Christians are not even aware of the raging battles in the unseen places. And even though angels and demons are mentioned throughout the Bible, and can be recognized in everyday living, few contemporary Christians, even pastors, expose the nature of these spiritual forces from God's perspective, or that of the bible.

Hidden from our earthly eyes are two kinds of spiritual warriors; God's faithful angels and Satan's malicious demons. Our sovereign lord uses his armies of loyal angels to help, protect and guide you according to your needs and his purposes, for all of our good. He uses the fallen angels, Satan's demonic rebels, to punish the wicked, to demonstrate his uncompromising justice, and in the midst of the battles, to test and strengthen your faith as we rely on him.

Of course, that short and simplified explanation only provides a glimpse of the ongoing battle. But remember this. When the devil rages against God's faithful people, our shepherd always wins. The book of Job illustrates it well. Notice how God allows Satan to test and torment his faithful servant before he saw the victory.

...the lord says to Satan, 'Have you considered my servant Job, that there is none like him on the Earth, a blameless and upright man, one who fears God and shuns evil?

So Satan answers the lord and says, 'Skin for skin. Yes, all that a man has he will give for his life. But stretch out your hand now, and touch his bone and his flesh, and he will surely curse you to your face!'

And the lord says to Satan, 'Behold, he is in your hand, but spare his life.'

So Satan moves out from the presence of the lord, and strikes Job with painful boils from the soles of his feet to the crown of his head.

Then, Job's wife says to him, 'Do you still hold fast to your integrity? Curse God and die, Job.'

But then he says to her, 'Shall we indeed accept goodness from God, and shall we not accept adversity?' In all this Job did not sin with his lips.

When Job's trials finally end, God richly blesses his faithful servant. But you, too, face challenges beyond your human understanding. And when you do, you, like Job, can trust our omnipotent savior to guide you all through the times of agonizing tests and anguish. Be encouraged by his words below:

'Do not fear any of those things which you may suffer. Indeed, the devil is about to throw some of you into prison that you may be tested. Be faithful until death, and God gives you the crown of life.'

Let us close and hand the floor over to Saint Bruno with prayer and preparation.

Let us pray that through your weakness God will show his strength -and his victory!

'...they brought to him many who were demon-possessed. And He cast out the spirits!'

'Amen, children… And thanks and praise be to God in the highest! AMEN!"

The Chosen, one and all, respond. "Amen heavenly ones, Amen."

Jesuette spoke more than she intended to. She returns to her chamber in heaven without another word.

CHAPTER TWENTY-ONE

Saint Bruno awards the chosen everywhere seven hours of well-deserved rest. He urges his patriots to imagine and dream of themselves in flight, obliterating the fallen with lightning speed, using their prowess, holy water and gestures. And destroy fallen attackers with the weapons and tactics he and Master Bruno awarded them. He assures them that upon awakening they shall feel strong, confident and well-prepared.

"Children warriors of heaven," Saint Bruno calls. "I shall call upon you when the time is come under the full moon to rise and fight.

Rest well, dear ones. Your victory is on the cusp."

Saint Bruno and Master Bruno review the aspects of battle facing their chosen.

"Organization?"

"Consider us the Commanders in Chief over all regional Generals, Commanders and their hierarchies."

"We have one Commanding General for every theater. Each Commander shall hold Field Marshal Rank over the Divisions, Brigades, Regiments, Battalions, Squadrons, Platoons, Squads and Fronts within their region."

"Very good Master Bruno," Saint Bruno listens carefully. "Please, go on."

"Our most mature, they being the first of all recruited by me or by you Saint Bruno, will hold the command positions. Divisions and all ranks in the hierarchy exist. All the combat troops are assigned and ready to report to their immediate ascendant. Reporting is well understood by all. Speak now?"

Saint Bruno is pleased. "I can add no more on this topic. Please continue, Master Bruno."

"The Special Daytime Operations Forces ascend on daytime activities as they seek-out and convert or jettison the fallen. We know the demons are recognizable by cosmetics or perhaps the jet-black hole in their souls, which our troops can visualize."

"Master Bruno! I am pleased you implemented that in the plan," Saint Bruno exclaims. "I thought that attribute got by you when first mentioned. I was feeling like I would have to feed you at the last minute. Oh, thank the Lordess!"

"You are being facetious, saint? Good...That means you are comfortable.

We plan to ascend and attack at the same relative time in every region of the world. That is, we attack the East Americas at dusk as it comes there, and so in the Central Zone in America, dusk there and so on around the world with attention on earthly time zone. This implies, however, that we start the nightly attacks at dusk two logical days before America in the Far East Pacific, then launch in the East, the Middle East, the European East, the European West, and finally in the Americas moving to the West in each region as we go."

"I also believe that is the best-planned coordinated effort, Master Bruno."

"Without prior discussion, please forgive me Saint, I created a second Special Forces Recognizance and Recovery Division." "Well,

Master Bruno...do you really believe I have no clue at all of this?" Saint Bruno chuckles. Master laughs along with him.

"We have data to show how the fallen are likely to attempt spirit to spirit combat. They will conjure machetes and attempt to sever the chosen's astral cords. However, we should bade well as the chosen can carry-out their orders from a fair distance away, that being aiming and firing the holy water and gesture at the enemy. Not to mention implantation of your more tangible weaponry."

* * *

Saint Bruno addresses the chosen. "My special, chosen Earth children and young people...The time is upon us. For, tomorrow evening you shall all rise toward the heavens in spiritual ascension into the dimension that is ours. This awesome space is yours to claim as you shall return one day, upon your death on the way up to the next plane; Heaven. All the heavens await your arrival with great eagerness, yet with patience, as they know all decisions are for the trinity to make, and not theirs alone.

You may find the coming days and nights slow for your preparation. That is because we are launching our holy assault without announcement, warning or declaration, by surprise. I assure you, so be alert to the all the possibilities; a warning from Master Bruno, because it will not be long until the fallen will act upon you and retaliate in attack after attack. You intend to make the effort to save them, but they are out to kill you… kill you anyway they can, and, they will. Not just you, but all those believers not yet recruited as chosen.

The fallen have many flaws in their being,

action, patience and fortitude. This is due simply to the inherent flaws ingrown in their leader, Lucifer. He demoted Ballard to the ranks, for example, on account of his evil greed and arrogance. Ballard is ripe for conversion, believe me, my chosen. We are doing well, as the path to this moment gave you the sacred training, weapons and courage you need. I commend you all on your diligence, determination, promise and accomplishments. Remain still and quiet for just a moment. Be keen."

Jesuette feels an intense love, even kinship toward the chosen aligned.

"All my children, children of heaven, my army of goodness, I, Jesuette, your almighty Goddess shower you with heavenly grace, and blessings upon your departure to represent me and the universal good. For, your departure on this dangerous journey and battle also represents your next significant steps toward the entry to heaven. So, go forth and conquer for the love of God the father, God the son, me, God the Holy Spirit, all the saints, Mary and Joseph and all the angels. Most of all do it for your mother Earth. We pour down upon you every tool of goodness within our realm. We award all who are fearful. Please take these gifts, rise up with your brothers and sisters. Be strong and go forth in concert with Saint Bruno's and Master Bruno's word. Bless you My Chosen."

The rally of chosen quite instinctually and without pessimism whatsoever, break into excited cheers and war cries. Saint Bruno gives them a moment more, then says:

"Chosen ones, rejoice in your message and blessings from the Lordess!"

The rally of chosen break into an explosion of thrilled optimism. Saint Bruno and Master smile on them. The two Brunos go on to review their teachings for the masses, all the mechanics of a coordinated approach to combat against the fallen. They are satisfied and so rest.

* * *

Satan rests comfortably in his laurels. He feels no inclination to rally just yet. He speaks to his ragged crowd. "Fallen ones of mine, your tasks, until I command different, revolve around exactly what you have been doing thus far. Keep going after our sleeping souls in the night and draw them into our fold. Use the tactics I have shown you. Wait two days. We shall introduce the element of surprise over the damned chosen."

They know the directive. And they are thankful for the two night rest, the very first extended rest they will have taken to date. Most of them sleep for the full forty-eight hours. The few who do not, stay at home, lying around just waiting for Lucifer's roust. Those who sleep, dream. They rest unsettled. They toss and turn discomforted in total. They feel unable to initiate a journey to attack whatever it is that is bothering them so.

Lucifer is blind and deaf to the fallen troubles brewing right under his dripping nose. Other fallen do not feel any change in climate as their counterparts suffer through the hours. The sleepers experience entrancing visions and actions through the night, the first… the second. In the midnight moments shuddering awake. Is Lucifer putting us through some nasty test? Is Ballard invading our heads to torment us in order to better prepare us for the fight?

No one knows and no one is talking, yet

the fallen who sleep suffer in agony without the means to control it. As they wake on the back-hand of terrifying, stinging dreams they feel engaged with something seemingly the opposite of what they practiced thus far. They surprisingly feel very good about it inside. They stay right here at home waiting to hear from the dream spirit for next steps and clarification... affirmation, drive and motive, once more.

CHAPTER TWENTY-TWO

Jesuette and Saint Bruno walk through the message they plan to relay to the chosen holy warrior children. Saint Bruno understands what Jesuette prefers and agrees in blessed goodness. The good Saint shall call upon their chosen to rise-up, and Jesuette shall fortify them. Those who await patiently, confidently and relaxed in nature, will know very soon the reality of heaven, love and purpose.

For what are heavenly moments and earthly hours, an appropriate call to arms takes hold and so shall be what the chosen will wake to in only a few short hours. Most chosen did take their rests right away a day and a half ago, and now sit, ready for the announcement from above. Ready to ascend and battle.

"Oh, chosen warriors of heaven:" Saint Bruno commences. "Wake now and heed these words. Upon the closing message from Jesuette, you shall be ready and enabled to rise and go forth. As this battle progresses, you will encounter more and more fallen ones in our dimension. You must convert and jettison immediately, do not contribute a single word to or in reply to the wicked ones. Remember that they are children and young adults just like you, but they are corrupt and degenerated into evil through the work of the devil Lucifer. Upon an encounter, hold up and out toward them your holy water and gesture, and kinetically recite to each the prayer 'Act of Love.'

No matter what they intend to do, any action toward you, they will stop and freeze upon your actions toward them. You must not let them get to you, for their mode of battle includes bladed weaponry. The goal they have is to slash apart your astral cord. If that happens, you will die. So, prior to rising, please say a prayer asking your soul be saved. Each of you have a ranking officer who will guide you through your duties day upon day and night after night.

Initially, you will obey this directive. Rise up and guard your territory, that is, do not wander far from it just yet. This night is somewhat crucial, in that the fallen are asleep in rest until their call from Lucifer. So, I am asking you for this night to fly low and visit any fallen you find and perform your conversion rites upon him or her. You can tell who is fallen by the absence of light, any light that otherwise will have shown from their souls. They can see you by the presence of light gleaming from your soul, for the Holy Spirit fills your soul as you say your prayers with pure white glimmering grace from the heavens above. You can also recognize each other by pure vibrations emanating from chosen to chosen from this point on forever and ever. So, my soldiers of Jesuette, go forth tonight and visit the sleeping fallen and convert."

Saint Bruno feels the feedback from the great army, and so performs his introduction.

"Chosen, you shall rise up as Jesuette closes her fortification of you."

In that second the chosen hear the most exquisite tones they have ever heard. Tones reminiscent of a Flugel or Euphonium horn. The tones play in an analog curve, rising, falling and issuing smooth arpeggios. The chosen, all, have their eyes closed as the light inside them warms and settles. It calms and sooths, yet also gives them ultimate cause and confidence. In the euphoric song, is a short message from the Goddess.

"As you rest, and as you rise, and as you contribute to this war of chosen good against fallen evil, you will know the presence, affirmation and strength directly handed to you from the Divine Trinity, Mary, Joseph, all the saints and all the angels. Hark and be hush as your warrior saint, and your superior officer, Master Bruno shows you the path to make, the fight to take and orders that will have ultimately come from me or Saint Bruno that lead to your concluding checkmate and win for the heavens. So, my children, rise up now and go forth in Godspeed. Rise! Rise! And praise the Lord!" Jesuette is done. She exhales a honey suckle breath.

Chosen everywhere feel a moderate breeze

and inhale the delicate scent of a sweet lovely flower.

The chosen army, save for the Special Forces, slowly float up, higher and higher. They move temperately as they pass fully into the higher plane. Each soldier stakes a circle of bailiwick and then purposefully dives below into the homes where the vibration of an offspring is identifiable, yet there appears not any sign of soul-shine. The chosen continue to discover many households that Satan has hit.

Groups of sleeping fallen are left easy to convert, as the chosen need only to hold the holy water and gesture out to him or her, and recite the prayer. The groups are dealt-with the way that the chosen converted those on the way to war. Here…where all roads lead. Hordes of fallen lie sleeping unaware. The chosen convert back many, leaving none on this first night of war, quiet as it is.

* * *

Lucifer sniffs the dense air. The odor chokes him. He falls over in collapsed shock and helplessness. He sits there, in the darkness of his sad and lonely space. He is unconscious, yet he, for the first time, dreams. Dreams that carry him far away to a place so attractive, positive and seductive. Longing to be in such a place, he luxuriates, basks and revels in the pleasure. Pleasure he has not felt since his existence in heaven. And not felt since his falling into hell. Then, he was adrenalized and high at his coming to his own heaven, where he is the boss...no loss... no, he is the king...the god.

Now, as he sleeps, the vistas of both places, side by side, he sees without a doubt the heavens above overfill with propriety, decency and nobility. It illuminates and shines with the unadulterated white grace of God. The other side reeks of dishonor, cruelty and corruption. The sleeping, dreaming mind turns back to the heavens from which he fell millenniums before. All the souls there illuminate with bright, white shining light. He feels warm, pleasant, glowing and snug there. Once again peering into hell he is enveloped in agitation, discordance and repulsiveness.

Lucifer lies there comfortably, yet he still feels somehow completely vulnerable. The scent is that of the chosen. They have risen, yes, but more so what is to him an odiferous strike, although it is actually the holy, sublime and lush essence of the good Saint Bruno. So, within the realm of dreamy sleep, the redolence turns from bad to very, very prepossessing and copacetic.

That alone, keeps the beast oddly at ease and feeling...believing that he is, indeed, in heaven enjoying his existence by God's side among his fellow saints.

As The Prince of Darkness lies there inadvertently rendering himself quite impotent, more and more of his sleeping fiends, those malignant spirits convert to chosen, right under that long, pointed, jagged nose of his. Hours pass, several... many, before Lucifer wakes to the tickle of dampness at his groin. He slowly wakes and eventually sits-up. He looks down and sees the crawling lice.

He raises his nose to the sky, and it hits him. His rogue army is breaking apart at the hands of the chosen, and he, under a spell of Saint Bruno's. A long, raspy groan escapes his mouth, as he stands, crooked over, and paces in circles, full of anxiety.

It is just before dusk when the fallen leader speaks to his minions. "Fallen soldiers! Followers of the fallen one. Tonight, you rise. Yes! Rise up now, you little fuck-faces, and go out and kill every chosen being in your path. Do it right…do it fast…and do it…now!"

The fallen warriors slept all they could, so now chomp at the bit. They want and wait for the go-ahead order. At varying times throughout sundown, fallen combatants rise. The chosen ones fly about at the ready, and so most of the fallen meet a throng, a scary pack of nemesis. As the fallen enter the realm, the heavenly plane, chosen ones, all, carry a holy water and make a strange looking hand gesture that none of the fallen understand. Understanding, however, does not matter, as one look at an armed chosen soldier freezes the fallen in space, a place without time. Within seconds during a culmination of prayer, fallen disappear from the sky.

* * *

So as calm as the dimension was just moments before, it now fills with the spiritual beings amongst the sounds of battle.

So, the war begins. Soldiers are now in full engagement.

Deacon fights-off a fallen boy that just tried to shred Deacon's cord. He receives an impromptu unexpected message from Billy.

"Wow, Deacon, that happened fast, eh?"

"Sure did."

"Are you doing okay, brother?"

"So far, so good, man. I can't even tell you how many of those fiends I have taken-out, so far."

"Yeah, I know...Me too!"

"Alright...Let's fight!"

"Right on, Deacon!"

The two carry-on in a successful melee along with their brethren. All around them float and fly comrades, most of whom flash their holy waters and gestures over and over, all around. Fallen victims vanish. It is the chosen army's interpretation that their enemy at the receiving end of the holy weapons will have mysteriously found themselves back to their rooms. They sleep, and when they wake they are fully converted to the chosen movement. The new converts feel nice and clean, safe, and good about themselves. Most initially pray their thanks and praise.

Saint Bruno and Master sense the battles beginning, and receive visions of the fallen, falling. The heavenly army is met with little effective defense. Even so that is true for tonight, they must prepare and regroup every day. The Special Daytime Forces stand at the ready. They are all up and impatiently waiting for the word from above that orders them to rise and fight the evil.

Saint Bruno advises Master of the expected turn-out for the skirmish upcoming today.

"Master Bruno, we may leave our daytime force as is until the third day. We might have too many out there for the number of fallen that rise in the light. However, perhaps too few for what is to come afterward, although I do not see it that way at this time."

"That is good news. We designated our soldiers pretty much on the mark, then, did we not?"

"With Jesuette's blessing, yes, Master

Bruno. I believe we are set for the foreseeable future."

"Great then, right?"

"For now, I dare say, however, we must be ready to re-distribute troops and, or, revise the battle plan at any given moment."

"I fully understand, Saint. Thank you."

"So, let us now talk upon a light note the possibilities given the scenarios, shall we?"

"On a light note? What do you mean?"

"As I explained a few moments ago, we need not take action right away. It would behoove us, though, to think about what we may be facing; try to cover all the bases we can envision considering the possibilities. Do you understand this, Master Bruno?"

"Yes, Saint. I have it now. Thank you."

"Good. Now...shall we?"

"Ready."

"Let us first offer a prayer for Saint Daniel, our saint of holy war."

*   *   *

Full of dismay and feeling quite badly beaten, Lucifer fixates intensely on this first night's outcome. He admits to himself that he is taken by surprise. His sleep and distant dream, he is aware, form the root cause of his problem today. He takes on a deeper shade of red and grows greasier. His hands and feet stretch...grow four inches in length, while his inguen coils-up tight in retraction to his lower torso. Lucifer feels sick and cannot get past the realization in front of him. He is ditched in a self-pitiful moment. He is frozen. He feels the hurt of loss, loss of children, but mostly loss of face.

He fights the urge to lie back down and

just dumb-out. He feels the slaughter that his underlings withstand. He realizes many of those young warriors disappear with each confrontation. Let the army run on their own. After all, he already taught them everything they need to know.

Ballard notices his mentor is gone, so maybe he should step-up and run the show. Feelings? Is the prince of darkness experiencing feeling? Oh no. He mustn't. He can't. He has no one to pray to. Prayer? Why is Lucifer considering wretched prayer… he moans softly, groans a little louder. He hears it from deep within. It echoes in the emptiness. Yet still, he rises over his droning hum there in the darkest depths of abyss. He is the sole being.

"Fallen army of mine!" Lucifer snaps awake and yells as loud as he has ever. Upon the sense that they are all with him, he continues.

"Listen to me. I will announce a change of plan, but not perspective. I want the fighters in the west up in the daylight hours. Fighters in the east, keep on track in the night. Now, you will hear this but once. You people introduce as much violence and aggression as you can. Draw upon the images with which I feed your head.

First, for example, go for their astral cords...sever it. Result? Instant death. That is what I want. That is what you must do. That, my fallen comrades, should be foremost in your mind's eye. Go forth now, and follow my directions to the tee. I watch and I listen, so do not fuck this up. Please me, and I will please you. OhhhhAghghghgh. Beleeeeeeeeve Meeeeeeeeee." Lucifer gnarls in a mumble, and

God forbid the children see what he looks like right now.

* * *

In the west, as night turns to day Commanders in each territory send emergency signals to Saint and Master Bruno. The two spirits sense and then see a potential issue just as they receive the cries of their Commanders. Yes, a momentous influx of fallen ones appear in theater this day. The chosen special daytime forces manage well, but they are indeed losing many more servicemen than in prior daytime battles. Saint Bruno speaks to the chosen clans people.

"We shall increase or forces by number a full fifty percent. Commanders, please do this now. Confer with each other to reassemble the teams to the best of our favor. May that be done now, immediately, please? Go!"

The chosen are extremely sharp. They act and in this case react smartly, intelligently otherwise beyond their earthly years. There are welcome attributes every day that both Brunos note. They are impressed and pleased at the absence of desperation and self-osmosis among their young chosen spirits. The soldiers in battle display diligent calm and rationale. The fight absorbs them, but not to the point of circular distraction. The war, the premise and yes, the prize imbedded in each shine like the elegance within their souls.

If there is just a single disadvantage to the shine, it reveals the chosen to the fallen on-looking. Yet it blinds them, as well. Upon encounter and showdown, the chosen must be quick. But, they must work hard to change their technique in a way to thwart the fallen plan to creep up behind them, in some occurrences, but barely unnoticed. When the fallen seize those opportunities a chosen child dies.

Other detriments among the chosen are the mechanics and combative nature of their fight. The chosen must face it and must have the attention of their adversaries for the sake of success over methodology. The piercing glare of the fallen provide the intake of the chosen emissions. So, the chosen spend the availability of every third warrior as they must watch the backs of their counterparts. This works well, even if it is not a perfect solution.

The Commanders continue to look on and consider all ideas and possibilities. They are given reign over decision making. That is, chosen Commanders are not required to get a blessing from Saint or Master Bruno with each and every augmentation. The latter two know when to intervene and reassign. The Commanders do report-in after the fact.

Considering the fallen fly by the seat of their pants, they perform surprisingly well. They are all fired-up and very much involved with the ways, means and the prize. Lucifer did not construct a top-down hierarchy chain-of-command. He is at the top and his troops are at the bottom. He lets them soar and kill, or be killed on their own accord and by virtue of the skills they develop as they go, no thanks to him. This leaves their side more and more susceptible, as they act out a haphazard plan of action if there be a plan at all. Kill or be killed. There is no consistency and no organization. It is quite amazing that they do as well as they do.

The fallen are a disgusting, mangy and ugly assemblage. They often initiate an unhealthy distraction among the chosen.

The chosen are a beautiful and graceful battery garbed in robe, holy water hanging low from their necks, ready for introduction to each and every attack.

The fallen do not have contained battalion anywhere over the Earth. Many live a meth addicted and dark life. They tend to feed their degenerating beings dose after dose often three to four days and nights at a time. Then, due to exhaustion they are only able to join the fray one day or night at a time before they crash. The army is an embarrassment to Satan, yet the little goblins' ferocity at the same time sooth the devil at the top.

The dedicated and devoted chosen stay true to their respective battalion and Commander. They receive consistent messages from Saint and Master Bruno. And they adhere to the directives given them. They are full of confidence and zest. They are strong and well-rested for every battle.

So, even though it is early in this grand war, the aspects, characteristics, facets, idiosyncrasies, and peculiarities serve each side well, if not in a queer way for the fallen.

CHAPTER TWENTY-THREE

The young angel lamb spirits in the west rise up at dusk. The plain is at capacity with fallen demons. They are thick in crowd and fly about playing with each other in what appears to be a game of Tag. Some of them play some kind of ugly version of Move Over Rover. The chosen feel an order from Master Bruno, who says to them, "Blessed chosen, please remain invisible and quiet until you each position yourselves directly behind an enemy soldier.

Once you are all set in place and posture, please sound-off with your trumpets. And as fallen ones turn to you, flash immediately your munitions. Initiate conversion. Understand this. Some of you may inadvertently be more vulnerable than some others. This is dependent upon the location of any given fiend of the devil. Please…it is extremely important you not leave your astral cord open to the enemy. I remind you all that if your cord is severed, you will die.

By the ethic nature of your attack, you shall move in a logical sequence, even if subconsciously driven, those inevitable next steps at the forefront of your mind. Each step toward victory fortifies you and strengthens you. Envision it. Feel it. You will operate in this manner, yet feel free to style your individual activities based on your very own awareness, talent and experience. Stay on course with battle plans put forth by your Commander. Now, you chosen sons and daughters, go forth and triumph!" Master is gone quickly and smoothly.

The throng of fallen in the west smell something sweet. Noses to the sky, and piqued, they hear the sound of trumpets; an ugly, piercing blow. As each in their own time pivots, hoping for discovery, instead face an instant blinding bright light before them. In an instant they turn paralyzed in frozen animation, transfixed on the holy water and odd-looking hand gesture directed at them. They are awash in warmth and feel cleansed, as they involuntarily drift slowly and easily back to their encasement....home.

In the East, the chosen receive the same message from Master Bruno. The daytime Special Forces rise to the morning sky. They find a large sinister population of fallen warriors. The eastern fallen are keen, however, in every sense, and so will not have been taken by surprise no matter how the chosen chose to enter the theater. Unbeknownst to the good, the bad slowly become aware of risings, even if they cannot see the chosen individually. Most are well-versed in martial arts, and so morph into super live spirits of a sort. A darker sort.

The chosen too in the East are masters in the eastern disciplines, but they must rise and fight and know there is little else they have to stop the immediate struggle and instant combat with the fallen. There is nowhere, no way to hide behind the live spirited fallen artillery troops. The fallen bring the fight to the chosen the moment of their arrival. Chosen Field Artillery spirits know the danger and face it like the heroes they are. Combat troops appear from behind.

The Middle East is glossed-over. The earthly situations and circumstances there require a completely different approach. So, the chosen continue to let them kill each other. Goddess promises strength behind the persecuted Christians in the territory. Saint and Master Bruno comfortably hold that promise in mind.

* * *

Lucifer was the Angel of Light, "The Morning Star," and a divine servant of God. He is related to all other angels, but especially his fellow archangels – Michael, Azrael, Raphael, Gabriel, and Uriel.

Surprising to most, Lucifer was God's most powerful servant, having no superiors other than God himself. All the other members of the heavenly hosts were subject to his will, including the other archangels. He was also, reputedly, the oldest and most beautiful angel in all of paradise. However, Lucifer's glory fostered arrogance, leading him to believe that he was a being of perfection. When God creates man in his own image, Lucifer refuses to bow down to them. Corrupt and consumed by his pride, the angel deludes himself into thinking that God is incompetent, and that he the supreme angel was the rightful ruler of the universe.

As a result, Lucifer gathers up an army of rebellious angels and attempts to storm heaven. In turn, God sends Michael - the only angel skilled enough to match Lucifer in combat - to meet the rebels in battle. Despite Lucifer's best efforts, Michael emerges victorious, tearing away Lucifer's wings before casting him and his minions into the pit of hell as punishment. His name is stripped from him, and he earns the title "Ha-Satan" (the Adversary). His treachery against the father earns him imprisonment in the lowermost circle of the inferno, where his bitter tears and the icy winds generate from his ruined wings created the Cocytus, a frozen lake.

Being trapped in the belly of hell distorts Lucifer. His inner ugliness, caused by his hatred and wickedness, slowly becomes a reflecting force in his outward appearance, and transforms him into a brutish, fearsome abomination. His fellow rebels also suffer, becoming the first members of his new demonic hierarchy. In time, Lucifer attains dominion over hell, plotting a means to destroy paradise, kill God, and drag the last of his beloved human race into the mouth of the inferno.

The first blow against God's plan, comes as Lucifer projects his essence into the Garden of Eden, where it takes the form of a serpent. In this form, he tricks the first woman, Eve, into presenting, and the first man, Adam, into eating the forbidden fruit of knowledge, knowledge of physical greed and sexual gratification, thus stripping the human race of innocence by granting them the knowledge of good and evil. From then on, every human is instilled with the nature to live sinfully, sentencing them to fall to hell upon death; the price of sin is spiritual damnation.

However, to Lucifer's dismay, God sends his only son, Jesus, to Earth. After being crucified in the name of all mankind, the Devine Trinity reclaim the souls of Adam, Eve, Abel, Abraham, Noah, and all others who had dedicated themselves to God in life, but who had died because of their sin. Upon Jesus's resurrection, the many souls saved from hell are raised into paradise, forcing Lucifer to find another means of achieving his vengeance. God and his son beat Satan down.

Over time, Lucifer lures many heroes to

hell to try and free him, including Alexander the Great, Attila the Hun, Odysseus also known as Ulysses, and Lancelot. However, their souls are not black enough to free him from the prison God banished him to.

Lucifer finally resorts to the ancient, muscular, supernaturally tall, humanoid demon with black skin. He has several glowing scars around his body. His eyes glow red/orange/ yellow. Two large horns on his head and small spikes on his shoulders and chest daunt. He wears a bronze/ gold armlet on his right arm in the shape of a serpent, and his legs appear to be those of a goat, similar to a Satyr. His angelic wings are torn off, with only smoking stumps left. But he still seems able to fly. He has a huge penis and testicles that flop around during flight and fight.

* * *

One by one, and swarm by swarm Lucifer grants the fallen children the ability to change shape. Some take on the default shape of a serpent, while others choose other sickeningly and unsightly monsters, mythical creatures and other images that represent typical human phobias. Fallen ones take on entirely grotesque shapes, faces, beings and things, but their weaponry is limited to arrows and blades.

Their erratic rise to battle is the most crippling aspect of the fallen army. There is no rhyme or reason behind it. It all revolves around individual whim fired by their human addictions. They consider the essence of the drug they believe lay within their reward. Try as Lucifer may there is no breaking his warriors out of the stifling, undermining behavior. He is no longer feared. The fallen act and react with only the call to war and the ultimate prize in mind. No matter disorganization, coordination.

Just prior to the second rise of the chosen, Jesuette reaches out another time to her army. "Children…chosen ones. Put on the full armor of our father, God, so that when the day of evil comes, you are enabled to stand your ground. And do stand upon it. Stand firm then, children with the belt of truth buckled around your waist, with the breastplate of righteousness in place, and with your feet fitted with the readiness that comes from the gospel of peace.

Also, take up the shield of faith, with which you can extinguish all the flaming arrows let fly by Lucifer's evil ones.

Take the helmet of salvation and the sword of the spirit, which is the word of God. And reach out to the Holy Spirit on all occasions with all your prayers and requests. Do this each and every time you rise to battle, and in everyday life routine. Bless you… My children."

And so, the chosen carry arms.

* * *

The chosen rise up and into the divine plane. First, they sense that rancid stench of the fallen, and then, they gaze at the vista crowded with the most hideous, horrid and beastly creatures. Subliminally, they hear Saint Bruno. "Children, the devil awarded his army of demons the power to appear as any deformed, disfigured and frightful freak they wish. Do not let this consume you. If anything, this makes the fallen ones even easier to identify."

Master Bruno takes mortal poetic license and adds. "Easier to 'pick-off'."

The chosen thought patterns snap back to the

mission at hand. Absorbing Brunos' messages exhausts only a second of time for the holy army to interpret. Unlike the young chosen forces in the east, the western territory assigned cherubs take an immediate lead. They now enjoy the element of surprise on their side. In the sacred dimension hundreds of thousands of chosen battlers light-up the heavens and execute a deadly assault to the targeted enemies.

A great myriad of fallen combatants simply vanish. A crushing blow to the fallen army does not go unnoticed, as Lucifer smells the severely arduous and distasteful essence he recognizes as defeat. In a moment, he rises to the eastern territory and up to the higher plane. Without the bother to aim, he lets go one-thousand infected, diseased and flaming arrows in all directions.

Upon their significant win over the devilish

adversaries, most the chosen retreat, and so most of the devil's arrows pierce very few, and fly to nowhere. A small number of chosen too slowly in retreat do get hit. They fold like wounded ducks, disappear and waft downward to their beds. They are once again impotent until they are converted again by a chosen one, divine or earthly. Lucifer nonetheless celebrates even this minimum step, but he knows deep down the chosen score a momentous victory in the west. And for the chosen hit tonight, help is on the way.

The next sunrise sends the chosen Special Daytime Forces up to the higher dimension. There, they spy the cloudscape to find fallen warriors absolutely nowhere. The chosen receive a short prompt from Master Bruno. "They are at rest here in the west, licking their wounds. Please stay on alert where you are until dusk." The faction in turn rest invisible, yet vigilant in the theater of war.

The night fliers arrive as the daytime forces sail and glide downward toward Earth. There are no losses on this day, but no kills either. Tonight, the fallen rise. They rise with newfound guts full of hostility and loathing. They break the seal of the fighting plane and advance with a campaign planned carefully by their vicious, villainous leader. As they snap the hem into the upper dimension fireballs fly all around. They appear to have nearly two dozen outlets each that repeatedly fire slim torpedoes of flame. The chosen hold up their heavenly shields and nimbly and rapidly spin so as to foster deflection from all angles. Very few are hit.

CHAPTER TWENTY-FOUR

After the initial onslaught from the eastern fallen, that theater is empty of the chosen army. The large warzone is overrun with the devilish eastern creatures. But the chosen recover from the one-sided battle the previous night. Their daytime forces did not fly this morning. Saint and Master Bruno are in deep thought and deliberation to discern what to instruct and what they can award their troops. They must also take a step back and issue specific orders to assure victory. They are not in a hurry. They carry out careful circumspection. There will never be a repeat of the prior night and evening.

The second night's non-attendance has the fallen one and his eastern army taking a victory lap, cheering amid celebration. Saint Bruno is sickened by the display but he is not surprised. He conferences with Lordess Jesuette and the saintly board on the subject of ultimate victory.

"And this with whatever means necessary?" Saint Paul asks.

"Yes, Saint Paul," Saint Bruno replies. "I believe that if we cannot readily convert, and, if we lose too many innocent souls in the thwarted process, then it is time to put into play additional munitions. And, the license to kill of course."

"I see. I believe we all understand." The table of saints murmur.

"I request only the permission to use artillery that is already part of the angel's arsenal going back to the divine creation of angelic beings. That is all, Saint Paul, board and Lordess."

Saint Paul responds. "I make the motion to award our earthly cherubs additional weaponry...however with care and earnestness."

"Yes, Paul, I would ask for nothing more," Saint Bruno is pleased. "I suggest the almighty sword, if I may. With an added augment."

"Please continue, Saint Bruno," Jesuette requests. "Tell us how that particular implement will make a difference."

"I see the chosen army, as it rises inconspicuously, carrying out an immediate charge to the adversary with swords drawn. Upon a touch the adversary instantly vanishes. Those that attain the wherewithal to attack our chosen will be struck, and then the otherwise earthbound individual succumbs."

"Succumbs?" Saint Peter asks incredulously, as he looks toward the Lordess.

"Yes, all," Saint Bruno wishes to conclude. "I pit that against the notion that good children who follow God and his own Jesuette, and you all, in fact, deserve that advantage. The other side of this coin, I remind you, means certain and cumulative death to our special chosen ones, and that just beginning in the eastern territory."

"GRANTED!" Jesuette loudly proclaims, a fist pounding down on the great table, thus putting an end to any further debate against Saint Bruno.

The Pacific Coast in the western territory rumbles long and hard with an earthquake measuring six point nine on the Richter scale.

* * *

Following the order to rest easy while they wait for more from Saint Bruno, the chosen all over the east comfortably adhere. The saint walks through developments and devises new plans with Master Bruno. Master has many questions, and Saint Bruno has all the answers. The saint brings to a close his message for Master Bruno.

"And with that final word," Saint Bruno smiles. "Jesuette puts an exclamation point on it with a fist to the table."

"Wow, really?" This impresses Master Bruno.

"It is not funny, Master, but it is important to note."

"You mean note that she is in full support of our imminent plan, ever-changing so?"

"Yes. It is quite out of the ordinary for heavenly beings to display animated declarations."

"Well, of course, that does not apply to the Goddess."

"True, Master...So true."

Saint and Master Bruno prepare to address the chosen. Master prefaces the saint's message by introducing the background and the intention before introducing the saint.

"Are you prepared, Master Bruno?" The saint asks.

"Yes, Saint."

"Whenever you're ready, young sir."

you're ready, young sir." "Okay."

Master Bruno has an outline of his speech in mind and he is confident that it is the right and most potent message he can pass down. He takes a deep breath and begins.

"Chosen angelicas all the world over, hark and be hush. Receive my message in openness and transparent understanding. Saint Bruno and I are acutely aware of the defeats recently suffered and witnessed. And those were due to the fallen having been given new strengths in the way of weaponry. We know they have taken to implement fire and flaming arrows in their fight against us. That is the background to this message coming from Saint Bruno. He will introduce to you a new weapon of our own. Now...Saint Bruno?"

The young chosen bestow a great round of acclaim and ovation.

"Chosen ones of Earth, hear me now and let this memo serve you well, as I deliver it straight from the Lordess, herself, and the grand table of saints. As Master Bruno stated, I am contributing this over the recent forceful defeats suffered, particularly in the eastern region.

Lucifer awarded his army the fireball and

the flaming arrow, adding to their arsenal. I fully admit we were all taken by an element of surprise. Lucifer is out, then he is in. Now, I shall grant to you a new weapon, the heavenly sword. I suggest you cease with underwhelming and listen to my rudimentary facts about the sword. The flaming arrows and fireballs are well-known tactics of the fallen angel in heaven, and I sincerely apologize personally for not introducing you to the threat. To my credit, I have not seen those devices in play since Lucifer's battle with Saint Michael. That said, let me tell you and suggest to you the essence of the sword, and a few ways to put the sword into appliance.

First, how to manifest the sword. You will see and feel the sword no matter the mode of your journeying soul.

Second, a suggestion for you all. Journey

in spirit, unseen and clandestine. Remember, the sword takes on your mode of being.

Third, a suggestion for onslaught. Once arisen, and immediately thereafter, charge at your foe, sword before you. Aim to slash the astral cord. Mind you, you need only touch the cord or any fallen target with the sword to make the consequence equal to your intention. Remember, children. When you reach your assailant, handle the sword the way you intend to. You may swipe, swing or touch your target. The sword, remember, will move by virtue of your holy intent and be unseen as long as you are imperceptible.

So, arrive, brandish your sword and attack. You deserve to know the result of this application of the sword in this particular fight. Upon severing a fallen astral cord, the dreaming spirit and the earthly encasement both die. Jesuette gives her blessing, and so do I, along with the entire table of saints. So do not fret. For the fallen are out to kill you and nothing less."

Suddenly, Master Bruno again leads the announcement. "Heavenly warriors, now, with all that in mind, return to the theater tonight and put forth your newly developed competence. We must retake any and all ground we have lost. Guilt is misplaced here, angelicas, as your enemy strives to serve terminal harm to you. They have orders to kill, so go out and battle for yourself, the world and the heavens above. My apologies saint."

* * *

The fallen rise and gingerly enter the higher arena. There is no light, no presence and no scent of the chosen anywhere. The demons float about their personal airspace impatiently waiting to wage another killing enterprise. They are extremely confident, now that they have witnessed themselves the ways of the fire and arrow. They are quite aware of the substantial defeat they handed easily the chosen over the past three nights. Lucifer even recognizes his army over the developments.

The fallen combatants all hoist and hold tight their implements whether it be at the ready with the fireballs and bolos, or setting up their arrow to bow. They are nonchalant as they waver at the ready. They are told to hover in their rightful place and sharply wait in observance for any possible recognition of their enemy. Most believe that the chosen are frightful to return because of the beating taken. For they have been absent ever since.

Many of the fallen launch their arrows and let fly their fireballs and watch as the flames climb into the atmosphere above and finally fizzle there or until the demons simply cannot see them any longer. Lucifer frowns at such naivety, but then again they deserve a night of impractical nonsense.

Some of them descend back to their rooms, tired of the down-time, but most heed the order to stay no matter the wait or boredom. "Was it that easy?" Many of the fallen ask. "Did we win the war?" Others ask. "When will we know?"

All questions go unanswered, which only fuel the gang with more and more assumptions and for some, celebration. Some small groups of fallen troops make up games to play against each other using ballistics fired. The others shoot the flames from the atmosphere above, like skeet. As ugly as the fallen adversaries appear, they continue to frolic in the airspace, completely inattentive, oblivious and distracted, not unlike ignorant toddlers. Fallen soldiers begin to fall sleepy in flight there, riding just above the edge between Earth and their second attention.

The chosen squads worldwide receive orders to prepare to ascend and battle. Also, within a new strategy offered by Master Bruno, they are ordered to enter the higher dimension in what he refers to as 'layers.' That is, for regional units within each territory, to form a ladder of goodness and enter the space above vertically, one warrior just above another, ninety deep. What would follow has already been communicated when the heavenly swords were granted. And now, following three days and nights out of action, the chosen are primed-up and ready to fly.

CHAPTER TWENTY-FIVE

The chosen slowly rise up and into the higher dimension. They rise in layers, each a rung on the ladder. As the top layer of chosen break the seal, shields held to the fore, they charge in a flash to the inattentive fallen reclining down low. Within a moment, chosen units around the world instantly kill tens of thousands of fallen.

The second, third, fourth and every angel top-down peel away from the ladder formation and set upon their enemy. Moment by moment chosen rip into the fallen fray. They savagely slash the enemy astral cords or touch them away with the almighty sword. The scene is unsightly. The agony of the fallen appears as though they are each blown apart by some kind of improvised explosive device. Their rancid, thick black blood splatters out from their evil dreaming encasements.

In frozen buoyancy, the expression on the fallen faces exhibit surprise, distress and sickness as momentarily they become jettisoned non-beings, finally just speckles of dust in the atmosphere, rendered forever helpless...hopeless. Many faces illustrate the hair-trigger sobs of the annihilated. As each top-down sequential layer of chosen come away from the formation and advance, multitudes of fallen explode and rocket up into nowhere.

The dark blood, weapons and body parts climb with the dismembered beings. It is a ghastly sight that disturbs the chosen, yet not to the point of deferral. The chosen soar further toward their next victims behind or above each fallen they shred. The fallen are perplexed by the consternation, revelation and shock. They have not even the time or chance to draw their weapons. Mouths open and eyes wide, over one half the demons in the air this night artlessly disappear.

Very few fallen are alert enough to carry out kills over the chosen. The heavenly army drives upward, forward and onward. Unit by unit the chosen descend from the higher dimension last in-first out on their ladders, seeping through the trammel downward to their beds. There is no doubt that this effort won them a victory and also, time.

As daylight breaks, the Special Daytime Forces rise and follow the battle plan of their night time counterparts. They find the destination free of fallen army, and rogue fallen fighters. Master Bruno instructs all to stay-put in vigilance but orders a return at nightfall. But, Saint Bruno interjects and orders the chosen grounded until they hear otherwise. Master forwards the message.

Upon twilight, the Saint observes the theater from above. Saints Peter, Paul and Luke peep over his shoulder. Master Bruno sits on the lip of mortality and keeps his eyes on the theater above. The higher space above and beyond the Earth is still in the entirety free of the fallen army. The five observers abide and hold their positions all the night long. Throughout the night there is occasional conversation, questions and answers among the cluster of holiness. "Do you have next steps outlined, Saint Bruno?" Saint Paul wants to know.

Jesuette would also like to know. She calls her saints to the round table.

"Does this not prove-out our theories discussed last century, to be true? ...that the more liberty awarded, the less responsibility there appears? When it is our intention to send the opposite message? As it remains true, always, to achieve total peace, is to know pure love. Saint Bruno...do you have next steps in order?"

"Yes, my Lordess. I have another offensive plan that is somewhat reminiscent of the highly successful plan carried out most currently. There is, however an element of further surprise."

"Just now, saints, we stand in the proverbial lead, so I declare and bestow this command. Go forth one more battle, my two Brunos. Implement your latest plans, Saint Bruno, then rest indefinitely as I deliberate over my observations and consider all cues from you and Master, the holy table and from God above. For this, is the word of God."

PART FOUR
THE STORM

CHAPTER TWENTY-SIX

Saint and Master Bruno have one last operation, a last ditch effort to wipe the world of as many fallen beings as possible. The announcement is made and the army is instructed to wait until the call. Saint Bruno addresses Master and their brigades.

"Ah chosen warriors, on behalf of our Lordess Jesuette: Given our casualties, regardless of those of the fallen, the Lordess orders us to take a last climb up and attack for an indefinite term of task. You will re-convert or kill as many fallen as you are able. And you shall keep on the offensive over evil until I call you down and away.

Given the directive from me, you shall again rise in the layered, ladder formation, yet this time first, third, fifth, seventh and ninth in each ladder of goodness attack bottom up vertically traveling. The second, fourth, sixth and eighth angelica in each ladder attack the fallen to the forefront horizontally traveling. Hold up strategically your shields, and hold out intently your swords. Charge, touch and slash. Eradicate all demons possible within your realm and circle of strength. Bring forth your talent and effort. It may appear painful to you good soldiers of the Lordess, but this is the only way to bring the battle to an end, presumably, hopefully victorious. Commanders," Saint Bruno conveys. "There shall be nine ladders in each vertical unit. That is eighty-one chosen soldiers each.

I expect to call on you tomorrow night. Expect to battle continuously, night and day. You may be in the field many consecutive shifts, depending on what I, Master and Goddess observe and sense. Daytime forces and night flyers shall merge. Be prepared."

Master Bruno is on cue at his home for questions and answers from the worldwide chosen army.

* * *

All anybody has to pray for is courage, strength, wisdom and health. It has always been this way. Yes...thanks, praise, request for blessings, and courage, strength and wisdom. The keys to a happy and successful life under heaven. Jesuette calls the board of saints back to the table. Saint Bruno appears.

"Saints, angels, please hear my holy family

views, which are based on the scripture. You will interpret my message in terms of kinetically relayed information using the names of territories and regions based on the current world map I put before you and on today's current events. Please close your eyes and receive:

Rising conflict in the Middle East stirs within me a sense of worry as I see numerous areas of human lives and condition affected greatly and negatively by what transpires in the region. Note terrorist activity throughout, and spreading around the world, the increasing danger of hostile regimes hell-bent on the destruction of the free world, the West, Israel and America. Even the rising resource prices. However, this should also awaken our awareness of bible prophecy and God's activity in the world as we near the return. Listen as I review.

The uprisings in the Middle East today should capture our attention, for several nations involved in the conflict today will play key roles in the battles which will take place in the end times. My purpose in this speech is to present a brief overview of the unrest occurring in the Middle East today and to explain their connection with bible prophecy.

I recognize that many of us are aware of the uprisings going on in the Middle East, but listen. The nations experiencing uprisings at this time are Algeria, Bahrain, Egypt, Iran, Iraq, Jordan, Kuwait, Libya, Morocco, Saudi Arabia, Somalia, Sudan, Syria, Tunisia, and Yemen.

Several factors have led to these massive uprisings. First, there has been a long history of growing unrest against the corrupt regimes whose leadership has left the majority of their people in poverty while only a small upper class enjoys the wealth gained in the oil trades. Second, the desire for freedom is a universal longing in all people. With greater access to the international electronic communication and resources network available to developed countries today, many citizens in these countries can now observe the freedoms other nations have and enjoy, and their desire to attain their own freedom grows. Third, this network provides the ability to communicate and mobilize large numbers of people for mass movements. When many of us were observing the riots in Egypt, it was often said this revolution was made possible by social networks that are so popular on Earth today. Fourth, with the varying decline and violent take-overs by the Soviet Union, and with the United States' lack of leadership in the Middle East conflicts, it is difficult for the western leaders to maintain stability in the region.

The upheavals seem disorganized with no clear leader, so is there a mastermind behind these uprisings? Is there an emerging leader? It appears that two influential powers are at work. Listen, absorb and learn.

First, we must understand a little about the Islamic world. In Islam there are two major divisions: the Sunni and the Shi'ites. The two groups have been at war for nearly fourteen-hundred years since the death of Muhammad. Ninety percent of the Muslim world is Sunni. The Sunnis believe Muhammad's successor should be the most committed and worthy disciple, while the Shi'ites believe it should be a blood relative. The first three caliphs were Sunni: Abu Bakr, Uthman, and Ali. After several internal wars in which Umar and Uthman are assassinated, the

Shi'ites were able to install Ali, a blood relative of Muhammad. However, shortly after this installation, he was assassinated. This fourteen-hundred year-old conflict between these two parties is intense and hostile.

The Shi'ites are primarily in the countries of Iraq and Iran. An important facet of Shi'ite Islam is the belief in the twelfth Imam, or the Mahdi, who Shi'ites believe was placed in hiding as a child by Allah in 941 AD. He is expected to bring about the golden age of Islam by arising, returning, and defeating the non-Muslim world when the world is in chaos and at war. There has been a movement in countries with large Shi'ite populations to overthrow Sunni led governments and replace them with Shi'ite leaders. There is also the desire to replace current moderate leaders with more radical Islamic leaders.

One country having an influential role in the midst of these uprisings is Iran. Iran has sought to be the major player in a region known as the Persian Gulf. Iran has the largest population, seventy-five million, of the Middle East nations, and the largest military force. Iran seeks to encourage countries with Shi'ite majorities to overthrow their Sunni governments. Its current president, as those passed, expresses the goal to destroy Israel, the West and America. These are Shi'ites who believe the twelfth imam will return when war breaks out.

Some ambassadors of Iran write this regarding Shi'ite view of the apocalypse: 'The appearance of the twelfth Imam can be hastened through apocalyptic chaos and violence by unleashing a holy war against Christians and Jews. It is within man's power to bring about the end of days.' Irani leaders believe the mission is to pave the way for the rise of the Mahdi. Iran has been and is a major leader in the spread of radical Islam. Experts on the history and politics of Iran, write in their books on confronting Iran, 'Iran is not simply a problem, it is the problem. It's not just a member of the Axis of Evil, but the founding member, the chief sponsor of state terrorism, or to use a more recent characterization, the central banker for terrorism. It is believed and accepted by now, that Iran today is the mother of terrorism. Tehran openly provides funding, training, and weapons to the world's worst terrorists, including terrorist groups, known as Hezbollah, Hamas, the Palestinian Islamic Jihad, and the Popular Front for the Liberation of Palestine, and it has a cozy relationship with Al Qaeda.'

I know Iran is working in the country of Iraq. With American withdrawal from Iraq, Iran seeks to influence the outcome of this nation. In numerous reports, military officials around the world claim to have compelling evidence that Iran is supplying training and arms to the insurgents. Western officials in particular are greatly concerned that Iran will exert itself and become a major force in shaping the future of Iraq.

Another country of great interest to Iran is the island nation of Bahrain, which has a Shi'ite majority. Bahrain is connected to Saudi Arabia by a causeway, and the United States' 5th fleet is stationed there. Iran is encouraging the Shi'ites to overthrow the Sunni government in Bahrain. The toppling of the Bahrain government by the Shi'ites would potentially encourage the Shi'ites in Saudi Arabia, the oil-rich nation northeast of Bahrain.

Another country of interest is Yemen. Yemen is a strategic country south of Saudi

Arabia along the Gulf of Aden, which controls the flow of oil from Saudi Arabia and other oil rich nations. Yemen is also a country where America had a naval presence. The fall of Yemen to a hostile regime weakens the United States Navy's ability to secure the flow of oil to Asia and the West. Although these are tiny nations, a change in the regimes could have worldwide impact. The Suez Canal, the Gulf of Aden, and the Straits of Hormuz are the three channels through which oil is shipped to Asia and the West. The rise of hostile regimes in Egypt, Bahrain, and Yemen could put a choke hold on these critical channels.

Now, another prominent group emerging in Egypt is the Muslim Brotherhood. The Brotherhood was founded in Egypt in the year nineteen-twenty-eight by Hassan Al-Bana. They claim that their intent to spread Islam is strictly philanthropic and spiritual.

Since its beginning the Muslim Brotherhood has aspired to reassert Islam through the establishment of Shari'ah law in all countries and to reestablish an Islamic caliphate and to destroy Israel.

The banner of the Muslim Brotherhood has the Koran with two crossed swords underneath and the Arabic word, 'prepare.' On the surface the motto may appear to be a peaceful exhortation, except that the Koranic reference comes from Surah 8:60, which states, 'Prepare against them as you are able of force and cavalry to terrorize Allah's enemies and yours.'

The philosophy of this Brotherhood is as follows: Allah is their objective. The Prophet is their leader. Qur'an is their law. Jihad is their way. Dying in the way of Allah is their highest hope.

Although they claim to be a charitable and

spiritual organization, they are in fact an international Islamic terrorist organization that has, over the last eight decades, given rise to the jihadist terror groups, Hamas and al Qaeda. The Brotherhood is involved in terrorism against all American interests in the Middle East and against Israel. The Brotherhood, an active supporter of Hamas, pledges violence against Israel whom they view as occupiers.

Doctors on this subject know as I do so write, 'The chief player in this stealth jihad in America today is the shadowy international organization known as the Muslim brotherhood. The Brotherhood is an international Islamic organization that has, in the course of its tumultuous eight decades of existence, given rise to the jihad terrorist groups Hamas and Al Qaeda.' So, it is written.

The earthly Center for Global Security

states, 'Hamas, which includes military and political wings, was formed by the late Sheik Ahmad Yasinat at the onset of the first Palestinian uprising or Intifada in the late nineteen-eighty-seven, as an outgrowth of the Palestinian branch of the Muslim Brotherhood.' Unfortunately the United States' National Intelligence Agency, states the Muslim Brotherhood is largely secular and has ignored the facts regarding this group.

What are the possible outcomes of these uprisings? The most desirable outcome is that peaceful moderates take over, and stable democracies are established. Another dangerous, but very possible, outcome is that civil wars break out in these countries allowing even worse regimes to rise to power in these nations. If radical groups, such as the Muslim Brotherhood, take over, their goal will be to carry out the agenda expressed by many Islamic fundamentalist groups and Iran to destroy Israel and the West. These regimes would seek to overthrow the leadership of other Arab nations and replace them with hardline Islamic leaders. These regimes could put a stranglehold on oil supplies to Asia and the West, and their leaders would continue to seek the destruction of Israel and her allies. Lastly, America and Israel have the ways and means to obliterate uncounted regions and territories, and they are capable of carrying this out at a moment's notice and to execute so swiftly that it would appear an act of the Heavens.

This is the situation in the Middle East today. Is there a connection to bible Prophecy? One famous passage is the prophecy of Ezekiel 38-39 which mentions several of these nations. I urge all of you to review his prophesies. And also, to realize this simple truth:

I fully admit to you that I near the decision to dedicate myself to the losses and foster a rebirth, if not through destruction. Test after test, the result is clear. It is by now painfully obvious that due to Islamic Extremism, our small planet cannot get out of its own way. The experiment now exhibits signs, and displays concentrically formatted patterns of failure. So much so that I consider, yes, driving the evil and possessed earthlings to completely destroy themselves, thus a beginning to abandonment of the experiment for those mortal sinners altogether. The ingredient of imperfection are the virtual boundaries, as I perceive them, and, as I currently look upon them.

Lastly, my brothers and sisters, realize the onslaught from the Islamic Extremist group ISIS. Born from an especially brutal al Qaeda faction, the Islamic State of Iraq and Syria has grown from relative obscurity in recent years to overshadow its extremist patrons. It now terrorizes large swaths of Syria and Iraq and Afghanistan has become the target of the largest U.S. military operation in Iraq and Syria in many years. With the public, cold-blooded execution of Westerners and others from around the world, ISIS dominates headlines the world over. That is exactly what they want.

Let us be clear about ISIS. They have rampaged across cities and villages, killing innocent, unarmed civilians in cowardly acts of savage violence. Table...no just God will stand for what they did yesterday and what they do every single day.

* * *

Upon a pointed wail from heaven, the chosen gather from around the globe and prepare to rise up in battle. The chosen review in mind the latest methodology, as the heavens above expect. Each unit breaks into eighty-one spirit squads and then they line up in vertical formation. They grip the weapons they plan to employ; shield, sword, those on top of the other fallen-stopping articles put into use from the start. And now, they wait with absolute initiative, for Saint Bruno's inevitable "Go" imperative.

The chosen spirits are there in formation, many trembling in anticipation, like nervous, cosmic Chihuahuas. The scene is intense as the army feels like it is about to advance out of themselves. And then, with no further a due, a message from Saint Bruno:

> "Chosen spirits everywhere, hear my prayers to the father almighty God and heed my orders for you all.
>
> O God, I beseech you, watch over those exposed to the horror of war, and the spiritual dangers of a soldier's life.

Give them such a strong faith that no human respect may ever lead them to deny it, nor fear ever to practice it. By your grace, oh God, fortify them against the contagion of bad example, that being preserved from vice, and serving you faithfully, they may be ready to meet you face to face when they are so called, through Christ our Lord.

Sacred Heart! Inspire them with sorrow for sin, and grant them pardon.

Mother of God! Be with them on the battlefield during life and at the hour of death, and grant that they may live and die in the grace of thy son.

St. Joseph! Pray for them.

May the guardian angels protect them;

Amen.

Soldiers of Christ and Jesuette, peace be with you."

"And also with you." The chosen feel showered blessings reigning down upon them.

"Amen."

"Children of the Lord," Saint Bruno continues. "This leg of battle will have been your finale performance in the name of Jesuette, the trinity and all of heaven. Immediately following my final note to this message, rise together in formation and deliver the holy barrage. If there exists a battalion that does not have the battle plan memorized, please reach out to me now."

All are silent.

"Magnificent. So, all you cherished spiritual beings, Go Now and Meet Your Nemesis."

With that, the ladders of chosen rise in perfect unison and they one by one percolate through the dimensional breach. Their swords point upward and their shields protect their spiritual mass. Like roman candles, the heavenly congregation of chosen platoons suddenly pop into the higher dimension. The even numbered soldiers shoot straight up slashing the astral cords of any, every, fallen above. And the others shoot outward dashing those before them.

There is noise of fright and cries as the fallen explode in a cloud of dark smoke, splattering black excretion all around. The screams fall off the chosen ears and the black tenebrosity dribbles off their shields. Fortifying fallen troops surface throughout the battle, yet the chosen are not taken by surprise. This first night brings defeat for the fallen, victory for the chosen.

Lucifer cannot explain to his force why the chosen can sense absolutely the fallen, while the fallen are blind. This advance granted the chosen is key to their overwhelming victories. Although the chosen do not entertain any such thoughts, they are keenly aware of their propitious elements. The fallen are dismayed and the chosen are emboldened.

The chosen Special Daytime Forces transude into the second attention to find and report that fallen soldiers now not only appear as the creatures they inhabit for the fight, but with the face of the addicted humans they break from every day in the course of the battles. The heads and faces are super imposed on each of the creatures are entirely monstrous and absurd. The chosen get by the humanoid head atop the creatures, but the facial expressions, the dark murky eyes, the disheveled hair, the scars and the sullen yet rapacious aura are so ugly that some chosen almost freeze in hypnotic spell.

But, as the youngest of the chosen glaciate, Saint and Master Bruno along with the territorial Commanders roust them back into action. The casualties are few among the chosen as they obliterate fallen ones thousands at every second in the holy stratum. Darting at frightening speed, directed by thought and intention, the chosen ones struggle not, as the fallen must explicitly make very specific changes to their respective sleeping, dreaming being to equate any movement whatsoever.

Throughout the following seven nights and days, the chosen carry out the onslaught.

The fallen continue to suffer heavy losses. The dimension is littered and blotchy with the final excreta of each fallen necrosis. Chosen forces sail right through the darkness, which appears as the thick seaweed on an August day on the Northwest Gulf Coast.

"Chosen angels!"

It is Saint Bruno at the ear of each heavenly warrior. "Delicately and discreetly retreat in descent and return to your homes.

Last-in-first-out. Wait there for my next message."

The heavenly plane is messy and nasty with imploded fallen gray matter carcass, but is free of chosen fighters.

* * *

Jesuette calls all her father's saints and angels to her sacred table. Within the instant, all her holy men, women and cherubs arrive attentively and settle into their space. She asks the robed and winged beings to join her in prayer:

"Lord hear our prayer…

Our Father, who is in heaven, hollowed
be your name.

Your kingdom come, your will be done
on Earth as it is in heaven.

Give us this day our daily bread

And forgive us our trespasses as we forgive those who trespass against us.

And lead us not into temptation and deliver us from evil…

Deliver us from every evil; past, present and to come.

For yours is the kingdom, and the power and the glory forever and ever.

Amen."

The session of those spiritual beings heave, "Amen."

"Thank you saints and angels," Jesuette begins. "Please welcome Saint Bruno, who joins us here, finally, after a victory of the chosen over the fallen."

Conveyed by the Holy Spirit, the crowd erupts in uncharacteristic applause.

"Unbeknownst as of yet but in announcing this now, may you all be aware that I call to an end, put to a stop, our earthly child chosen army strategy in battling Lucifer. And thus, I relieve Saint and Master Bruno of all combative responsibilities. Unannounced to all until now is an indefinite retreat orchestrated by Lucifer, as well.

That order standing, I say to all you angels here before me to go to, and remain with each of your respective earthly assignments. Stay with them always and sooth them, guide them and love them. Now, you angels covering the Middle East regions and territories in the world, as described in my previous review to you, have additional responsibilities.

Lucifer empowers a deep and broad throng of anti-Christian, and anti-Muslim, so-called 'non-believers.' They fight, take over cities and towns, and kill anyone and everyone in their path. They seek world domination at any cost to either side. The world leaders we coach, now dismiss the calls to action by the virtue of simple goodness and peace, surprisingly so let alone their supposed faith in God, Allah and Mohamed. It is a flawed ideology. It is also a flawed ideology these evil terrorists hold close, for they are no less bigoted and violent than the Nazis of mid-century Earth."

CHAPTER TWENTY-SEVEN

Jesuette relays a suggestion to listen, envision and feel what she struggles with today. "Heavens close your eyes, open your minds, and see:

Islamic music plays. It lilts and sways. Islamist militants knock at a policeman's door. It's the middle of the night, but the cop soon answers. He's immediately blindfolded and cuffed. They take him to the bedroom. And then, they decapitate him with a knife.

Militants with the Islamic State of Iraq and Syria herd hundreds of boys and Iraqi soldiers down a highway to an unknown fate. 'Repent,' the Islamic extremists tell inhabitants of its newly conquered territory. 'But anyone who insists upon apostasy faces death.'

Death is everywhere in the otherwise sacred city, and a strategically vital oil hub and the country's largest northern city. People speak of 'rows of decapitated soldiers and policemen' on the street.

The stories, the videos, the acts of unfathomable brutality become a defining aspect of the evil extremists, who control a nation-size tract of land and is pushing the country to the precipice of dissolution. Its adherents kill with such abandon that even the leader of the largest other terrorist groups disavow them. But in terms of impact, the acts of terror are wildly successful. From beheadings to summary executions to amputations to crucifixions, the terrorist group is the most feared organization in the Middle East, if not the world. All this outside of the nuclear threats. That fear is evidenced by fleeing soldiers and residents, five-hundred-thousand at a time, and plays a vital role in the group's march toward the capital city. Police and soldiers literally run, shedding their uniforms as they go, abandoning large caches of weapons.

You angels shall escort your Christian, Muslim and Jewish assignments to safety.

'We can't beat them,' soldiers repeat. 'We can't.'

The commitment to shocking violence is at the heart of both the extremist's recruitment and appeal. To radicalized Islamists around the world, there's something enticing about this group. It attracts at least thirty-thousand fighters — thirteen-thousand from the West — since its inception.

It's difficult to say what spawns such fealty to violence. There is absolutely nothing in Islam that justifies cutting off a person's head. But just as the bible discusses the beheading of John the Baptist, so does the Koran talk of beheadings. An example from the Koran: 'When you meet the unbelievers in the battlefield, strike off their heads until you have crushed them completely. Then bind the prisoners tightly.'

The act, despite its religious underpinnings, is massaged into terrorism. The purpose of terrorism is to strike fear into the hearts of opponents in order to win political concession. Islamist terrorism has already gone through several phases: hijacked airlines in the nineteen-seventies through to the twenty-first millennium, car and suicide bombs in the nineteen-eighties and nineties. But the shock value of each inevitably wears off, giving way to something new to maximize shock and press reaction upon which they thrive. What once garnered days of commentary now generates only hours. Decapitation becomes the latest fashion. In many ways, it sends terrorism back to the future. Unlike hijackings and car bombs, ritual beheading has a long precedent in Islamic theology and history.

Increasingly, Islamist groups conflate non-believers, combatants, and prisoners of war, which, coupled with their claim to Islamic legitimacy, provides them with a license to decapitate. Fear is the weapon of all terrorists.

Solemn Islamists and Muslims do not want to be taken by them, so they literally run away. The extremists give chase, all masked, and capture most of the fleeing innocents, who shout loudly to get the attention of the crowds of people. No one knows what they have done to reach such an ugly and unfair place. And people look, but no one says a word. They are all crippled and killed by fear.

Extremist fighters capture tribal militia Commanders, often along with sons, daughters and wives; entire families. The prisoners are forced to dig their own graves. Then the jihadists slit their throats.

Torture, flogging, and summary killings are rife in secret prisons run by the Islamic State, an armed group that currently and utterly controls large areas of the major cities within countries. The Islamic jihadists claim to apply strict Islamic law in areas they control, but they have ruthlessly flouted the rights of hundreds of thousands of local people. Those abducted and detained include children as young as eight who are held together with adults in the same cruel and inhuman conditions. Detainees face a shocking catalogue of abuses, including flogging with rubber generator belts or cables, torture with electric shocks or forced to adopt a painful stress position known as 'scorpion,' in which a detainee's wrists are secured together over one shoulder. Some of those held are suspected of theft or other crimes. Others are accused of 'crimes' against Islam, such as smoking cigarettes or sex outside marriage. Others are seized for challenging extremist rule or because they belong to rival armed groups opposed to the jihad. There is no shortage of detention. Many children are among detainees and even they receive severe floggings. Anguished fathers have to endure screams of pain as their captors torment family members...wives and children in nearby rooms. The standard flogging, for all, including children is more than ninety lashes during interrogations. Children, are repeatedly flogged over multiple days. Flogging anyone, let alone children, is cruel and inhuman, but the entire world is sadly paralyzed against action. Detainees are seized by masked gunmen who take them to undisclosed locations, where they are held for periods of up to sixty days. Some never learn where they are. Islamic State extremists continue to carry out scores of execution-style killings, including cruel and inhumane punishment of men, women and children.

Even men believed to be members of the Islamic State, who were accused of banditry, or some other crime, are tied by their arms to a cross and then shot. Other men, accused of homosexual acts are thrown off a rooftop. The ruthless murder provides another terrible example of the kind of monstrous disregard for human life that characterizes the Islamic extremists. Other cases include women who are killed for refusing to treat Islamic State fighters, female lawyers in different cities are also executed, and women are stoned to death, accused of adultery.

Scores of teenage boys are machine-gunned in public. Islamic State gunmen kill over accusations of cooperating with enemy forces, shooting them in front of a large crowd. Many other execution-style killings include husbands killed as punishment for their wives' failure or refusal to adhere to dress codes, while women are subjected to grotesque beatings for dressing improperly. Rule in areas under Islamic State control as characterized by the sheer brutality of its attacks on the most vulnerable sectors of society; women, children, and ethnic and religious communities."

"Lordess…Jesuette…Why must we hear this? Why must we be reminded of these atrocities… In so much detail? Please." Saint Peter cries out.

"Peter, and all you saints and angels, I want you to be aware, very aware of the horrific situations that I am dealing-with on our mother Earth. When you learn of my actions put forth for the betterment of Earth and man, you will have no question as to why, so listen as I continue.

Recently, a pamphlet made available by the militant terrorists lays-out justification for taking women captive, whether and when it was permissible to have sex with them and how they could be treated. It is permissible to buy, sell or give as gifts, female captives and slaves as they are but property that can be disposed of.

So, <u>this</u>, my brothers and sisters," Jesuette closes her message. "Is out of hand, out of control and cannot be tolerated under these heavens any longer."

The angels quietly whimper and the saints

whisper back and forth. All pray...for the world below and for Jesuette above.

The sound of a one-thousand pound gavel on Mahogany thunders and resonates throughout heaven.

Thunder blasts deafeningly over America.

CHAPTER TWENTY-EIGHT

A single drop, water is it, falls onto the gloved hand of the executioner. It is so uncanny in this region that he does not think twice. It is probably a droplet of sweat from his prisoner. The militant is covered-up completely in black; black high-top basketball shoes, black shirt, jacket and slacks, black gloves and black head cover. The eyes are the only part of him exposed. The prisoner is draped in an orange jumpsuit from shoulders to feet. He has sandals under foot and his entire head is exposed.

Chopping off someone's head or sawing it

off or slicing it off is about gore. Blood. Pain. Grotesquerie. Death by the blade is about shame, suffering in an animal slaughterhouse. It's the most repulsive theatre, understood by man.

To be hanged, drawn and quartered is about fear, terror, a word liberally used around the globe with the exception of one western country called United States. It still is. The most judicious, accurate and gruesome executions stink of terror. The black clad man stands to the left of the prisoner, and a little behind him, the executioner focuses upon his quarry.

The sword is drawn back with the right hand. A one-handed back swing of a golf club comes to mind. The down-swing begins. How can he do it from that angle? The blade meets the neck and cuts through it like a heavy cleaver cutting through a melon; a crisp, moist smack. The head falls off and rolls a little. The torso slumps neatly. This is why terrorists tie wrists to feet. The brain has no time to tell the heart to stop, and the final beat pumps a gush of blood out of the headless torso on to the plinth. Good show on behalf of the terrorist regimes.

The executioner turns and walks away, seemingly to nowhere, however when the videotaping ends a jeep rolls-up and takes him back to his camp. Two more militants in a small pick-up truck load-up the dead prisoner's head and headless body. They take the two bloody masses to an obscure location a distance away from their hidden camp and place each item a relatively short distance from each other.

* * *

Another small team of dedicated jihadists

work swiftly, yet carefully and judiciously to edit the video. The process is difficult and tedious, but the work is fairly professional. However, deep analysis of any given execution not a fully edited video would expose other jihadists standing around in the background, fully identifiable, as well as vehicles and baskets of weapons.

A sixteen minute horror video takes seventy-two hours and costs two-hundred-thousand dollars to produce. The strangely modern production of the videos reflect the versed talent behind the terrorist forces.

Prodigious groups of extremist murderers stand at the ready for any order passed down from regional command. They hide themselves just behind the field artillery and combat forces. The special operations groups are far enough away to keep their anonymity but close enough to move up to the given captured land and prisoners in order to carry out well-planned executions.

Mass murders are commonplace now. The executioners behead, burn to death, bury alive and crucify the meek and spiritual inhabitants along with the helpless foe who try to battle them. Coalitions of the sympathetic conduct air raids against the extremists, but offer no ground forces whatsoever. The Generals call for them, but the Commandersin-chief do not heed.

* * *

The heavens are aghast at the modern day behavior of battle cries reminiscent of old. This type of onslaught, killing in the name of religious belief, ethnicity and race, is outlawed, now for centuries. The only altercations of late are those in the name of humanity and humility; civil rights on behalf of the civilized world.

Jesuette is dangerously close to taking her hand to the unholy, atrocious and gruesome acts of the one-sided war raging in the Middle East territories on her sacred Earth… the hallowed Earth of her father: God. While this is a contemplation in spirit, our Lordess openly asseverates. When does the time come announced? How is the situation to be dealt-with? What is she to do, in preparation, and again in task? Who besides God is on her side in complicity? Where will any action strike, in particular? And why aren't these questions answered axiomatically? She prays to her father incessantly, uninterrupted. She pours and yearns perennially.

"My daughter and Lordess Jesuette," the father responds to Jesuette in a comforting voice barely above a deep hushed tone. "Be still in your deliberations. Be steadfast and clear. Be good to yourself for the heavens. It is up to you, my dear, to enforce a decision that both serves the purpose, and, is seen below as a natural, even if unheard of event in the end. The Christian masses and others will in eventuality, adopt the event as a miracle of the heavens. Now, go to your circumspection with care yet with also, determination and resolve. For you will rise to this earthly occasion. What you decide will be for the better, for all."

Jesuette returns to her thoughts with a new sense of confidence. She receives a message from her brother. "Dearest Jesuette, Please help."

This gives her ever more a sense of security and strength in where she tends to lean at this point. Jesuette weeps over the conundrum. She never wanted to have to face anything like this. Though, she has always known this day would indeed come. Still, this does not deliver her beyond it, even though hearing from her family eases her mind and softens her thoughts.

* * *

The long onerous dream paralyzes Lucifer even deeper within his coma-like dormancy. He is days deep into this arduous, agonizing trench of abyss. He growls, moans, groans, drools and spits throughout the ever changing scene before him. Every scenario within are connected, and they are representative to the inert, inactive ogre as some inevitable dooming cataclysm.

Before the beast lay the vista of a panoramic powder blue sky. There are wee and pure white cloud puffs scattered about, where white doves drift and dip slowly, casually about.

High above are soft bright rays of light reigning, as if through a prism, through the clouds and beyond reaching the soil below, consecrated as God's land. The star above is not pleasing to Lucifer's eye. He screams in pain as he attempts to spy it from below.

The beast is on the rise. He drifts upward and hovers there a moment. In a flash, he is in the midst of a ferocious battle. His fallen children explode in the sky, one by one, two by two, three by three. It is a never-ending display of contemptible defeat at the hands of the chosen. Lucifer must look away, howbeit he cannot. The scene is a most mesmerizing and hypnotic exhibit wrenching the devil's glare toward it, around it and into it.

In the dreary, lenitive slumber also comes a discomforting apathetic deadness and immobilization under which the king of darkness cannot escape. The blackened splattered detritus of his followers stain his coat and slap against his skin, his face. It yanks cruelly at his groin. Tears seep from the eyes and instantly stiffen and thicken, as they fall down and roll off his snout to disintegrate into powder; the plane out there impregnated and permeated in sanctity and holiness.

All around him darkness falls to light and the chosen army surround him. Lucifer is terrified wrapped in his helplessness like no time ever in his existence. He looks up at himself and instead of rejoicing in viciousness, he weeps in embarrassing collapse. A dark gray nebula of gloom hangs, lilting, moving gently. A buoyant mist of fog among the flying chunks of his own children.

The chosen army there above Western Europe threateningly creep toward the devil and advance all around surrounding Pazuzu. With a collective breath exhaled through pursed lips, they blow the fallen king away. The fiend vaporizes, vanishes in a cloud of white refinement that envelopes every speckle of black gloom and squeezes him like a worm in a vice.

* * *

Lucifer wakes with a start and jolt, with an impending feeling of defeat before realizing he is safe in the pleasing, sedative, hot steaming mess of his cavern. He sweats fire. He deeply pants flame. He sits in the middle of a pool of lava. He is home.

The fallen devil forces his scruffy mind through a self-conscious review of the phantasm now behind him. Is it an inner vision of events to come? The slaughter of his army over the past twenty-seven days and nights fuel his thoughts as they did his dream. Time is here to decide next steps. Lucifer feels the nightmare is a warning and he accepts it as such. His scabby mind sinks even lower as he tortures himself into thoughtful planning. But the never ending sink to his entire abysmal career overtakes all else.

There is no future in haphazard evil. There has to be a target. He makes an effort to contact Ballard, but to no avail. Ballard is now chosen and inaccessible. Ultimately, Lucifer places and keeps two inevitabilities in mind. There is the intention to call his worldwide army to rise and fight, for the duration, until the end. But, the latter thought is much more attractive to the devil, so he spends the rest of the review focused on it.

The fallen ones, caught by surprise, adjust

to the call from their leader. Most, still in bed and neutral since the last series of defeats, barely listen and hardly care. They are justly and understandably very scared, their spirit dead. None of them want to climb up again amidst the risk and danger. Their desire is to be chosen, and they are on the cusp of conversion as the chosen file through the defeated ranks.

Fallen loyalty sinks completely when they realize Lucifer has no plan or further direction to bestow them. They all will have been paid a visit from the chosen, they know. And then, they will be truly free. Is there is a chance of actually winning, they reason, what is the sense? What is the answer? The answer is 'No.'

Lucifer speaks to his drove. "The answer is rise and fight, you cowards. We wait until the chosen ooze into our space and then encroach upon them. The element of surprise is on our side this time. I will tell you when….just be ready because it can happen at any minute, any day. Those who decide to ignore me? You die!"

The devil departs as quickly as he appeared. The fallen units all around the world conference and discuss, the elder teammates take the lead and facilitate. Try as they may, their underlings warily sit by and let each word puff into and then out of their heads, their minds. Most feint the words, just as they did Lucifer's. The elders surrender.

*　*　*

"Chosen angelicas…we have orders for you," Saint Bruno commences with his unannounced speech. "Even though we may have entertained the thought that our tasks are complete, we must follow-through with a finale to be."

True to form, the heavenly cherubs stand with peaked interest, wanting and ready. They listen intently on the plan for the upcoming battles. The ultimate plans describe a braid, a welcome twist and a new challenge.

The chosen rise but in limited numbers. They understand that they are the bait. The plan is to lure the fallen back up to the plane, then barrage them with the remainder of the chosen fighters; the switch. And true it be that, upon recognition, Lucifer alerts his army to immediately attack in the higher dimension. The leftover sympathetic, small and scattered fallen do as they are told. The rest pray for deliverance from evil and forgiveness of their sins.

"Here they come, my children..."

As the fallen enter the war theater, nimble chosen soldiers buzz all around them with swiftly. The fallen cannot compete with the chosen aeronautic soaring and flawless aerial navigation. As half the units in part continue the acrobats, the other half rise and attack in the confusion. The chosen outnumber their enemy by ten-thousand-to-one. And with every span of shredding, all of the fallen feel it deep within. They explode in this upper atmosphere into dark, leftover muck.

Wave by wave the fallen rise and the chosen massacre.

Jesuette leads a prayer for the heavens to pray:

> "Oh divine eternal father, in union with your divine son and the Holy Spirit, and through the immaculate heart of Mary, I beg you to destroy the evil spirits.

Cast them into the deepest recesses of hell and chain them there forever. Take possession of your kingdom which you have created and which is rightfully yours.

Heavenly father, give us the reign of the sacred heart of Jesus and the immaculate heart of Mary.

Let us repeat this prayer out of pure love for you with every beat of my heart and with every breath I take.

Amen."

CHAPTER TWENTY-NINE

"All the heavens and all my chosen: I commend you for your exemplary display of righteousness and sacrifice. Saints and angels you guide your assignments with a depth and breadth I have yet to witness, until now. And now, I hereby relieve you of the duties relating to our latest theater of war with the fallen one and his horde of demons. The fallen army is in retreat and no longer pose a threat. Most of the dark army is either deceased or in-line for conversion to the holy chosen side.

So now, my chosen children, I leave it up

to Saint Bruno, Master Bruno and you all to visit those fallen who pray for forgiveness and convert them with friendly means, and welcome them in celebration for their unselfish and wise decision, late in coming as it is. There need be no desperation in haste, as they no longer pose any imminent threat. They want you. They need you. They long to know me.

I have work to do on Earth, in the Middle East regions. So, beginning now, let all communications flow to my board of saints… Saint Peter residing.

Saint Bruno, Master Bruno, please carry-on the conversion effort."

With that, Goddess Jesuette ascends further on high and into her own private sanctuary; her chamber.

* * *

The executioner looks up to the sky as he begins a prayer to the false god. A rain drop falls into his right eye. He lowers his head with a stinging jerk then uses his sleeve to wipe away the unfamiliar moisture from the socket. A deep thought speeds through his mind and evaporates as quickly as the drop of water is gone. There is no prayer this morning, after all. He turns to the media team that set-up the shoot and he waits for the director's cue.

The orange clad captive kneels before the black draped killer. He is helpless. An under soldier fastens the subject's bound wrists to his constrained ankles. He commands the prisoner to be still.

"Keep your head up!"

A grip raises the cue-card. The director orders, "Action!"

The executioner holds his Bowie knife up and outward as he reads the words in white print on the black cue card. He stumbles through the narrative and is told to perform and read again. He repeats the procedure seven times before the director announces, "Done!"

The crew immediately rolls out the vignette in support of the next scene. The assistant director coaches the young killer. They repeat the details of the upcoming shoot five times through before they are both satisfied with the assassin's performance.

The director orders, "Action!"

The assistant director points at the armed man in black. Three seconds pass, and then the slaughterer reaches around the prisoner's forehead, holding it in a tight grip at the crook of his black-sleeved, muscled right arm. He is sure he has a firm headlock on the prisoner's head so he bends it back. The knife comes from the left and swiftly slices through the captive's throat in an explosion of blood and gore. The executioner slices hard again, and then saws through the rest until the head is severed from the body. The body twitches but for a second, and rests. The killer lets drop the head on to the sand.

There is only one take to get this shot.

A third associate bags-up the headless body, separately the head, and drives them out to some uncharted location, yet one where the separated corpse will be found. He drives away. Hiding between the van's side doors, the executioner changes from the bloody garb into a clean uniform. The crew jumps into their van and the actor and director step into theirs. They shake hands and exchange praise of success. Smiling faces of the guilty, sipping on hot water.

CHAPTER THIRTY

Jesuette outlines the countries within the fallen Middle East region and identifies other nations under the siege of Islamist extremists. She kneels and silently prays to her father. He appears to her in spirit, and she weeps.

"Oh Jesuette, my child, my pride, envelope my soul as I reflect upon all you accomplish fighting back Satan. As you move to your next leg of the necessary, I understand you leaning toward eradication. I bless the action and I bless you in the quest. I have abundant faith in you my darling, and your decision-making."

"Thank you, father. I pray now that my decision turns-up a positive, meaningful and evil-ending result."

"I know. Bless you, Jesuette." God drifts away in a mist of white which evaporates as he nears the brim under his mighty alter.

She meditates within the soft tornado of thought behind her impending actions centering on limited territories, yet all-encompassing therein. The Goddess is pleased and she feels soothed. Yet, she whimpers slow-falling tears of sorrow and prayer, thanks and praise.

A light slow uncharacteristic drizzle sprinkles across the swath of desert nations.

The cumulative tasks form a sensible sum, and this comforts her. Her plans take shape.

She wants measured gradual steps to leave space for adjustment, refinement and escape based on progress and projection.

"Angels please," sublime, wonderful, mellow music fills the heavens. "Hear this and heed this imperative rule. You shall gather in your charge's territories and descend upon your respective assignments." She pauses.

"The overall heart of the mission is to prompt the meek, mild and peacemakers. Granted, prompting the innocent is possible even while the hard-edged extremists are untouchable. Regardless, simply perform what I suggest to you to the highest degree. Clearing the way for my imminent action in the region shall constitute your reasoning. Angels over the chosen…remain with the innocents and guide and protect them for the duration of the procession.

Now, go and save our peace-making community

of humankind in this harsh, wicked region of the world. Walk to the borders. That is all, now...Go!"

Christians experience the miraculous vision of the angels. There are no nagging questions or doubt. For they are the faithful, the believers, the hopeful and the saved. They prayed all their lives for a moment like this. They follow the guidance of their angels without query, simply driven by an element of fundamental Christianity, brotherhood and love. There are a smattering of Christian souls residing or trapped in pockets within the confines of damnable occupied cities and towns. Difficult challenges face those unfortunates, for if they attempt to migrate out of the region, the vicious and demonic troops will slaughter them. And if they stay put, the evil-doers may still torture and execute them for the sake of display and terror. Those angels assigned them must offer by any means direction, relief and calm.

Islamic extremists experience dreams of terrific light, safety and reconcilement in the presence of their angels. However, these fiends are so ultimately devoted to their false god and cause that even in sleep they fight away the goodness of heaven, presented by the visiting holy. Lucifer's fallen that successfully thwart the angels' plea understand their just desserts from their prince of darkness.

Nothing. Just life. A damned life. Lucifer comes to them in the forms of Mohammed and Allah. And they are easily convinced they are invincible as long as they continue with their global initiative to rid the Earth of infidels, establish the caliphate and vie for world domination. They are non-believers and they dismiss with ease the coaxing attempts of the lit, heavenly messengers.

Abu Omar al-Shishani addresses the fighters over which he commands; all Islamic extremists everywhere. "My fighters of the Koran, we near an unplanned victory of land-space. A visit from our divine being discloses to me that a mass exodus is about to take place. Non-believers of Islam, infidels will walk from our lands at their will to migrate into the surrounding nations of sympathizers representing the western coalition. Let them walk. Let them walk!

This only further secures a more immediate land conquest for us and ultimately leaves those who walk just as vulnerable to our invasions to follow this, our current mission, our holy re-patriating."

He proceeds with a linear strafe of propaganda that is broadcast worldwide. The

West shrugs at the nonsense they perceive. Yet the West continues with their bombing campaign over Iraq and Syria in an effort to stall the ever encroaching middle-eastern march of evil. There is some success therein, but this Islamic State, constituted by Iraq and Syria ISIS fighters continue to enslave, torture, execute and over-trample town by town, city by city. They represent by far the most resilient terrorist group ever known to man. They taste the first establishment of the Islamic State coming.

* * *

"Behold, for I am your familial guardian angel," each angel begins. "I will guide you, and protect you, as you walk to freedom. We shall hike to our nearest outside border to safety within the arms of our brothers and sisters. You represent one family among the mass exodus to take place. Rejoice in the heavens and in each other, for you children are saved from further persecution. Believe and follow, you men, women and children. Follow me, as I am of your Lord."

Non-conformists everywhere across the region pack as many belongings as possible for the trek. Some neighborhood families own mules or camels, yet most do not. The show of camaraderie is not surprising to the angels leading the way and walking with all those they came to save.

"You shall be released. You shall be delivered in peace unto the presence and goodness of your Lord."

Jesuette puts all her trust in the heavenly spirits while she awaits for the saved exit from horror. A glance encourages her further… mellows her. She prays incessantly for the walking believers amid the non.

"Oh you powers of heaven, deliver them from evil."

* * *

"Although several rogue terrorist groups, as they are referred to by the West, continue their own brand of attack and murder, the fighters for the Islamist State are strangely quiet and unseen." The political NEWS around the world report in like.

"One has to survey what they may be thinking, or worse planning during this apparent lull. Innocents continue to flock to safety in waves without interference from the killers."

* * *

Refugees cross the borders to asylum and safety, as Jesuette ponders her next steps, even in review. She prays to her father, "I beg forgiveness, father, over what I am about to do."

And God says, "I assure you, my dear Jesuette, that heavenly acts of overall good need not cry forgiveness."

CHAPTER THIRTY-ONE

The air is cool over the flatland expanse of desert. Temperatures ring fall even though it is almost summer. A light chilly breeze develops throughout the region. The population wear layers of robe and woolen headdresses, which make the climate change hardly noticeable, although they can feel the gentle nip upon the face. Noses redden and run.

Skies are gray, unlike the days leading to this one, and before. The color darkens, smudging the clouds with each passing hour. Tribes below are too preoccupied to dwell. They have enough on the plate. Militants across the territories continue their encroachment and conquests, stealing life out of all who do not conform.

Sands of the arid sterile terrain rise at the surface in waves and drifts. Killer armies trudge against the wind and stinging sand. They lean forward, trudging, heads covered and turned in an effort to brave the elements. Fighting eventually becomes impossible in the face of what is. For there is next to no one left to encounter. So, the fighters rest underneath the cover of blanket, fray and cold, lonely sky.

* * *

Jesuette points a finger downward and notes the atmospheric climate. Is it ripe enough yet to support the imminent charge? No. No, not just yet. She patiently waits. She prays.

Her angels over the militant army units report that none of the target assignments took to conversion. Hunger for the Islamist State outweighs the promise of heaven, by and large a Christian concept.

Three days into the storm, the evil ones are hunkered down in the sand. Many lose their shelter and tents to the wind. They struggle to keep at all comfortable. Jesuette smiles. The time is right. Now. She balls her hands and gently wrings them as if daintily holding a fallen chick from a nest. The crease at the bottom of her clasped hands open...a little more...a dite wider. And there they are; small orbs of marble and alabaster. She beholds the wavy patterns and host of colors. They drop onto her lap.

Concentrating, Jesuette, through her will and by God's grace, the precious little miraculous balls turn a key toward the next condition. First, she rests and observes. Her careful thought and prayers help initiate the very action planned upon and necessary. Are the temperature and conditions in the contiguous cut-out regions on Earth's Middle East acceptable? She dips a finger downward. She brings it up and touches her inner arm, then the tip of her nose. Yes, the spirit moves. "Yes."

Leisurely and lingering, Jesuette takes care in her walk-through. One small hail stone drops into the middle of each country below. She turns away but notes the marble does not melt in the atmosphere, nor does it on the ground.

So, two days pass and then Jesuette returns. She spies. And she is satisfied. The stones survive.

Jesuette conjures nine large fabric pouches of small, Agate and real marbles. She picks-up and cups each handful one-by-one in her hands. The marbles drop slowly into a tight mass on her lap. She repeats the action until all of the marbles have sifted through her hands and have fallen into the pocket formed by her robe just below her tummy. The Earth just below her deliriously quivers. Viewing it offers but a translucent look as the larger hailstones fall densely from the sky.

* * *

Still under inclement conditions militant units nonetheless take to the roads again. Field Infantry and Artillery lead the way toward the next village. Armed combat troops follow with more heavy weaponry; Howitzers, tanks, mortars, propelled grenades, cannons, fifty caliber vehicle-mounted machine guns. One half day into the march forward, amid a surprising barrage of frozen balls of sky, the procession stalls. Men cannot walk and wheels cannot roll. The soldiers blither in dismay and chatter nonsense with each other. They are ignorant to the conditions. Never before had they ever felt a pelting to the face under such ache and hurt.

Their Commanders order the units to once again dig-in, urging all to request the help of their highest. The militant leadership is at a loss for the first time since their initial calls for jihad into the Islamist State years ago. Never before has anyone ever dreamed of such an event, never mind witnessed such an event. Tents spared before cannot be pitched. Under the bare shelter of layered clothes and blankets, some fighters endure the unending rapid array of pops made all around them, and onto them. Some die. It is a barrage the like of which they have no experience. All they can do is hide from it, and that just barely.

* * *

Jesuette lets the hail fall. The small circles form a lawn of ice six inches deep and puddles deeper across the target areas.

* * *

CHAPTER THIRTY-TWO

Lucifer oozes into the lethargic fallen minds. Fear is nonexistent among the warriors for the Islamic State, but they hear and feel the ferocity and fury. "So, you let the nonconformists walk? Ohhhhhhhhhhhh...be happy that your hope did not disappear with your fear. I understand you put your dreams of the caliphate ahead of my desire and desideratum, and I do not like that. Don't you realize that I can wipe you all off the planet in a matter of moments? Fools. Fools!"

The Islamist Militant's commanding spokesman steps-up and remarks, "Devil, certainly you realize that the installment of the Islamic State implicitly, yet imminently means decimation of all targeted infidel pockets...No?"

"Do not mock me, you mortal piece of shit, you. Of course I see your point, but now instead of being able to move out of this region upon your settled state, you will have had to start right here before moving ahead."

The command is confused. "We also will have grown in number, thus affording us the balance to forge ahead beyond our borders as well as the capacity to continue cleansing the localized infidels."

"Are you blind to the threat of Western nations?"

"No, we are not."

"What makes you think you have instilled

enough fear into them? To keep them passive and at bay until your state is established and your numbers higher?"

"we have faith and hope, Lucifer."

"Eeyooh…Oiyuh…" Lucifer stutters. "You Are On Your Own!" The devil coughs as he fades and sinks back down into his impious, unsanctified and dark under-cave. Defeated once and rejected once more Lucifer sulks and pouts in the hellish corner in the unhallowed hole. Flame seeps out of Satan's evil black pores. He slumps where he sits, hands to his sides, and head lolling back on his necks and shoulders. There is no thought, no intention, no hate and no filler to the void being. He is nothing more than the fallen, dethroned angel of eons ago. And at this time there is no inclination to fight.

The militant armies share and spread the latest word. The devil is out. And the larger message here is contained in a directive. Remain under until the storm exhausts itself. Every time the falling, solid moisture slows, they pack-up and prepare to begin marching and fighting again. Then, inexorably the storm rages again, more forcefully, pushing them back into cuddling in the ice.

The Commanders and other leaders keep their eyes on the weather and forecast from inside their resident stone homes in Syria. On the ground the hail rises to almost ten inches, and there is no sign of a foreseeable term, let alone an end. For the first time ever, leadership is dumbfounded and fearful.

* * *

"There is a 'Weather Accurate' special presentation at seven o'clock tonight. It will showcase all things hail, and also explain the coming forecast," the NEWS anchor closes. "We hope to see you there."

Looking like a winter scene with bowing, shabby trees and flora, the weather special looks back at the second afternoon following the very start of this curious event. The weather man slugs on. Three inches of marble hail drop overnight and the afternoon temperature is at thirty-four degrees.

"Temperatures on the cool side are not all-together uncommon in the region, but prolonged conditions are. Hail storms are particularly a strange occurrence in these Middle Eastern territories. Of course, driving is a real nightmare over roads of loose, hard stones," the show host stupidly continues.

A field reporter adds, "The severity of damage caused by a storm like this depends on the wind speed while the hail is in progress. Storms that produce high wind in addition to hail will crack windows and damage siding. Regardless of wind, other outside structures and vehicles are extra-prone to damage."

The incredible storm opens and falls down onto the northern, southern and eastern most borders of Iran, the northern and southern borders of Iraq, and the northern, western and southern borders of Syria. The lines of the storm are murky, but now it is fairly clear that the front slowly encroaches in and upon the inner-most regions from the borders where it began.

"We call it a smart storm...the interior forecast calls for continuous storms, which could bring with them more hail," the weather man says excitedly.

"Hail is precipitation in the form of lumps of ice that form in some storms." He explains. "Hail forms when thunderstorm updrafts are strong enough to carry water droplets well above the freezing level. This freezing process forms a hailstone, which can grow as additional water freezes onto it. Eventually, the hailstone becomes too heavy for the updrafts to support it and it falls to the ground.

Hailstones are usually round, and vary from pea size all the way up to softball size. So, again, hailstones generally form in thunderstorms between currents of rising air called the updraft and the current of air descending toward the ground, called the downdraft. Large hailstones indicate strong updrafts in storms. The larger the hail, the stronger the updraft, needed to hold it aloft in the storm."

The queer attribute of this wide-reaching storm is that it spreads, it does not travel. Teams of tornado chasers arrive on the scene. Local guides join the handful of daredevil possess. They all struggle to catch-up and keep-up with the front. But it keeps moving. They report that the massive hailstorm before them shows no sign of clearing from any direction. No one dares predict the breadth or depth of damage that will occur to property before it's over.

* * *

Jesuette kneels in a state of meditative hibernation, the prayers flowing through her and out of her to the father, an immaculate form of white smoke, in his plush throne.

"'Our Father forgive my sins. For I started and I shall finish. Bless me, father.

If you are willing, take this cup from me, yet not my will, but yours be done.

Father, I thank you that you have heard me. I know that you always hear me, but I say this for the benefit of the earthly people standing there, that they may believe that you sent me.

Now my heart is troubled, and what shall I say? Father, save me from this hour. No, it was for this very reason I came to this hour. Father, glorify your name! Glorify it, and glorify it again.

Father, the time has come. Glorify your daughter, that your daughter may glorify you. For you granted Jesus and I authority over all people that we might give eternal life to all those you have given him. Now this is eternal life that they may know you, the only true God, Jesus Christ and Jesuette, whom you have sent. I have brought you glory on earth by performing the work you gave me to do. And now, father, glorify me in your presence with the glory I had with you before the world began. I have revealed you to those whom you gave me out of the world. They were yours. You gave them to me and they have obeyed your word. Now they know that everything you have given me comes from you. For I gave them the words you gave me and they accepted them. They knew with certainty that I came from you, and they believed that you sent me. I pray for them. I am not praying for the world, but for those you have given me, for they are yours. All I have is yours, and you have what is mine. And glory has come to me through them. I am not of the depths any longer, but they are still in the world, and I am praying to you. Holy Father, protect them by the power of your name--the name you gave me--so that they may be one as we are one. As I am with them, I protected them and kept them safe by that name you gave me. None has been lost except the one doomed to destruction so that scripture would be fulfilled. I am praying to you now, but I say these things while I am protecting the world, so that they may have the full measure of my joy within them. I have given them your word and the world has hated them, for they are not of the world any more than I am of the world. My prayer is not that you take them out of the world but that you protect them from the evil one. They are not of the world, even as I am not of it. Sanctify them by the truth; your word is truth. As you sent me into the world, I have sent them into the world. For them I sanctify myself, that they too may be truly sanctified. My prayer is not for them alone. I pray also for those who will believe in me through their message, that all of them may be one, father, just as you are in me and I am in you. May they also be in us so that the world may believe that you have sent me. I have given them the glory that you gave me, that they may be one as we are one. I in them and you in me. May they be brought to complete unity to let the world know that you sent me and have loved them even as you have loved me. Father, I want those you have given me to be with me where I am, and to see my glory, the glory you have given me because you loved me before the creation of the world. Righteous father, though the world does not know you, I know you, and they know that you have sent me. I have made you known to them, and will continue to make you known in order that the love you have for me may be in them and that I myself may be in them.

Amen."

* * *

Hail storms show no sign of slowing or stopping. The hail is golf ball-size. It makes one to two foot splashes when they hit the ice-ball tundra below. The bombardment spares nothing and no one bearing the storm protected and unprotected. Businesses, houses, vehicles and crops are slowly jack-hammered down.

"Storms of this intensity are uncommon everywhere around the world and naturally unheard of in the Middle East." The acting, concerning television host says.

* * *

The persecuted refugees are fully migrated to the bordering asylum countries. Television and radio stations within the three targeted countries are off the air indefinitely. The support infrastructures collapse, flatten and are ruined. Islamist militant leadership lose all lines of communication with their army. Those troops, most without shelter begin to succumb to the surrounding ice beds formed all around them. Many are suffocated alive, or die from hyperthermia. Those inside the abandoned tents and mud buildings, homes, are no longer safe, as those safe havens built upon ground level dirt and sand ultimately fill up with the marbles of deadly hail.

The strongest roofs overhead now sag down causing a lumpy implosion inside and about all those huddling inside.

The experienced chasers know not to get in the wake of the old super cell. Swinging wide to the multiple fronts before making a run for the inflow area saves time, but not lives. Early spring storms riding on a one-hundred-fifty knot jet stream speed away leaving chasers spinning in the ice.

The tank-like vehicles of the few still-active chasers become largely immobile. Maneuvering in the hard hail, unlike snow is like trying to drive on contained, gigantic ball bearings. Much of this renders the chase over. Images are captured in the desolate provinces in center territories inside of Iran, Iraq and Syria. Chasers seek over the wide open swaths with few obstructions to limit the view of the clouds and skies. But a common row of high lines are a detriment to cloud photography. The isolated areas of even the higher plains over those inner-most parts provide the chaser with limited views of the sky. There is simply no more for them to see.

* * *

Hail in the wake of the tornadic super-cell thunderstorms continue to cause severe damage to roofing, siding and windows and automobiles. Houses crush down to the thick ice floors. The hail strips indigenous bush and trees of all leaves, buds, fruit and small limbs. Baseball-size ice orbs drop from thirty-thousand feet with speeds reaching one-hundredthirty-five miles per hour crashing to the ground. That, coupled with the last chasers' travelling at seventy miles per hour under the big ugly clouds, becomes lethal. The heavily armored tornado intercept vehicles are rendered helpless.

Hailstones make different sounds depending on how hard they are, and their size. The little ones go click, crack or pick, the marbles announce whack or smack. The golf balls say bam, especially when they are hard enough to bounce off the pavement. Bouncing ice, that's an amazing concept. The baseballs actually hit hard enough to hurt your ears, ka-bam extremely loud. Then comes what the chasers call gorilla hail. Imagine the sound of a sledge hammer smashing the top of the roof in.

Headliners pound across the chaser's vehicles. Glass shatters from the front windshield into the back seat. Surviving chasers absorb the impact as their whole vehicles stall and shake amidst the onfall. Directly in front of one of them, four high priced BMW's are sitting in the middle of the road under the overpass, the passengers dead. The local leaders pulled to the side of the road mid-storm.

Baseballs litter the roads. The arm of the hook is less than a mile ahead. Only one chaser still has a windshield. A tornadic super cell crosses Esfahan, Baghdad and Lebanon. Tornados come to and come down, the hail inside pry to get out. The back side is not rain wrapped as usual, it is a frozen front that delivers the large deadly hail quickly. Since the largest hail is just northeast of the miles-wide tornadic mesocyclone and sometimes wraps around it, this is a sure and deadly sign the chaser is close to perhaps more than he bargained for in 'core and hook punching,' the big taboo of storm chasing. Everyone says don't do it. Yet, still some do.

Jesuette heaves another breath and peers downward, surveying the scape.

Another colossal meso-cyclone churns about two miles to the southeast. The chasers are on a roll but this is the high risk move chasers seldom get away with. Today it blows up in their faces, literally. Safety glasses are a must, but they still eat glass. And the barrage leaves dark, oblong circular bruises around their eyes. They see even larger stones just to the south. The east wind is now very strong. With the windshield in their laps, they give up on the super cell. Victory is only the sight from afar. A string of tornados fill the low sky from the south. They turn away from the wind and ride out the core.' The day is lost. They are lost.

* * *

Hail storms cause an incredible amount of damage to property and crops across the entire landscape. In just sixteen days hail causes over a billion dollars in damages, not to mention thousands of lives. Then, the costliest severe hailstorm in history strikes the southern metroplex. It causes intense loss, due to the large and growing hail.

In storms that cause tornadoes, hail often falls directly to the northeast or east of the path of the tornado. The strong updraft is associated with the part of the storm that produces the tornado. Hail very rarely kills anyone, until now. Of course, the best way to keep safe in hailstorms is to immediately seek shelter. But the efforts to keep safe are thwarted by the massive storms that deliver larger than life hail and winds.

There are now large hailstones falling

from tornadic super cells throughout the Northwest Territories to the upper Midwest and South. The stones leave paths miles wide littered with grapefruit-sized stones, over a six foot frozen bed. The hail falls from dark clouds in onerous loud explosions to the south of the new developing meso-cyclones. No rain or thunder occur in those immediate areas. The stones are coming down hard and fast. Further to the northeast, more large stones fall blocking anyone further from reaching the belching tornados.

The last chasers left living retreat and flea to surrounding cities, Balkanabat, Elaziq and Cyprus. While waiting for their flights out, they transmit photos and affidavits that journal the storms so far, that is, as far as they were able to keep up. Chasers witnessed and collected golf ball, baseball and grapefruit sized stones before abandoning the chase. As they depart the frozen countries, a few get a glimpse and shot of the monstrous hail as yet, and their last seen.

"Note the irregular shape of some of the stones," one weatherman from New York points out. "The one on the left is elongated with small spikes, and others that fell more recently are jagged. Near this location particularly large stones fell. They measure seven and one half inches in diameter." The reporter goes on to show photos of hail captured within the past three days. The hail is ridiculously large... the size comparable to a ten-pin bowling ball.

Damage from the hail usually depends on the hardness of the stones and the angle of the impact. Occasionally a motorist can get lucky and get hit with a large soft stone when temperatures aloft are warmer. The soft stones crack apart absorbing the impact. In this case the stones are rock hard. And they are grossly huge. These gorilla hail stones are the largest ever recorded, the heaviest ever fallen and the hardest and most dense of any hail ever. People in the States are terrified from thousands of miles away.

Jesuette keeps the temperatures everywhere down and the atmosphere consistently perfect for the hail to start at a marble and grow to a grapefruit, then bowling ball size and beyond.

The deep hail easily worsens ice-flood situations. The giant ice orbs sit atop of smaller hail, which clogs drainage paths, culverts and grates. In flat country of the Middle East, water, mud and hail combinations cover, layered over the roadways. It brings perpetual blockage.

*   *   *

Lucifer is trapped in frozen animation below.

CHAPTER THIRTY-THREE

Jesuette slowly lets sift through her long slender fingers more pouches of three inch Aggies, some marbles larger. As they fall through her hands and land in her linen covered flexure, new storms of the most colossal hail descend upon the entirety of her targeted countries. Millions of kilometers in land mass lay underneath a deep ice cover over thirteen feet high of giant hail. The hail storms continue, while Jesuette addresses the holy table.

"Saints...Angels..." she begins. "I brought

forth my wrath down upon the devil-infected countries of our Middle East earthly region."

For most, this comes as a surprise. They have been busy with their respective assignments, the chosen in the West, shoring-up following the war experience. They were not privy to Jesuette's action, regardless.

"The wretched area now lay beneath more than five meters of frozen rain…hail. The region is near null of any sign of life that is all things and beings. I shall continue the purge until I am sure…positive that the root of the Islamic Extremists is decimated. Do not fret with what is about to take place. I believe it is for the best."

On the conclusive heavenly day of her extended blitz, Jesuette kneels and prays to her father, God almighty.

"In your name I pray. Dear father in

heaven, you are aware of my actions against Satan and his deadly gaggle. I am saddened that this occurred in some of our very own Holy Land. People are crying out in prayer, offering thanks and praise, however our souls are eaten up with fear. For they realize the obliteration is and was, by me, an act of God.

Therefore, I beg of your consideration to perform what I feel is an end-delivering and monumental step. I near the last, the action I seek to plan with you."

She goes on to explain what she believes are non-discretional tasks, and then rests. Jesuette lies back in her soft, plush chaise. She awaits her father's reply.

* * *

Jesuette kneels. She holds her two hands up high in prayer. Her hands come down slowly,

482

inch by inch separating until they rest on her either side.

Below, the frozen ground under the boulders of ice separates. The sound though muffled by the toppings, is awesomely, dreadfully and incredibly loud. It is loud enough to be heard hundreds of miles away. The blasts commingled with roaring, creaky, crammed and crackling sounds drone on in tandem, like that of an incredibly long and intense earthquake. And the inner Earth swallows the fallen and all trace of their being. Hell is indeed frozen-over.

And so she sits still, satisfied.

* * *

The root cause nations are gone, and now it is time to take from the streets all those rogue, lone-wolf and sub-capo groups, ridding the world of threats that otherwise will have been thrown. The western allies immediately follow the obvious cue and conspire to take down every potential and known killer-threats hidden in their inner-city pockets. Wave by wave of arrests follow. This is an iterative process that westerners hope and pray will virtually rid the globe of most extremists and terrorists.

Asmodeus attempts to recruit more fallen, but he is powerless. And now that the world population agree Earth is touched by the almighty above, evil is no opponent to the much greater good. People are united now. They possess faith, hope, and charitable strength with the unquestionable holy rescue. People from all around the globe drop Satan, as he is no more than an irking imp and one who they despise. He is dismissed easily and so he falls, slithers downward through the lawns, the soil, gravel, sand, silt…he helplessly bleeds through crust, mantle and outer core. Through the inner core he settles with a mortified splurge, a flat splat into the bowel…though the kernel of God's Earth.

He lies there in a rank and rancid bubbling puddle of molten blood, each fallen orb explodes into a fizzling spark. With each pop comes a wretched and painful cry. The pool of putrid polluted malevolence swirls gently, not violently, like hot simmering oil. The heart and spirit disappear to liquidity for the next two-thousand years. And there he sits, frosted and iced-over. He lost again.

* * *

On the new moon, people everywhere heed a call to gather. Jesuette, Jesus and God the father appear in the sky in a panoramic sequence, so they may be viewed by everyone, everywhere around the world. Jesus is on his father's right side and Jesuette on his left.

Jesuette speaks. She delivers an introduction of sorts.

"Brothers and sisters…children on our great planet Earth, please allow me and listen. I am Jesuette and I appear here with my brother Jesus and our father, God almighty. We have brief announcements for you, upon the wake of the unholy force we recently decimated.

In an attempt to rise to power, Satan once again waged war between his fallen empire and us, you and me, of God's heavens. We are chosen. Through the power vested in me by God the father, I gathered armies of young chosen people to beat the devil back down by combating his recruited soldiers. We won those battles, and thus, the holy war. The compassion and faith of the world leaders today disallow them to advance further, even toward our worst enemies, in the name of goodness, but also not even in the name of

God. Personal greed will have fueled that, and so their failures, as well. But now, after witnessing God's power and will over such heathens and evil-doers, we hope we struck the final stake for the sake of peace, the mild, the meek and most of all the peace-loving, peace-keeping, God-fearing people of the Earth. I shall continue to cleanse your souls, and then fill them with holy white grace from heaven, every night by the Holy Spirit. Jesus?"

"I wish to remind you all," Jesus continues the sermon. "I, Jesus, God the Son sacrificed myself to beat Satan eons ago, and to forgive you all from sin. I did lay the path of the Christian life before you, for you to follow. I lay a path before you all, each and every one of you, every day as you wake. You stumble, you fall and you ignore me. However, I have faith in you, always. And so, gentle people of our Earth, please hold close your faith in me. Father?"

"Children," God the father begins, in beautifully deep, comforting, warm tones. "I am the almighty creator. The creator of all things, all beings. I provide life and support life – my greatest gift – with the means for you all to follow suit. The miracle of child-birth...I am proud of my Jesuette's acting all for fairness and love of heart, soul and life itself... for being holy. We shall restore the Middle East region now. I urge you to practice patience. You will know the signs. Please continue what you are doing in your lives. I love you. We love you. And people of Earth... our love must have no parameters. Just love."

Many people faint. Some praise, hands in the air. Many fall to their knees, and almost all weep. But everyone bears witness. Everyone owns a newfound base of faith, hope, charity and strength. They know full confidence and have the knowledge. Love. So, the divine trinity vanishes away unto the heavens in a translucent vapor, disappearing, and then reigns across the sky a magnificent show of colorful clouds, trails and contrails.

* * *

The skies above the Middle East finally fall completely still three days following the miracle in the sky, the spirit in the sky, as it has become to be known and termed. An itchy song from decades ago continuously plays over the radios everywhere.

The Middle East region is completely and neatly buried under twenty feet of ice. It shall stay in that state until all traces of evil have vanished from below. No one offers to explain how a frozen being of any kind does not surface in suspended, frozen animation.

No one cares. The people left living once again feel renewed, secure, rescued, protected and free.

PART FIVE
THE
REBIRTHING

AFTERWORD

Sublime space

Yes, but the foul being

Immortality gone

Ailing, infirm, lame, sickly

Naked before God.

All mortals

Age-old sing-song

You cannot petition

Our Lord with prayer.

James A. Landry

After storm calm

Days over on end

Miraculous orbs

By now rained.

Ridden the world

Everywhere, and here

Without of itself

God appear through.

Hearts, souls, conscience

His children again

In defeat the fallen

Down in a hole.

Goddess breathes

In the center

-God created Earth-

Yet there is no life here

The surface waters

In frozen darkness.

The Spirit of God

Brooding over tundra.

So, Goddess breathes

Let there be light

Upon this barren land

And warm bright light

And blowing wind

Through and through

In her heart

James A. Landry

Only God's goodness.

See the light

It is good

So separate the

Light from darkness

-He called the light Day-

The darkness Night.

And Goddess breathes

Let Us expand

Middling the waters

Let separate waters be.

-God brought forth-

Atmosphere the provider

Sky and Earth

Lick and shore.

And Goddess beckons

Let the Earth here sprout

Vegetation, plants, seed

May tree bear fruit

Goodness live animate.

Then Goddess breathes

Let God's light appear

In the sky above

Divide day from night

Let them be.

Brightly upon Earth

Bright light by Day

James A. Landry

Radiant the Sun

Dim light at Night

The heavenly stars.

And Then Goddess breathes

Let waters abound

Moving creatures

Sea bread

The sky winged creatures.

Goddess resides, ponders

Great living creatures

Every living creature

Move and live

Abundantly so

In waters, air

She sees

It's good.

Goddess prays blessing

Be fruitful multiply.

Goddess exhales

The Earth bring forth

Living creatures

Walking, crawling

Tame wild.

Goddess again breathes

Bringing forth life

Father's image

Prevail over all

Fish, birds, cattle.

Goddess breathes

Male and female

Bless them so

They multiply

Sublime, subdue.

And Goddess trumpets

"Behold;

We have provided every seed bearing plant on the Earth, and every tree with fruit and seed for your nourishment.

Also, to every living creature of the Earth, to the birds, and to everything living that crawls on the Earth, we have given all the green plants for your nourishment. And beyond recourse, it is so."

And He sees everything that He and she had created in Earth's

Middle East, and it is, indeed, very good.

From darkness to light, Jesuette rests in repose.

James A. Landry

Of the scroll

Lay with babe

Linen parchment

Bronze end-lets

Maroon tassels.

On the scroll

Upon unnumbered page

Written in longhand

Perfect chirography

Rolled neatly

Tied in compass

With light colored

Blue ribbon

And Raffia twists,

It is written:

Israelis behold

Christians believe

Muslims unite

A tender

Meek mild

All powerful

Baby girl

Of supreme parents.

He and She

Creations of Goddess

Small child be

Of their seed

Believe this one

Such as the last

A protector

James A. Landry

Beyond medicinal

She sees

She wills

She lives

She breathes

The air as do you.

But hark

Now, and listen

To the Earth

Walk the virgin turf

You repatriates

This land is

Once again God's

Once again yours.

So believe

Believe in goodness

Believe in meditation

Believe your scriptures

But behold this

The new chapter

Amends your teachings

So they may

Reflect the almighty

Riddance of evil

Giver of life

Exquisitely sharing

Returned these lands

Rightfully so

Absent of evil

Let it remain.

And this time

You have a blessing

James A. Landry

Spare none nothing

To beat down

To destroy

To decimate

True forces

Of Satan.

Yes, behold this child

And see

How just as Jesus

Lays the path

Upon the commandments

Of sweet life.

She shall wander the region

As age comes and goes

Fearless and righteous

Offering Herself so

To others and all

That we may see

The goodwill

The graciousness

The honesty

The integrity

The kindness

The mercy

And the morality.

Prophesize then

She will not bear

Any child for

It is She

Who is the giver

Giver of soil

James A. Landry

Giver of air

Giver of bread.

The giver of legged

The giver of winged

The giver of love

The giver of life.

The answer to all

It is simply-complex

Your right discovery

And practice, and see

All good and needs

The others around

Who cry out

Never desperation

Always with need

Whether you see

Or not.

Let us not

Our belief system

Fail our savior

Nor ourselves

So that we not

Hate, despise or covet

So that we not

Overthink problems.

Let the rain flow

Let the flowers grow

Let the righteous

Mind of eternity

Blossom with age.

James A. Landry

We shall not

Wish the bliss of youth

Over the wisdom of age

Rather celebrate life

Miraculous births

With the profound

Natural love

Love connecting

All things

Earth

Atmosphere

Creature

All living things.

Man

All humans

Hearts Spirit Soul

Across obliterate

Borders, beliefs

Flatten thresholds

Attitude, disposition

For the sake of all

For God's sake.

Shake the hand

Wash the feet

Applaud the band

Join together

Dance to words

Dance to vibrations

With the band

The band of faith

The band of hope

James A. Landry

The band of charity

Make it be good

Make it righteous

Make it be shared

Make it now.

Beyond all belief

Blind you not

Of love

Of peace

Of understanding

Of harmony

Between all men

All beings

And all things

Seen and unseen.

Live for the joy of it

Apply willfulness

Be understanding

Be a true mate

Be a match

Be an all-out lover.

Yes and be

Just be

A giver

A lover

A peacekeeper

A communicator.

With all of these

Attributes in constitution

Attitude

Disposition

Persona

Attractiveness

Foresight

Level-headedness

With morality

Fine values

Fine standards.

And

Love of God

Confidence

And confidence in sexuality

For it is good

Rejoice in togetherness.

Make bread

Share bread

Practice understanding

Empathy

Respect

Truthfulness

Openness

Honesty

Be humorous and

Behold a keen sense of humor

Be faithful

And know you are loved

Of self by all.

Shy from lies

Cheats

Thieves

And pray for them

Teach them

Show them

Show them the reward.

Show Love

Shy from conflict

From violence

From inflexibility

Confidently dislike hate

In all forms

Teach over it

Always for better

Share.

We do not gossip

We do not embrace ego

Keep just enough

For confidence

For presentation

Of work

Of lesson

Of self

In thoughtfulness.

We do not judge

For we are not qualified

Adore voice

Adore music

The language of all

Adore arts

And the artists

And writings

And writers

The professors

The wealthy

The poor.

Help all things

Help all beings

Just be

You be.

Behold the gorgeously adorable

The natural

Nature

Its giving

Its offerings

All better

Than synthesized.

Appreciate the bohemian

Vagueness

Specificity

Softness

Be not superficial.

And yes take

Yet what you need

Though of the rest

Not taking

The favorite.

What you have

Can be made

Perfectly

Impeccably

Unselfishly

Yours.

And squander not

The gifts

Of life

Of love

Of miraculous birth.

Love of ones' self

Love for each other

Beyond reproach

Of one another

Or just one other.

Celebrate it

Not in parade

But in heart

In words

In actions reflect.

Cause joy

Wherever you may

Share yourself

Your side

Welcome too

Other views

Other ideas

Other mindsets.

Do not be afraid

Scared

Woozy

Threatened

Simply understand

And rejoice

Rejoice the likeminded

The different

The alternate.

James A. Landry

Be not threatened

We all be friends

We are all one

Without containment

Constraint

Censorship

Taught roping

Pining.

For we may adhere

To our thoughts

Our minds

Our praises

And not encroach

Or Force into

Another's in kind

Or not.

Share

Be not boastful

Be not belligerent

Defensive

Redundant

Stay clear

Concise.

Do not let

Or let negativism

In your way.

Let conscience be

Your guide

From within

A gift from God

Reflected in Spirit

James A. Landry

For your soul

It does steer

Into the right direction.

Witness

Sanctify

Live just enough

On fringe.

Feed your mind

Feed your senses

Take it in

The sights

The sounds

The reality.

Be humble

Appreciative

With respect

For yourself

For all things

For all beings.

Take pride

In righteousness

In self

And family

In work

In others

Hold true

Your word

Your advice

Your council

Each step

Beyond

Backward

In keel.

Yet feed confidence

Within self

Unto all others

And spread the word

And also your wares

Kindness

Your brand.

Help

See

Under ably equipped

Take comfort

Let loose

And then let

Be taught

Be wrong

Be right

Be clothed

Be naked.

And in others

Be tuned

Be they welcome

Be attentive

Learn from

Take from

Give of

Again share all

Simply be nice

Be kind.

James A. Landry

Form rhythm

In life

For sleep

And wakefulness

So to be

Punctual

Or not.

For health

In work

In play

In repose.

Practice virtues

Like patience

In others

With nature

In general.

Ask why not

Or why

Study foreign rule

Decide for better

For God

For the Son

For the Spirit.

Be not swayed

By the self-absorbed

The loud

The obnoxious

The negative.

Wait your turn

For water

To speak

In turn

James A. Landry

Thus sharing

The positive.

Abandon negative

The harsh

The hurtful

The overbearing.

Just pray

Pray for a chance

A chance to teach

A chance for them

A chance to comfort

In their ears

From the word of God.

Lead even

In line

Following must

Keep true though

To the right

And not sin

With eye upon

Honorable prize

Yours or others

Conscientious

Ethical

Law-abiding

Noble

Pure

Spiritual

Upright

And virtuous.

Resist temptation

And evil

Of past

Of present

That to come

For here within

Is the power

The glory

The kingdom

For ever

And ever.

And Hail Mary

Of the present

She is full of grace

Blessed is she

Among humankind

And blessed be the fruit

Of her womb.

And honor Joseph

Of the present

His being full of grace

Blessed are his hands

Among humankind

And blessed is the light

Of his soul.

Pray, yet still

Give thanks

Give praise

Declare your beliefs

And ask only blessings

Over you

Your children

And the planet

James A. Landry

All things

All beings

And for

Relief from evil-doers.

Be the instrument

For peace

Where there is

Hatred, sow love

Injury, pardon

Doubt, faith

Despair, hope

Darkness, light

And sadness, joy.

Seek not consolation

As to console

To be understood

As to understand

Be loved, as to love

For it is in

Giving that we receive

Pardoning that

We are pardoned

And in dying

Born to eternal life.

Admit sin

Please yourself by God

Please God by yourself

Live life

For yourself through God

Bear sorrow

Have fun

James A. Landry

Ask forgiveness

Do not shy

From reaching

Reaching for friendship

For repentance

Any kind

For love.

Feel sorrow

It's alright

Believe in others

When in disbelief

Standing or in mind

Note success

But note effort

Ask

Be asked

For we do not control

we know.

Pray for spirit

Discipline and love

Smile on your tasks

On the tasks of others

Go where sent

Deal with arrival

Open your heart

To you

Open others'.

Believe in solution

For the good

In the name of love

Listen to scripture

Listen to man

James A. Landry

Listen to nature

Travel

Wander

Gaze

Wonder

Imagine

Believe.

Know you are heard

Know the journey

Envision destinations

Be not satisfied

For then there is nothing.

Decisions impact

Fate is formed

All roads lead to here

Walk alone

Without fear

Walk with others

Do not be bogged

Do not be dragged

Into the too much

Or the mire.

Remain a servant

Of man

By God.

Center amidst chaos

Bring calm to argument

And peace to fight

Form importance

With eyes on all

Know importance.

James A. Landry

Resolve conflict

Yours and in life

Of all

Enter hearts

Stop fussing

Find peace

Make peace.

Stand

Inhale the air

Feel sunlight

Sing songs

Remember

Forget

Give thanks

For family

Friends

Loved ones.

I have come

In the name of revelation

Revolution

Evolution of spirit

Of law

Of society

Of the divine trinity

My holy spirit is

With Father above.

But also receive

Receive me here

Allow inspiration

You share me

When sharing yourself

James A. Landry

Seek to bring

Bring all to me

When need be

Yet do

Think for yourself

Unfiltered

Nor destructive.

Equality is key

Between lovers

And friends

Children

One and all

Between one and all

Deliver calm

Among storm

Balance the scales

No one is above

Nor they below

Equality

It matters not

Where they be

Actually

Inanimately.

Look into the eyes

Of all those you face

And with whom you speak

Open your soul

See theirs open too

Speak the language

Of the mighty

Of the mild

James A. Landry

Of the child

Of the elder.

Realize diversity

In beings

And things

In wonderment

In actuality

In shape

In size

In color

In ways

In person

In all.

Shun not the sick

The weary

The marked

The foreign

The unknown

The unlike

The different

The shy

The boisterous

But see those

As equal too

As the god-like

As you.

See through the eyes

Of a child

Of an elder

See wonder

Excitement

James A. Landry

Darkness

And light

See happiness

It's what we need

So bad

It is a lonely

Lonely time

A walk

A streak

A river

A road

It is winding

It is treacherous

It is the unknown

But keep walking

Till the cross

And you may decide

Which way you're on.

Need we repeat

That which is written

That which is spoken

That which is practiced

That which is thought

What is the truth

We may have ignored

Yet likely not

That simple cliché

That simple imperative

That simple phraseology

That simple statement

Whether it's thought of

James A. Landry

Whether it's dwelled upon

Whether it's taught

Whether it's believed

Yes now confident

Think

Speak

Spread

Loud and clear.

Let us all be disciples

As twelve Saintly

That were

Yes now people

Love

And love of all

Abounding

Underneath

Love

Children

Ancestors

Descendants

Time fore

Time on end

Each other

Love.

Coin the sentiment

Not afraid

Believe it

That yes

Yes

Yes:

Love is the answer.

The answer is Love.

And appended directives state:

These words are simple. These words are truth. The very essence of every stanza is built into second nature among those who are born of love, learn love, and follow the way of love.

Take this scroll and live from it. Copy it. Share it. Share not only within your family and friends, but with all those around the world. As this represents the new and lasting testament. It is free of analogy, melodrama, metaphor and fear. It reflects the way of the world. Yes... as seen by and is designed by God, the trinity, but with only YOU, in heart, in spirit and in soul.

So, as we follow this blueprint of a lovely world, we shall never need or use defense in posture no matter the sense. If we all can do this, my friends, it becomes our implicit intention, and the light of our way.

The divine gives to you as you are one of our own. It is true. We are all as one under the lord thy God. We have faith in you as you do of us. We love you unconditionally, in hope that you may love in every phrase with the word, freely and unconditionally, as well.

God imbeds an ounce of greed, to foster motivation. But the people gorged, feeding it, they grew fat and got lazy. That was the downfall. But now we have the opportunity to change all that. People can change their ways for goodness sake. While every child born of this new colony call Middle East shall be void of greed.

We are the authors of our lives. We write our own story. This fact, not cliché. So, contrary to myth, people can indeed change... that is, if they so desire. So, counter greed with generosity. Counter power endowment with equality. Marry technology with spirituality. Let one compliment the other.

Parents know your children, and children know your parents. Stand together one and all, as one. Know your neighbor.

So, whereas of the disciples of Brother Jesus:

Peter was crucified, but felt himself unworthy to be put to death in the same manner as his Master, and was therefore, at his own request, crucified with his head downward;

Paul died under suspicious circumstances the same time and location as Peter;

James the son of Zebedee was put to death;

John died a natural death;

Andrew was crucified;

Philip died a natural death;

Bartholomew died a natural death;

Matthew died a martyr;

Thomas died of natural causes;

James son of Alpheus was thrown down from the temple by the scribes. He was then stoned, and his brains dashed out with a fuller's club;

Simon's death was natural;

Jude (Thaddeus) died a martyr;

Judas Iscariot died shortly after the death of Christ. He killed himself by hanging.

The heavens call. Children! Fear not! Your death shall be not an end, nor a beginning. Your death will be an event of continuity. As it is a part of life.

So, behold this heavenly child. Practice the messages in the announcement scroll. Know the child, the being and the intention.

Believe and live the life born of God and confirmed by the spirit. Yes, behold this God-child, and look in wonder and praise. For she is the young Goddess, Jesuette.

LIFE.

CREDITS

Portions of monologue and narrative are loosely based on, or inspired by various biblical writings and sermons analyzed, and by contributions from:

Zukeran;

McCoy, Cumming-Bruce and Amnesty Intl;

Fisk;

J. Daniel.